"Are You Telling Me the Truth?" Drew Asked.

"You haven't been with anyone since you left me?"

Lynn's throat constricted and she could only nod.

"Why?" Drew asked gruffly.

"I don't know why! What difference does it make, anyway?"

"All the difference in the world," Drew told her, pulling her around to face him. Moments later she was in his arms.

SONDRA STANFORD
wrote advertising copy before trying her hand at romantic fiction. Also an artist, she enjoys attending arts and crafts shows and browsing at flea markets. Sondra and her husband live happily with their two children in Corpus Christi, Texas.

Dear Reader:

Silhouette has always tried to give you exactly what you want. When you asked for increased realism, deeper characterization and greater length, we brought you Silhouette Special Editions. When you asked for increased sensuality, we brought you Silhouette Desire. Now you ask for books with the length and depth of Special Editions, the sensuality of Desire, but with something else besides, something that no one else offers. Now we bring you SILHOUETTE INTIMATE MOMENTS, true romance novels, longer than the usual, with all the depth that length requires. More sensuous than the usual, with characters whose maturity matches that sensuality. Books with the ingredient no one else has tapped: excitement.

There is an electricity between two people in love that makes everything they do magic, larger than life—and this is what we bring you in SILHOUETTE INTIMATE MOMENTS. Look for them this May, wherever you buy books.

These books are for the woman who wants more than she has ever had before. These books are for you. As always, we look forward to your comments and suggestions. You can write to me at the address below:

Karen Solem
Editor-in-Chief
Silhouette Books
P.O. Box 769
New York, N.Y. 10019

SONDRA STANFORD
Love's Gentle Chains

Silhouette Special Edition

Published by Silhouette Books New York

America's Publisher of Contemporary Romance

SILHOUETTE BOOKS, a Simon & Schuster Division of
GULF & WESTERN CORPORATION
1230 Avenue of the Americas, New York, N.Y. 10020

Copyright © 1983 by Sondra Stanford

Distributed by Pocket Books

ISBN: 0-671-53591-9

First Silhouette Books printing May, 1983

10 9 8 7 6 5 4 3 2 1

Map by Ray Lundgren

America's Publisher of Contemporary Romance

Printed in the U.S.A.

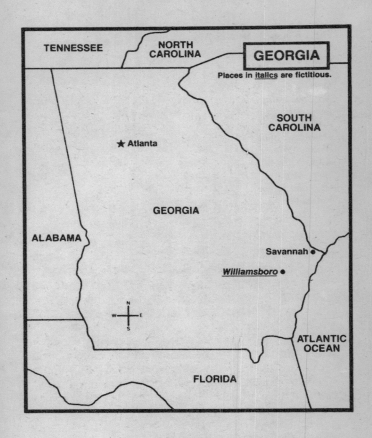

Chapter One

It was a brilliantly sunny afternoon in April when Lynn Marcus drew her small car to a halt in front of the day-care center. A light breeze wafted across the city from the Atlantic Ocean twenty-odd miles away, and despite the sunshine the air had a faint chill about it.

But it wasn't the cool air that caused her to hurry from the car and into the building. Despite the enormous amount of work that faced her during the next few weeks, excitement and even a measure of pride bubbled inside her and she looked forward eagerly to the challenge.

"Hi, Lynn," the day-care director greeted her as she entered a large room bustling with children. The woman smiled at her. "Joy tells me this is the big day."

Lynn smiled back, unaware of the glow that

radiated in her clear gray eyes. She bobbed her head, then smoothed back her long, brown curls with one hand as she replied, "Yes, it is. The movers were supposed to deliver everything today and my sister, Gwen, was going to be at the house to meet them. I'm sure that by the time I get there everything will be complete chaos." She sighed. "I dread all the work, but it'll be wonderful to get out of that cramped apartment and have a home of our own." She glanced around the room, her gaze searching for a familiar dark-haired child and she added, "Is Joy ready? We've got a long drive ahead of us."

"She's helping store things away," the director answered, "but she can go with you now. Don't work too hard and have a nice Easter."

"Thanks," Lynn said. "You, too." Then she crossed the room to join her daughter.

As they went outside together, Joy skipped along the sidewalk. Her long brown locks billowed away from her head and excitement danced in her sky blue eyes. "Hurry, Mommy," she insisted as she paused at the end of the walk and turned to glance over her shoulder. "I want to see how Mary Louise likes our new bedroom."

Lynn laughed as she reached the car and opened the door for Joy to scoot inside. "I'm sure Mary Louise likes it just fine," she replied, referring to the doll named after the great-aunt who had given it to Joy last Christmas.

Joy didn't exactly bounce, but she did squirm impatiently on the seat beside her mother as Lynn headed out of Savannah toward the interstate. Lynn cast a sideways glance at the child and chuckled inwardly. She knew that it wasn't her concern about Mary Louise's acceptance of their new home that possessed Joy's thoughts as much as the thrill of moving to the country, just down the road from her cousins, not to mention the fact that her Uncle Cal had promised to give her a puppy of her very own just as soon as they were properly settled.

No puppies for me, Lynn mused as she reached the interstate, but there were other rewards for her. She would be living near her sister in a healthy country environment, and she was now the proud owner of a farm of her very own! On second thought, she decided a bit sheepishly, she was probably even more impatient than the ebullient four-year-old beside her.

The next six weeks would be the hardest. There would be the long drive each day to and from Savannah as she finished the school term at the elementary school where she taught second grade. The early rising and long drive wouldn't be easy on Joy, either, but they would manage somehow. There were also the multitude of things that would need attention at their new home . . . settling in, having a garden tilled and planted, seeing that fences were repaired and, she hoped, if the money held out, building a barn.

By summer, though, the pace shouldn't be quite so hectic. Although there would still be plenty of work to do around their new home, at least there would be the free time in which to do it. And fortunately, next fall she would be able to teach in the small community of Williamsboro, only ten miles away, while Joy attended kindergarten.

"Do I still go to Penny's grandmother's house tonight?" Joy asked, interrupting Lynn's reverie.

Lynn smiled and nodded. "Yes. I know you're eager to try out your new bedroom, sweetheart, but it won't be ready tonight. There'll be boxes stashed everywhere. But by the time you get back day after tomorrow, I promise it will be finished, and then you and Mary Louise will feel right at home. Okay?"

Joy nodded. "Okay. Can I bring my puppy then, too?"

"Let's wait a few days on that," Lynn suggested. "We need to get things livable for ourselves before a puppy comes to live with us."

It was after five-thirty when they arrived at their new home. Lynn swung her red Chevy into the dirt drive and parked in front of the garage next to Gwen's station wagon. They got out of the car and while Joy scampered toward the front porch of the white frame house, Lynn flexed her slightly stiff muscles and paused long enough to gaze around her with immense satisfaction. In the front yard stood a mimosa tree and beyond the fence stood a sentinel of pines. Behind the house was the open space where she intended to have a barn and a garden. Beyond that were more pines, hers, and beyond them, though it couldn't be seen, a field.

At last her gaze returned to the house itself. It was not large or elegant by any standard. But it was sturdily built and had ample room in comparison to the apartment they had just vacated back in Savannah. A few yards from the house was the large garage, and built on the back of it was a separate bedroom and bath. Near its entrance stood a peach tree.

Slowly, Lynn made her way across the lawn, up the steps, across the front porch and into the house. Just as she had expected, she encountered a scene of total confusion, with boxes and bags stacked everywhere. Four children also occupied the room. On the sofa were Joy and Penny. In a cleared space in the center of the floor was Patrick, Penny's twin, and their two-year-old brother Kenny. Patrick was attempting to help the younger boy build something with blocks.

"Hi, kids," Lynn greeted them. She bent to ruffle Pat's cotton white hair. "Where's your mom?"

Pat shrugged. "In the kitchen, I think."

Lynn unzipped her large purse and extracted a paper bag. "I brought you all a little something," she said as she handed the sack to Pat. "Now everybody share, okay?"

"Candy," Kenny said plainly, eyeing the bag with a gleam in his hazel eyes. "Give *me!*"

Lynn headed toward the kitchen, leaving the children to divide the candy and knowing it would be done with mathematical precision by five-year-old Patrick. Already he showed an aptitude for numbers and with his even-tempered and fair-minded personality, he would make certain that each child received an equal portion of the treat.

Gwen Jennings, dressed in slacks and a flowery maternity smock, was stacking bowls into a cupboard. Her short brown hair was slightly mussed, as though she had not found the time to comb it, but her smile was serene and calm as she looked up to see her twin coming through the door. Except for the fact that Gwen's middle was quite large, due to her being seven-and-a-half-months pregnant, and that her hair was cropped a manageable short length instead of long like Lynn's, the two women were identical in looks. Still, Lynn never quite thought so. In her estimation, her sister, at twenty-seven, appeared a bit younger and more innocent looking than she did, even though it was Gwen who was the mother of three children and would soon have a fourth. There had always been a gentle air of dewy-eyed wonder about Gwen that Lynn lacked.

Now Gwen paused in her self-appointed chore.

"You must have burned up the highway," she said as she peered at her watch. "I didn't expect you for another half hour."

Lynn grinned. "I suppose I did, a bit. Joy and I were both eager to get here. Did everything go all right with the movers?"

Gwen nodded. "No hitches. They were here by ten and, as far as I can tell, not a single thing has been broken or scratched. Of course I haven't had time to unpack all the boxes."

"I didn't expect you to unpack *any* of them," Lynn scolded. "Sit down and rest right now. You know all I wanted you to do was just be here to show the men where to place things."

Gwen laughed softly even though she obediently sat down on a kitchen chair. "If I'd been home all day," she pointed out in a reasonable tone, "I'd have been working, so I couldn't see any point in just *sitting* in the middle of all this mess. Besides, I really didn't do too much. I found some sheets and made up your bed, stored a few major necessities in the bathroom and unpacked a few dishes. That's all, I swear."

The fierce scowl that had been on Lynn's face faded and she sank into a chair on the opposite side of the table. "Well, thanks, sis. You're great. It was a big help. I just don't want you getting too tired, that's all."

"I'm fine," Gwen insisted. "I stretched out on the sofa for about an hour after lunch while the kids were napping. Speaking of which," she added as she lifted her head in a listening gesture, "I don't hear any. Did they go outside?"

Lynn shook her head. "I brought candy. Their mouths are probably too stuffed right now for them to make any noise."

"And right before suppertime!" Gwen complained. "Really, Lynn, sometimes you're just as bad as they are!"

Lynn grinned unrepentantly. "Well, today's special. I knew they'd be here with you, and Joy is so excited about coming to live near her cousins. I figured it wouldn't hurt to spoil them just a little."

Gwen grinned back. "I suppose it's all right for once," she relented. "They'll be a little late having dinner, anyway. Cal promised we'd stop and buy hamburgers before heading to Valdosta. By the way, I've already packed Joy's clothes."

"I appreciate your taking her along," Lynn said. "I'll be able to get a lot more done around here without having to concentrate on keeping up with her."

"Of course," Gwen said simply. "And you know Cal's mother doesn't mind. She just thinks of Joy as another one of her brood of grandchildren."

Lynn nodded. Between Cal and his four brothers and sisters, they had already presented Mrs. Jennings with fourteen grandchildren. "It's too bad you can't stay there for Easter, though," she commented.

Gwen shrugged. "It doesn't matter. At least we'll have a couple of days with her like this. I'd rather come back home anyway before Cal's sisters and their children get there. I like them all, but can you imagine how wild it would be with that many people in one house? She only has one bathroom and we'd even have to *sleep* in shifts!"

They both laughed at that. Then Lynn said, "I would have enjoyed going to Atlanta and visiting Aunt Mary for Easter, but I just didn't see how I could afford the time and get settled in here, too."

"I know," Gwen replied. "But she understands

how it is, even though she was disappointed that neither of us could make it this time. I talked with her a couple of days ago. Which reminds me," she grimaced, "our phone has gone on the blink again. Cal was supposed to report it when he went into town today."

"They're supposed to install mine next week. Maybe they'll fix yours at the same time and make one trip out here to do it."

"I imagine so," Gwen agreed. She glanced around the room at the stack of unpacked boxes. "I hate to go off and leave you all alone with all this."

"Don't worry about it," Lynn said. "I'll get it all done eventually. And John promised to come up tomorrow for the day and help me."

Gwen frowned and studied her twin's face intently. "John Simpson is a nice man, Lynn. I like him. But I really don't like the situation. It isn't right and you know it."

Lynn tensed. Her sister was touching on a sensitive subject and it made her uncomfortable. "I haven't done anything wrong," she said defensively.

"I didn't mean to imply that you had," Gwen told her. "All the same, you know deception is wrong and I think he really cares about you. The point is, what are you going to do about things?"

Lynn averted her eyes from her sister's probing gaze. "I'll deal with that problem when the time comes." Quickly, in order to change the discussion to something less guilt producing, she asked, "Has Cal decided yet when he'll be able to start plowing?"

"Probably Monday afternoon, maybe Tuesday. It depends on how much work he has facing him at the shop."

Lynn nodded. Her brother-in-law, who farmed his own land, had leased hers also. Besides the timber crops, there was also a field in which he planned to grow soybeans. But Cal also worked part-time in town as a mechanic of farm implements, so his time was divided between his various jobs. "Has he heard of anybody who might be willing to come to work for me yet?"

Gwen shook her head. "No, he's been asking around, but to tell the truth he thinks it might be difficult to find someone willing to work full time on a temporary basis. You may have to wait until school's out and hire some teenaged boys to help you." Awkwardly, she struggled to her feet. "I'd better leave. Cal's probably home by now and ready to pack the car and get on the road."

Lynn felt a strange sense of abandonment after her sister and the children were gone. The unfamiliarity of her new home and the deep silence of a country night combined to stab her with unaccustomed loneliness and a feeling that something was lacking in her life . . . some vague, unnamed thing. *It was ridiculous,* she chided herself. Only a few hours ago she was filled with elation over her new home and the new life she would lead in it. Now, completely alone, the shining happiness had dimmed.

She didn't like the niggling, unsettled feeling and, with an effort of will, she shook it off as she immersed herself in unpacking. She had far too much work to do to waste time on introspection. For the rest of the evening she worked hard, finding places for the things she unloaded from boxes. By the time she stopped, just after midnight, and finally settled down to eat a solitary supper of bread and canned sausages, she felt satisfied at what she had accomplished and eager to get some rest.

The next morning she got up early, donned a pair of jeans and a long-sleeved plaid shirt to ward off the early morning chill and, after a breakfast of coffee and toast, set to work again. With the coming of day the senseless, unfathomable yearnings of the previous night were entirely banished. Her spirits were high and she hummed happily to herself as she hung frilly pink curtains on the windows of Joy's bedroom.

They were going to be happy here, she thought with sudden intuition. *Really* happy. This was a good place to live a life of usefulness, a place where Joy could grow up in a wholesome atmosphere and develop a deep love for the beautiful nature that surrounded them. Savannah had been a lovely place to live in for the past few years and Lynn was grateful for the opportunities it had provided for her, the friends she had made there and for the gracious charm the old part of the city still imparted, but somehow she had never had the feeling of permanence and belonging there any more than she had had before in California.

At ten, the honking of a horn in the driveway announced that John had arrived. Lynn smoothed her hair with her hands and ran outside to meet him.

"Hi," she called out cheerfully as she descended the porch steps. "Your timing is perfect. I just put on a fresh pot of coffee."

"Sounds good to me," John said as he came toward her. Like her, he was wearing jeans and a long-sleeved casual shirt. His light brown hair looked golden beneath the sunny sky and a smile stretched his lips. "I'm already missing you," he told her as they met in the center of the lawn.

Before Lynn could react, his arms slid around her waist and he pulled her into his arms and kissed her soundly. When they drew apart a moment later, laughter danced in his brown eyes. "Ah ha," he teased. "I caught you off guard. Are you glad to see me?"

Lynn disentangled herself from his arms as she smiled. "Very glad to see you. I need a good, strong man to help me rearrange the furniture that the movers put in the wrong place."

John scowled at her. "I figured as much. All you want is a useful workhorse," he complained.

Lynn laughed. "True, true." She turned toward the house. "Come on in. I can't wait for you to see it now that I've got my things in it."

Inside, John duly admired the house he had only seen once before, when it had been empty. After a brief tour, they went into the kitchen where Lynn poured coffee.

John was an accountant in Savannah. The two of them had met at a dinner party a few months ago. After that it seemed that they were constantly running into one another at an art show or at a restaurant, until finally John invited her out. Lynn had been dubious about the wisdom of it, but he had badgered her into accepting. Since then they had grown to be close friends. She knew all about his divorce and she had confided to him her dream of a country home for herself and her daughter.

"Seems awfully quiet around here without Joy," he commented idly as he spooned sugar into his coffee.

"Too quiet," Lynn said ruefully. "Of course I'm able to get more work done without her interruptions, but I sure did miss her last night. I didn't like sleeping here alone."

"You should have given me a call, then," John said dryly. "I'd have been delighted to come and keep you from having to sleep alone."

Soft color stained Lynn's cheeks. "That's *exactly* why I didn't call you," she shot back. "Besides, I have no telephone yet."

"A whole wasted night when we could have been alone together," John lamented. "I should have followed my impulses and come last night, after all." The teasing tone was abruptly dropped. "We've known each other quite a while now, Lynn. Don't you think it's about time we . . ."

Like a skittish colt, Lynn jumped up from the table and carried her empty cup to the sink. "Please, John," she pleaded in desperation, "let's not go into that now. Not now."

There was a heavy silence behind her and then at last she heard him sigh, scrape back his chair and stand up. "All right," he agreed quietly, "we'll shelve it for the moment." Then in a lighter voice he asked, "What do you want me to do first?"

For the remainder of the day both of them worked hard. John was a great help to Lynn by doing the things that would have been too difficult for her to manage alone and by late afternoon she realized she wouldn't have been able to accomplish even half as much work that day if he hadn't been there. He shifted furniture for her, unpacked boxes, hauled empty ones outside to burn and carried things she didn't need to unpack right away to store in the room just off the garage.

At dusk, Lynn prepared for them a simple meal of broiled chops, baked potatoes and a salad, and they both ate as though they were starved.

Afterward, John wiped the dishes for her as she washed. They shared the task in companionable silence as thick darkness stole over the countryside, cutting them off from the rest of the world.

"I really like it out here," John said as they left the

18

kitchen and moved into the living room. "It's so quiet and peaceful. I can see why you wanted this place."

Lynn nodded and sank wearily onto the sofa. "It's a whole different world from living in a city, isn't it? No traffic, no hustle and bustle. Just fresh air and solitude." She yawned involuntarily. "I bet I'll sleep well tonight."

John nodded and sat down beside her, stretching out his arm along the back of the sofa behind her shoulders. "So will I. I'm tired, too." He paused and then added in a different tone, "I suppose you want me to leave?"

Lynn turned her head to look at him with apologetic eyes. "I'm sorry, John, but I . . ."

John cut her off and his eyes were dark and serious as he met her gaze. "You didn't want to discuss it this morning," he pointed out. "Nor the last time I brought it up. But we have to talk about it, Lynn. I've been very patient with you up to now, I think, letting you really get to know me, not pushing you in any way. But we can't go on forever like this and you know it." His hand left the back of the sofa and fell lightly on her shoulder. "I love you, Lynn. And I want to marry you. And because I really care about you I haven't pushed you. I didn't want to scare you away. But I'm a man, Lynn, with a man's needs. I want to sleep with you, to make love to you. Surely by now you've had plenty of time to make up your own mind about how you feel about me. I won't be put off any longer."

Hot tears rose up in her eyes. Tears of regret and of frustration. She had known that the day of reckoning would come sometime, and she had told Gwen only yesterday that she would deal with it when it arrived. Well, she thought, here it was, and

Lynn was no more prepared for it than she ever had been. And yet John was waiting, watching, demanding with his quiet gaze an answer that he most surely deserved.

But as much as she cared for him, Lynn could not bring herself to tell him the truth that she had so carefully concealed for years. She lowered her gaze from his face, unable to look at him anymore and stared down instead at her tightly laced hands while she struggled for words. "You're a wonderful man, John," she began in a soft voice. "And I'm deeply honored that you want to marry me. I care a great deal about you, I honestly do, but I'm not sure that what I feel is love. I *want* to love you," she lifted her eyes briefly to his face before lowering her lashes once more to shield them, "but I have to be certain before I make a commitment of any kind. You have been more than patient with me, I realize that, and I know I can't expect you to keep coming around forever when I'm not ready to let our relationship grow. But I just can't. Not yet, anyway."

"Are you telling me that you don't want to see me anymore?" he asked in a tense voice.

Lynn forced herself to look at him again and she shook her head. "No," she said earnestly, "because I do. I enjoy being with you. But there are reasons why I can't marry anyone just yet . . . or go to bed with you. So . . ." She shrugged wearily. "Whether we continue to see each other under the circumstances is entirely up to you. I can't blame you if you don't want to see me again."

John rubbed his forehead with an agitated gesture. "You're not making sense, Lynn. Why can't you marry me? Why can't you let me make love to you? You're a grown woman and you should live like a woman is meant to live. It all sounds like delaying tactics to me. Is there another man? Is that it . . . that I'm competing with someone else?"

"No!" Lynn stated emphatically. "You're not competing with anyone, believe me! It's just . . . I just can't explain right now. But maybe some-day . . ."

"That's not good enough!" John got to his feet and glowered down at her. "Someday isn't good enough, Lynn! The problem is that I've been too easy-going, just letting things slide and not pushing you to make any decisions you weren't ready to make, but no more. I'm going to leave now. Maybe a couple of weeks apart will give you a better perspective about your feelings for me and whether we'll have any sort of relationship after that. If so, fine. If not, then it will be good-bye. But that's my time limit. A vague someday just isn't going to work."

Without another word, without giving her any time to respond, John turned and went out the door, into the night.

Lynn checked the urge to run after him. She hated their parting this way and yet, she acknowledged to herself, perhaps it was for the best. John deserved better than she could give him and if she went after him there was nothing she could say that could make things right between them.

She sighed as she heard his car leave the drive, but she made no effort to move from her position on the sofa. He had given her two weeks. Lynn hated ultimatums, and yet in her heart she couldn't blame John for issuing it. He was within his rights when he said their relationship couldn't continue on the same course it had taken thus far. No man could be satisfied for long with only hand holding or an occasional kiss, and it was unrealistic to expect it. And yet, things being as they were, she knew that in two weeks time her answer would have to be the same as it had been tonight. John was a good man, and she was going to lose him and she couldn't do a single thing about it. She needed time for that . . . time he wasn't going to give her.

She should have taken some sort of action years ago, instead of just allowing things to drift along. But she had felt she had no choice if she wanted to protect herself and Joy. And yet she had probably been foolish. Bringing things out into the open might never have mattered at all. It was only that she had been afraid to take the chance.

Soon, though, she really would do something. The truth was that while she was really fond of John Simpson, she wasn't in love with him, and though she would miss his presence in her life, she really didn't care enough to tell him the facts and ask him to wait for her. But one day a man might come into her life—a man she could love—and the same situation, the same problem would exist. Then what?

She had no idea how long she sat there lost in thought, but she knew that some time had passed before she heard the sound of a vehicle pulling into the drive. Lynn jumped swiftly to her feet and went toward the door. It could be John returning, she speculated, though after the angry way he had departed it rather surprised her that he would come back. Still, it didn't sound like his car.

All at once she felt a twinge of fright as she realized just how isolated and alone she was here. She didn't even have a telephone to reach the outside world if she needed help. Then, telling herself that her fears were ridiculous and that if she were going to be a country woman she would have to become brave and self-reliant, Lynn squared her shoulders, flipped on the porch light and stepped outside. More than likely it was someone coming to apply for the job of temporary help.

An unfamiliar pale blue pickup truck had come to a stop in the driveway and it gleamed like silver ice in the dim illumination that spilled from the porch. A man opened the door and stepped down to the ground.

Something about the shape of the tall, lean body struck a chord in Lynn's memory and, when the man turned slowly to face her, she gasped in utter shock. A chill crept up her spine and for an instant she swayed. Her legs went so weak she thought they might buckle beneath her.

The man placed his hands on his hips as his eyes took in the sight of her standing beneath the glowing porch light. For a long moment neither of them spoke and then, at last, the husband she had not seen in five-and-a-half years said mildly, "Hello, Lynn. Surprised to see me?"

A feeling of helplessness swamped her as though she were struggling in a frightening nightmare. *And surely this was just a bad dream,* she told herself. But still, there he stood, looking solid and real, as fingers of light touched his face and arms.

"What are you doing here, Drew?" she asked ungraciously when she finally found her voice. "What do you want?"

He shrugged his shoulders. "Nothing particularly."

"How did you find me?" Lynn's voice was cold and curt, masking the fear that quivered within her.

A slow smile flitted across Drew's mouth. "Your Aunt Mary told me when I visited her in Atlanta. I decided I'd like to see you, so I bought this truck," he waved a hand to indicate the vehicle in the drive, "came down, asked directions in town and here I am! The man at the service station told me that you're looking for a hired hand."

"So?"

"So . . . I'm your man," he replied calmly, just as though he might have been speaking of the weather. He turned, reached into the bed of the truck and lifted out a suitcase. Then he strode purposefully toward the house and back into her life.

Chapter Two

"You are," Andrew Marcus queried pleasantly, "going to invite me in, aren't you? Surely the least a man can expect after not seeing his wife for so many years is a cup of coffee?"

Bemused, Lynn suddenly realized he had spoken. For endless moments after he had mounted the porch steps and joined her, she simply drank in his unexpected appearance. He wore dark corduroy slacks and a creamy white polo sweater. His thick, jet black hair was slightly mussed, lending a rakish air to the face it framed. Reinforcing that impression was a crooked, mocking smile on the full, sensual lips and the teasing squint of dark blue eyes beneath quizzical eyebrows. He was just as she remembered him: so tall that she felt absurdly tiny by comparison, so strong with rock-hard shoulders and a wide chest that he seemed almost overpowering. His long, lean legs, tapering down from narrow hips, gave a suggestion of unleashed energy. He had scarcely changed at all during the years since she had last seen him, except that perhaps now the creases that dented his cheeks when he smiled were a bit deeper than before and there were a few more faint lines across his forehead.

"It looks like the cat's got your tongue," Drew observed with a hint of amusement coating his voice. "But," he added, "I'll bet I've got a surefire way to help you find it." Swiftly, like a pouncing panther, he dropped the suitcase, moved across the space that separated them, pulled her into his arms and before she could react, soundly kissed her.

The shock of it jerked Lynn out of her reverie. In protest, she shoved against the hardness of his chest and twisted her body in an effort to free herself from his grasp. The pressure of his lips on hers was intense and though she struggled, she could not move her face away from his because one of his hands had firmly secured the back of her head. The assaulting kiss seemed to go on forever despite her efforts to end it. A surging warmth began to spread slowly through her being, a tingling sensation that she had all but forgotten could even exist. It was a silent call from deep within her, a responsive chord that could not be quelled.

Gradually, she relaxed against him, ceasing the futile struggle. Drew, sensing the change in her, loosened his punishing hold on her. Now his hands caressed her back and his kiss grew gentle and sweet. Lynn's lips parted, now returning his kiss with instinctive gladness as her arms slid around his chest. Her heart was thudding as though she had just raced up a hill and against her breast she could feel the answering throb of his own.

At last they drew apart and gazed at each other

wonderingly. A tiny half-smile was on Drew's lips as he looked at her. "Well, well," he said almost in surprise, "now that's the sort of greeting a man dreams about. If I didn't know better, I'd almost be inclined to think you were happy to see me."

The mocking tone of his voice brought Lynn back to her senses and she was suddenly appalled at what had just happened. She lifted a trembling hand to her lips, as though to wipe away his kisses and then she said stiffly, "You caught me off guard, that's all! And let me warn you, Drew, you'd better not try anything like that again!"

"No? And if I do?"

Hot anger swept over her. "You may think it's nothing but a funny joke, showing up here out of the blue like this and shocking me half to death, but I'm not laughing." She pointed toward his suitcase and added, "You certainly can't stay here, so why don't you just say what you came to say and be on your way?"

"What's the matter, darling wife?" Drew taunted with maddening composure. "Are you afraid of what might happen between us if I do stay?" Insolently, his eyes raked over her, noting the tight fit of her jeans over full hips and the stretching fabric of her shirt that curved over her breasts.

"Not at all," she snapped. But she was afraid— deathly afraid, though her fear had nothing at all to do with the physical attraction that he had just proved still existed between them. It came from another source altogether.

All at once, Drew dropped his bantering manner. His eyes grew serious and the teasing smile faded. "We have to talk, Lynn. Even you have to acknowledge the truth of that."

Lynn swallowed hard. A lump was lodged firmly

in her throat and defeat sagged her shoulders. He knew after all. Incredible as it seemed after all these years, Drew knew the truth. She supposed he must have learned it from Aunt Mary and now she felt utterly betrayed. She would have staked her very life on her aunt's loyalty in keeping her secret for her, just as she knew that Gwen would never tell. *So why now?* she wondered. Why had Aunt Mary exposed her now?

Drew waited quietly for her response and at last Lynn nodded and said dully, "All right. Come in, then, and we'll talk. But after that, you'll have to leave. You can't stay here."

Drew didn't answer. He picked up his suitcase and followed her inside the house where he deposited it beside the front door. Then he paused and glanced around the room.

"Nice house," he commented idly. "I understand you've just moved in."

"Yes. Only yesterday as a matter of fact."

Drew nodded. "It looks very homey, very comfortable. Quite different from our house in Los Angeles."

At that, Lynn laughed shortly. "House? Mansion is my word for it." Curiously, she asked, "Do you still live in it?"

"Yes, I do. Well," he gave her an encouraging smile, "what about that coffee? I really could use some. I'm pretty stiff after the long drive from Atlanta."

"All right." Lynn went toward the kitchen, glad to have something concrete on which to center her attention.

She scooped coffee grounds into the basket and poured water into the coffee maker. When she turned around it was to find Drew leaning against the door frame, his arms crossed as he lazily observed her every movement.

Nervously, she managed a grin. "No Mrs. Watson here to wait on us or to serve fresh-baked pastries. But I do have a bag of store-bought cookies. Want some? Or maybe a sandwich?"

Drew shook his head, pushed himself away from the door and went to sit down at the table. "No, thanks. I'm not hungry." His gaze flickered around the large, old-fashioned room with its linoleum-covered floor and white-painted cupboards and at last it came back to Lynn as she set out cups and saucers. "This house suits you, I think. More than the other house ever did."

"Meaning I was a field primrose in an orchid hothouse environment?" she asked tartly.

"Touché." Drew grinned. "It wasn't what I meant, however. You always looked perfectly beautiful in the gilded setting. But you hated it all, didn't you? You'd prefer this instead any day of the week, wouldn't you?" His hand swept in an arc, indicating the room.

Lynn shrugged and quickly turned her back to him. She reached into a cupboard for the sugar bowl. "It wasn't that I didn't like the house, exactly," she admitted slowly. "But it didn't need me. It had Mrs. Watson and the maids and the gardener. I felt like I was only an ornament there, something to be picked up and dusted occasionally."

"Is that the reason you ran away?"

The question was dropped like a small bomb and Lynn went rigid. Did that mean he *didn't* know after all? *Perhaps he really didn't,* she thought with sudden hope singing in her heart. Surely if he did he would already have brought up the subject by now. She relaxed a little and some of the tension left her.

She should have know that Aunt Mary would never give her away. Thank goodness there were no telltale toys strung around the house yet, and what a good stroke of fortune it was that Joy had gone away with Gwen's family just at this particular time! If she was careful, she just might get away with keeping her long-held secret.

The coffee was ready and Lynn picked up the server and carried it to the table where she poured both cups full of the steaming, aromatic brew. She sat down opposite Drew before replying.

"At this late date I really don't see much sense in going into reasons and rehashing the long-dead past. It's over and done with."

"True," Drew agreed unexpectedly. "I wouldn't bring back the past if I could. Only today, now, this minute has any importance." Leaving his coffee black, he lifted the cup to his lips and took a sip. "So," he continued in a light, conversational tone a moment later, "tell me how you've been, Lynn? Are you teaching again?"

"Yes. Second grade in Savannah. Next fall, though, I'll have a job teaching in Williamsboro, so that will be nice because it'll be close to home."

"I remember that teaching was very important to you," Drew mused thoughtfully. "Maybe you'd have been happier in L.A. if you'd had a job there."

"You didn't want me to work, remember?"

A twinkle lit Drew's eyes, the deep, sky blue so incredibly like Joy's. "I remember a lot of things," he said. "Like how it felt with you beside me in bed and the way you had of curling up into a little ball next to me like a kitten and . . ."

Soft color stole into Lynn's cheeks. "That's quite enough," she said with a harsh grate to her voice. There were certain things she had long since put out of her mind and she was not about to sit here and allow Drew to dredge up old memories that were best forgotten. "Tell me about yourself," she commanded. "Are you still involved with all your real estate ventures?"

Drew nodded. "We just recently completed a new high-rise office complex."

"Congratulations," Lynn said a bit dryly. "I suppose by now you must be one of the wealthiest men in the entire state of California."

He shrugged indifferently. "I suppose I am," he acknowledged. "But wealth by itself doesn't have a lot of meaning for a man who is without a wife and family to spend it on."

He was deliberately baiting her and Lynn resented it. To gain time, she picked up her coffee cup and took several sips. Then, with a casual laugh, she said, "I'm sure that isn't an insurmountable problem. There must be a lot of beautiful women who are delighted to allow you to spend your money on them."

"Perhaps so," he conceded. "But I'm certain that probability doesn't bother you in the least."

"Why should it?" She shrugged.

"Why, indeed, since you're the one who did the leaving. Was our marriage so distasteful, Lynn, that you had to run away from me?"

She couldn't meet his eyes. She feared that if she did he might be able to read the truth in hers. "It wasn't exactly distasteful," she murmured as she gazed down at the table. "But I just didn't fit into your life, Drew, and you know it."

"I know nothing of the sort," he contradicted flatly. "We seemed to get along all right. Our sex life was grand. We enjoyed each other's company. As to fitting into my life, you seemed to do that perfectly.

You were a superb hostess and you got along well with my friends and business associates."

Lynn shifted uncomfortably in her chair. Drew wasn't buying her explanation and it was essential that he do so. "I may have seemed to fit in," she said, "but I did so with an effort. Learning to play bridge and spending idle days with your friends' wives, playing golf or tennis or going on endless shopping jaunts. But there was nothing concrete in my life, Drew. There was nothing important with which to fill my days."

Drew laughed harshly, and the bitter sound of it surprised her into looking at him once more. There was an unpleasant curve to his lips. "Most men I know work hard to give their wives that kind of life-style because it's what they want and expect. I had to go and get a woman to whom it all meant nothing. Even my love for you wasn't enough to hold you."

"I'm sorry, Drew," she said simply. And she was deeply sorry that their marriage hadn't worked . . . sorrier than he would ever realize. She had loved him, too, and oddly enough, in spite of the necessity of leaving him, she had never once doubted his love for her. She had also never doubted that she had done the right thing by leaving him. But still, there was a twinge of pain over all that they had lost.

There was a long minute of silence while they both became engrossed in their own private thoughts about the past, about what might have been and yet never could be. The only sound was a slight breeze stirring the leaves of a tree near the opened window above the sink.

After a time it was Drew who shook off his thoughts first and spoke again. "Well, I could go for another cup of coffee." He stretched his arms outward from his body in a weary gesture before brushing his hand across his eyes. "I guess I'm more tired than I thought I was."

Lynn, glad at the interruption of her thoughts, picked up the coffee server and poured. She mustered up the polite smile of a hostess and asked, "Are you sure you wouldn't like something to eat?"

"I'm sure," Drew said as he pulled the saucer and cup toward him. "Thanks, anyway." In a tone of voice that was casual and completely unrelated to the intimate subject of a few minutes ago, he asked, "Tell me, what made you decide to buy a place like this in the country?"

Lynn spooned sugar into her own cup of coffee. "Mostly for an investment," she replied. "I never had used the money Dad left me. And also, I like it here in the country and now I'm close to Gwen. She and Cal have their own farm only a half mile down the road."

"That does make it nice," Drew acknowledged. "At least you won't ever be really lonely. But what are you going to do? Surely you aren't seriously intending to farm this place alone?"

Lynn laughed and shook her head. "No, I know my limitations. I've leased the fields to Cal. He'll farm my land along with his. And we're hoping in time to make the timber acreage pay off."

"If Cal's going to use your land, then why do you need another man to help you out?"

"I only want someone temporarily," she told him. "There are some fences that need repairs, I want to have a garden plot tilled and get a barn built. Things like that. As busy as Cal is, I couldn't possibly ask him to do all that for me."

Drew nodded with understanding. "It sounds like there's a lot of work ahead of you."

"Yes, but I don't mind. I enjoy staying busy and I think this will be a good place to live. I'm even planning," she added with sudden laughter dancing in her gray eyes, "to raise some poultry."

Drew chuckled appreciatively. "The egg lady, hmm? I have to admit, Lynn, that you've got depths to you I never suspected even existed."

Lynn giggled. "Let's just say I *hope* the depths are there! To tell you the truth, I'm a little bit afraid I may have taken on more than I can handle." She sighed. "I suppose only time will tell whether I made the right decision or not by buying this place."

"You probably did," he told her. "As far as I'm concerned, real estate is hardly ever a bad investment. Even if you discover you don't want to live here later on, you're bound to make a nice profit if you sell it, especially after you've made improvements."

"Thanks," she said with genuine gratitude. "I've been saying the same thing to myself, but it helps to hear it from an expert."

Their gazes met and held. Some emotion Lynn could not define darkened Drew's eyes and a strange yearning rose within her, squeezing at her heart. They remained sitting across the table from one another, their bodies not touching and yet an invisible bond imprisoned them with a glance. The years melted away. This was the only man she had ever loved in all her life, and though she had told herself many times that the love must be dead and decently buried so that she could get on with the business of her future without him, suddenly she was not so certain that she had actually accomplished that objective. Old desires and poignant longings tugged at her senses, betraying the wisdom of the decision she had made so long ago. And yet, she knew if she had to make that choice again she would do the exact same thing she had done before when she walked out of his house and out of his life. For Joy, every sacrifice was justified.

At the thought of her daughter, renewed fear crept over her like a chilling fog. Lynn wrenched her gaze from Drew's with a determined effort. She picked up her spoon, eyed it blankly, then replaced it on the saucer. "Why did you come here, Drew?" she asked bluntly. She tensed with dread and nervousness, waiting for the answer that would surely come, even though only a short time ago she had almost convinced herself that she was safe. Now she had to know. "Have you come to tell me that you're going to file for a divorce? Or that perhaps you've already divorced me? Or did you come for an entirely different reason?" She caught her breath and held it as she waited. She couldn't possibly have given him a better opening.

Drew's gaze on her was pensive, as though by studying her face he could read the secret she had held so long. The silence became, for Lynn, almost unbearable and she thought that if he didn't answer soon she would scream from anxiety. But at last he gave his head a slight shake and shrugged his shoulders with indifference. "I haven't been bothered by the peculiar marital state I've found myself in . . . married, yet not a husband. But I have wondered why you never set legal action into motion. After all, you're the one who decided you didn't want to stay with me. How come you've never done it?"

Now it was Lynn's turn to shrug. If she acted casual, perhaps Drew would suspect nothing, if in truth he actually knew nothing. "I just never got around to it, that's all," she answered, striving for a light touch. "But I assure you I won't stand in the way of a divorce if you want it."

"Is that what you want?" he asked quietly.

Was it? Lynn was taken aback by the question. It was something she had never really bothered to ask herself. In the beginning it had been impossible, of course. And later a nagging disquiet had kept her from ending their farce of a marriage. She had been terrified that if she initiated proceedings he would find her. But he had done just that, anyway, despite her careful efforts to hide.

Abruptly, she laughed. "At this late date it's immaterial to me, Drew. We haven't lived as man and wife for a long time now. Like you, I haven't felt constricted over the limbo state of being married, yet not married. Suit yourself. If you'd like a divorce, then by all means, get it. I won't contest it and neither will I ask for any settlement from you. I've managed just fine all these years without any of your money."

"That's right, you have," he agreed blandly. But a flicker of anger flared in his eyes and his mouth took on a set, bitter look. "From the day you walked out, you've never wanted anything at all from me . . . neither my support nor my love. I'm amazed that divorce or no divorce, you're still going by the name of Marcus. I would have thought you'd have discarded it along with everything else about our marriage."

"And how do you know I didn't?" she asked tightly.

Drew permitted himself only the smallest of smiles. "The man at the service station in town knew your name," he explained. "Also, it's painted on the mailbox by the road."

36

Lynn had no intention of getting into a discussion concerning her reasons for maintaining his name. Her nerves were stretched tautly and she felt she had endured enough for one evening . . . first the scene with John, then the overwhelming shock of seeing Drew again . . . all of it piled on top of a long and arduous day of work. She pushed back her chair and got to her feet.

"It's getting late," she said pointedly. "I've had a hard day, I'm tired and I want to go to sleep. It's been nice seeing you again, Drew, but I think you should leave now."

Drew also got to his feet but in a more languid fashion. Amusement played across his face and lurked in his eyes as he rounded the table until he stood just in front of her. "You're uncommonly anxious to get rid of me, aren't you?" he asked with a little laugh. "I wonder why?"

Again, the cold fear of discovery climbed Lynn's back. With desperation, she tried not to show it. "Does there have to be a reason?" she countered. "You're not part of my life anymore, Drew. That's all there is to it."

"Correction," he said softly. "I'm still your husband." He lifted a hand and brushed her hair away from her face with a feather-light touch. "Have I told you," he asked in a voice that was barely above a whisper, "that I still think you are most beautiful?"

His gaze was hypnotic and Lynn quivered as his fingers traced the contours of her face. "Please, don't," she pleaded faintly. "Don't do this, Drew."

"Don't do what?" he murmured quizzically. He was bending toward her, his lips, soft and sensual, dangerously close to hers.

"This!" Her voice was sharp. "Don't touch me or say things like this!"

"Who has a better right than your husband?" he asked. All the same, he drew back and his eyes glinted with mockery. "You *are* afraid of me," he said. "I felt you tremble just then. You're afraid to be with me even after all these years because you know that I've only got to touch you in the slightest way to make your body respond with unbridled passion."

His disturbing proximity made Lynn breathless. *And damn him*, she thought crossly, *he was right*, though she would have died before admitting the truth of what he said. Strength, borne of both anger and fear, rose to the surface. Roughly, she pushed his hand away from her face and her eyes were stormy and determined as she glared at him. "Leave me alone, Drew! Go away from here and leave me alone. Our marriage ended a long time ago and so did the passion. They're only cold ashes now and you can't fan them back to life just because it suited you to breeze in here and try. Like I said, I really am exhausted and I want you to leave so that I can go to bed."

An implacable expression came to his face. Drew crossed his arms and nodded. "Fine. I'm tired, too. But if you think I'm driving all the way to Savannah tonight just to hunt down a motel room, you're quite mistaken. And I doubt Williamsboro even has one. So, unless you want to share your bed with me, I suggest you offer me another. I imagine you've got a spare bed I can use for just one night."

She saw that he meant what he said. A feeling of utter helplessness washed over her. She had completely lost control of the situation, here in her very own home, and yet Lynn knew there was not one single thing she could do about it. Drew flatly refused to leave tonight and it was a physical impossibility for her to force him to do so. They both realized that.

At last she sucked in a ragged breath and nodded. "All right," she agreed dully. "I'll let you stay in the spare room behind the garage. But only for tonight," she added with a hint of steel in her voice. "The first thing tomorrow morning, you have to leave."

Giving her a mock salute, Drew grinned engagingly. "Whatever you say, Mrs. Marcus. Whatever you say."

Chapter Three

At five-fifteen in the morning, Lynn awoke. Her eyes were gritty with fatigue, but her mind was sharp and clear with the primal instinct of a hunted animal that knows its life is in danger.

She had slept fitfully, awakening several times throughout the night and each time the thought had come to her as a fresh shock. Drew was here; he had found her. And there was the ever-present fear lurking behind the thought. Why was he here? What did he want? What did he intend to do? How much did he know?

Now in the predawn darkness the questions caused Lynn to toss restlessly. Every time she had asked him last night he had neatly avoided giving a direct answer. She'd realized she had been out-maneuvered once she had finally been alone in her own bedroom after she had gone with him to the spare room attached to the garage and put fresh sheets and a blanket on the bed there.

Did he or didn't he know about Joy? She could scarcely assume that Aunt Mary would have betrayed her and actually told him, and yet for the life of her she could think of no other reason why he had come here. He had admitted he hadn't come to seek a divorce, and if that were true there could only be one other reason! But surely if he knew about his daughter's existence he would have at least mentioned it, wouldn't he?

Aunt Mary and Gwen had both told her through the years that she was wrong to conceal from Drew the knowledge that he had a child. Logically, she had always known that they were right, that a day of reckoning might someday come, but even so she had never been able to bring herself to the point of telling him. At first it had been as a measure of protection for her unborn baby, and later it had been to protect her own self-interests. She hadn't wanted him to know because she hadn't wanted to contend with any claims he might have made.

And yet she had told herself at least a thousand times that it was a foolish concern. Drew had not wanted children. He had made that emphatically and unequivocably clear after they were married, so in all likelihood he would never make problems even if he did learn that he was a father. But she couldn't be sure about that and that was what held her silent all these years. There was just no way of being certain how he would react.

Lynn flipped over onto her side, closed her eyes and opened them again at once. It was senseless to stay in bed when she knew that she would not sleep another wink. Wearily, she thrust back the covers, switched on a lamp and got up. Her thoughts chased one another around in her mind like a squirrel in a cage. She might as well allow them the free rein they demanded while she at least enjoyed her morning coffee.

She pulled on her robe, slipped on her house scuffs and went into the kitchen. While the coffee brewed, she moved mechanically to stand before the kitchen window and gazed out. It was still dark, but even so she could make out the blacker outline of the bedroom behind the garage. No light shined from its windows. Unlike her, Lynn thought with sudden bitterness, Drew apparently had no troublesome thoughts to hold his sleep at bay.

Turning impatiently from the window, she glanced around at the peaceful, homey room. Then she nearly laughed aloud. *It was so ironic,* she thought. She had bought this place with the feeling that at last she had found a safe, secure haven for herself and her child. Yet practically the moment she moved in, the one man she had hoped never to see again abruptly reentered her life, smashing to bits the illusion of safety like a bulldozer destroying an unsound building.

Lynn poured her coffee and carried the cup into the living room. She dropped into a comfortable armchair next to a window and watched the sun rise while her mind went back to the brief months of happiness when she had first met and married Andrew Marcus.

She had just finished her first year of teaching in Atlanta when a friend asked her to go on a blind date with a business associate of her fiancé's. Lynn had gone with trepidation because she was leery of blind dates on principle, but she did it as a favor to her friend. Drew had been in town on business and the four of them went out to dinner together. Surprising them both, they had instantly hit it off. She had been overwhelmingly attracted to the strikingly good-looking man from California with the excellent sense of humor. After that, it had been a whirlwind romance, with Drew lingering on after his business was complete and concentrating only on winning her.

Not that it had been at all difficult, she mused now as she watched vivid orange and pink streak the morning sky. She had fallen desperately and completely in love and within a month, despite Aunt Mary's disapproval and Gwen's and Cal's pleas to be sensible and not rush into anything, Lynn and Drew were married. She had answered all their arguments that the two of them scarcely even knew each other with the assurance that they knew everything that was important . . . namely that they loved one another.

And they had indeed loved each other. Their nights together had been ecstatically happy. Drew was a superb lover, a patient teacher, and she, a more than willing pupil when it came to learning the art of lovemaking. She had given herself to him with a delicious sense of wantonness while he gave to her the thrilling fulfillment of being a woman.

Or almost fulfillment, she amended to herself as she sipped at her cooling coffee. Certainly Drew had given her completion in the act of love, but the rest of her life quickly became empty and meaningless. Drew was a wealthy, influential man and he had expected her to live the idle life of a rich man's wife. When she had suggested going to the university to become accredited to teach in California, he had vetoed the idea at once. His wife had no need to seek employment. Lynn had meekly submitted to that decree and because she had wanted to please her new husband in every way, she had taken lessons in bridge and golf and had begun playing tennis again. But even those pleasant diversions could not occupy all of her time, energy or intelligence and she had soon grown bored and restless.

But looking back, Lynn knew that somehow she could have managed to be happy in her new life. She could have found other means to occupy her time and she would never have left him if it had not been for Drew's inexplicable attitude about having a family. Shortly after they were married she had idly brought up the subject one night in the afterglow of lovemaking and he had astonished her by his vehement objections. He didn't want children, he told her. He wanted her all to himself. Lynn had been shocked and devastated by his strange aversion to having a family of their own and she had hoped that in time he might change his mind. She had very much wanted the experience of motherhood first-hand.

However, the one thing she did not have on her side was an abundance of time. They had been married only a bit over three months when she became pregnant. It had not been a deliberate attempt on her part, but all the same, it happened. A doctor confirmed it two months later.

The news had brought to her conflicting emotions. She was both exhilarated at the knowledge that a tiny flame of life was growing within her womb and, at the same time, nervous and filled with dread at having to face Drew with the absolute fact of it. Instead of just coming right out and telling him, she had once again brought up the subject in a general way and that time he had actually become angry with her. His words were burned into her mind for all time. "For God's sake, Lynn, can't you get off that subject? Lots of people have wonderful lives without feeling the necessity to reproduce themselves. Seems like everyone I know has problems with their children, anyway. Someday you'll thank me for sparing you that! If you're so crazy about children, why don't you do some sort of volunteer work with them? That ought to take care of your maternal instincts!"

She had spent two agonizing weeks wondering what to do before she finally made her decision to leave. It was the hardest thing she had ever done in her life, but Drew had left her no choice. He wanted no children and Lynn had had no intentions of bringing her baby into a home where one parent resented the child's existence!

She left while Drew was away on a business trip. She took none of his money, for she had savings of her own besides the money her father had left her at his death. And in her carefully drafted letter to Drew, she made no mention of the child she was going to bear. She had led him to believe that she simply was unhappy with their life in general. Only she knew what that little lie had cost her, or how many tears she had shed as she had written it.

With a start, she came out of her reverie. Inexplicable as Drew's attitude had been, she had sensed that it must have had something to do with his childhood. His mother had died when he'd been too young to even remember her and he was raised by a stern, unaffectionate father who had never remarried. When he died, Drew was still young, barely twenty, and though Mr. Marcus had left his son a fortune, he also left him the legacy of a thoroughly masculine background, untempered by a woman's gentler touch. *Perhaps,* she thought now, *the whole problem had been that Drew simply didn't under-stand a woman's outlook on life.* He had been deprived of a feminine viewpoint while he was in his formative years and certainly it had been evident in more ways than one while she had lived with him. Her desire for routine and continuity escaped his understanding; he thought it hilarious that she actu-ally cared about their food budget and he honestly couldn't understand her objections to either throw-ing a dinner party without notice or packing for an impromptu trip. Drew might have loved her, but he had never understood her . . . nor really even tried.

Sighing, Lynn got to her feet and returned to the kitchen for a second cup of coffee. Morning light now streamed through the window above the sink and a glance at the clock showed that it was past seven. *Drew would probably be waking soon,* she thought, *and coming to the house for breakfast.* And before he came she wanted to be fully dressed. Some inner certainty told her it would be a great deal easier to deal with him this morning if she were clothed in something more substantial than a night-gown and a robe.

Back in the bedroom she dressed in brown slacks and a cotton brown and white striped shirt, which looked somewhat businesslike. Then she quickly brushed her long, dark hair and left it swinging loosely against her shoulders. She didn't bother with makeup, contenting herself only with a light coating of lipstick. She returned to the kitchen and began preparing breakfast.

There was still no sign of Drew by the time she had finished cooking the bacon, eggs and canned biscuits, though the sun had long since been up. Lynn's memory of her life with him reminded her

that Drew had always been an early riser. He must
truly have been tired last night if he was still sleeping
now.

She sat down to eat her own breakfast, keeping
Drew's warm in the oven. But when she had finished
eating and washed the dishes, he still had not come
into the house.

At last, shrugging indifferently, Lynn set to work
in the living room unpacking a box of books and
lining them up on the built-in bookshelves. But
when she had completed that task and unloaded yet
another box that was filled with an odd assortment of
items ranging from sewing needles to stationery to
an outgrown pair of Joy's shoes, she began to get
uneasy. A glance at her watch showed that it was
now past ten. *What on earth,* she wondered, *could be
keeping him?*

Giving in to her curiosity, Lynn left the house and
crossed the few yards between it and the garage. The
air had a clean scent of pine and the sun was warm
on her skin, but she did not pause to enjoy the treat
of a country morning. Resolutely, she approached
the door to the room where Drew had gone last
night.

She knocked loudly. If he was still asleep, then it
was high time he was awakened.

Immediately, Drew responded with a shouted,
"Come in!"

Lynn opened the door and entered the dim interi-
or of the room. The shades were pulled down low
over the windows, blocking out the sunlight, and it
took a moment for her eyes to adjust to the darkness.

And then she saw that Drew was still in bed. Two
pillows were propped beneath his head and his arms
were crossed over the sheet that covered him.

Unexpectedly, her heart lurched. Familiar memories of the time they had lived together assailed her. He looked exactly the same as he had then, when they awakened together, wrapped in each other's arms. His coal black hair, tousled from sleep, was strikingly vivid against the white pillow. His skin had a warm, sleepy flush to it while his eyes drooped languidly. A faint, bluish shadow above his upper lip and along his jaw testified that he needed a shave. And those hands, those strong, capable hands that she knew could be so gentle on a woman's skin, captured her gaze and commanded her fascinated attention.

With a quick, indrawn breath, Lynn regained her composure. She stood rigidly straight beside the door like an alert rabbit ready to dash into hiding at the first hint of peril.

"Do you have any idea what time it is?" she asked in a tone of reproach. "It's already past ten. I made breakfast two hours ago."

"I know," Drew replied. He shifted slightly, as though he were about to sit upright, but then he sank down against the pillow again and moaned. "I'm sorry, Lynn. My wretched back has gone out on me and I just can't get up." Now his voice contained a responding reproach in it. "I thought you were never going to get around to coming out here to check on me."

"Well, how was I to know?" she flared irritably as she moved further into the room. "Darn it, Drew, you *have* to get up. You've got to leave here today. This morning." Renewed fear dried her mouth. This simply couldn't be happening. Joy would be home this evening and Drew *had* to be gone before then. She stared down at him in helpless dismay.

"Tell my back that," Drew muttered testily, "and

I'll be happy to oblige you. I can't say I fancy the idea of being stuck in a garage room for days on end."

"Days?" Her eyes widened now with pure panic.

"You know it could happen," he snapped. "Or have you forgotten everything you ever knew about me?"

His words drew her up short. He did indeed have a trick back. Once it had given out on him when he had lifted an extremely heavy box and that had put him in bed for three days. Another time he had had a spasm that lasted for a day and a half, although not quite so severely that he had needed to stay in bed. In those days, they had laughed about it, for in spite of his pain, Drew had found humor in it, as he had in most things in life. He had said that it wasn't nearly so bad with a wife around to pamper him and to cater to his needs and to give him massages. But this time it was far from amusing. It was the worst possibility Lynn could imagine.

"How did it happen?" she asked in a tight voice.

Drew waved a careless hand toward his trousers that lay in a crumpled heap on the floor. "I had gotten up and was about to get dressed," he told her. "My pants were draped over the back of that chair. When I reached for them they slid to the floor. I bent over to pick them up and that's when it snapped. Now look," he added gruffly as he eyed the displeased expression that was plainly on her face, "I don't like this situation a bit more than you do. How about giving me a massage the way you used to? Maybe that'll help." He quirked one eyebrow at her as he waited for her reply.

Lynn visibly hesitated and she looked at him with suspicion. *Was he really in pain this time,* she wondered, *or was this all some sort of a trick?* There was an odd, devilish gleam in his eyes that she didn't quite trust and yet it was true that her massages had seemed to relieve his pain the other times. She sighed deeply, knowing she had to do it. If he *had* injured his back and if there was a chance that her massage might help speed him on his way, she had to try. She could not bring herself to think about what might happen if he were still here when Joy came home.

With extreme reluctance, she approached the bed. "All right," she said at last. "Turn over. And no funny business," she ordered firmly.

Drew chuckled, but it quickly turned into a moan as he flipped over onto his stomach. "Do I," he asked innocently, "sound like a man who's capable of any funny business?"

Gingerly, Lynn sat down on the edge of the bed. Her voice was tart. "I wouldn't put anything past you," she said.

"No?" The deep, rich voice sounded alert and interested. "Why is that?"

"You convinced me to marry you in short order," she pointed out sternly. "Against all prudent and sensible thought." She knotted her hands, studied them for a moment and then slowly unwinding them, at last placed them on his broad back.

"Umm." Drew closed his eyes as her hands began lightly kneading the smooth, silky skin of his upper back. "Your hands are so soft and warm," he murmured with deep contentment. Then, with a little laugh, he reverted to the topic under discussion. "I'll bet marrying me was the only impulsive thing you ever did in your life."

In spite of herself, Lynn felt the beginnings of a smile. She bit it back, although there was no danger of his seeing it while his eyes remained closed. She had an excellent view of his profile as he reposed against the pillow. "I suppose you're right," she agreed. "You did sort of just storm into my life and sweep me off my feet."

"Just like the fairy tales, only we didn't live happily ever after, did we? You had second thoughts later on. A few months of marriage and you had discovered that you'd made a horrible mistake and married a monster."

"Don't be absurd," she chided softly. Her hands moved in a rhythmic motion over his back, pressing down over corded muscles. Her fingers tingled with strange sensations at such intimate contact, and Lynn struggled to keep her mind off what she was doing. "I never thought you were a monster. You were very good to me, very generous."

"So generous that you were careful to go away without taking a single thing I'd bought you, so good that you couldn't even bear to live with me a full six months." There was a bit of accusation to the words, but not even the slightest hint of hurt or pain or loss.

Lynn nibbled agitatedly at her lower lip. "Let's just say," she hesitated an instant before going on, "let's just say that I had my reasons, Drew, and leave it at that."

"Don't you think," he asked point-blank as he opened his eyes wide and turned his head slightly so that he could look at her, "that even after all this time you might owe me an explanation?"

Her heart hammered as their eyes met and Lynn struggled to maintain a surface calm she was far from feeling. "Perhaps I do," she acknowledged softly, almost more to herself than to him.

"Well?" he prompted after she fell silent.

Lynn shook her head and gave him a faint ghost of a smile. "Not now," she said.

"Then when?"

"I . . . don't know," she admitted truthfully. "Tell me," she hurried on in a desperate attempt to change the subject, "is this helping your back at all?"

"Tremendously." Drew sighed and closed his eyes once more. "I always did say you had velvet hands. Remember?"

"I remember," she said quietly.

"Do you also remember the showers we used to take together?" he asked amiably, just as though he might have been discussing something of no more consequence than taking a stroll on a summer's day. "The way we would soap each other until we were slippery as eels and then we would . . ."

"That's enough!" Lynn's voice was as sharp as a knife's blade. "There's no point in bringing up such things as that."

"Why not?" His tone was mild.

"Because it's in the past and has no bearing on anything now, that's why," she answered emphatically.

Abruptly, Drew turned over on the bed so that he was facing her. Without warning, his arms encircled her and brought her down to his chest. His face was incredibly close to hers so that she could see the widening black depths of his pupils centered within the clear blue irises. "Do they bother you?" he asked softly. "Those memories? Do they remind you of how much we loved each other, how much we enjoyed each other's bodies even to the point where we sometimes had trouble restraining ourselves from touching whenever we were in the company of others? Do they make you wonder whether you should ever have deserted me?" His face came ever closer to hers.

"No!" Lynn gasped, and the sound of it was ragged.

Drew chuckled. The vibrations of it caused the bed to tremble beneath them. "Little liar," he said fondly. "They do all that and more. Just the thought of those times, as well as the fact that I'm touching you right now, is heating your blood." He lightly rained a few kisses on her unsteady, vulnerable lips. "Deny it all you want," he murmured sensually as his mouth brushed softly over hers, "but right now, this very moment, you're wanting me just as much as you ever did."

To prove his statement, his mouth claimed hers once again, now with strength and implacable persistence. Forcibly, he got his way, parting her lips so that his tongue could reach the passion and warmth of hers. One hand caressed her neck and his fingers threaded through her hair at the nape while his other hand slid with ease from her back around to cover her breast.

Flames leapt in Lynn's veins so that instantly she was caught up in the swirling vortex of a moment's passionate excitement. Her hands moved restlessly over his bare chest, rubbing against the crispy dark hair. A shudder raced through her as Drew stroked her breast and even beneath the cloth of her blouse and bra, brought the nipple to a peak.

But he was soon dissatisfied. Using both hands, he tugged her shirt loose from the waistband of her slacks and unbuttoned it. He released her lips long enough to see what he was doing when it came to removing the blouse and the bra. Bemused, Lynn watched him through lash-shuttered eyes as he took one rosy nipple into his mouth while he caressed the other.

She was aroused by the hungry sensations she had long denied herself and an intense ache spread through her lower limbs. She needed desperately to have the craving assuaged, to be released from this burning agony. Her fingers gently ran over his arms and shoulders, then back to his chest as waves of ecstatic, torturous delight swelled and crashed over her.

Drew, with seeming reluctance, at last released her breasts and his eyes smoldered with unbridled desire as he looked at her. He reached up to place a hand lightly behind her head and brought her down for another kiss. As he did, his other hand began fumbling with the snap on her waistband.

Lynn's hand strayed down beneath the sheet in an instinctive movement. It met bare, warm flesh, momentarily surprising her. She had not realized until now that Drew was completely naked.

He was having some difficulty with the zipper at her waist and now he pushed her up and away from his body only slightly and murmured, "You'll have to help me, darling."

At that precise moment, they both became aware of a loud sound outside that intruded upon their drugged senses. It was a vehicle.

"Damn!" The expletive came from Drew. He reached for Lynn. "Just ignore it, baby," he whispered softly.

But before he had completed the sentence, Lynn was off the bed, fumbling hastily and awkwardly as she attempted to hook her bra. She was shaken and for some odd reason had the uncomfortable conviction that she had just narrowly escaped being caught in a terrible mistake.

In only a minute more her shirt had been buttoned and tucked into her waistband and she lifted her hands to smooth her hair as best she could. She moved toward the door and glanced back toward Drew only long enough to say, "As soon as I can, I'll bring you some breakfast." And then she was gone.

Outside, the bright glare of sunlight assaulted her. Lynn was breathless as she skirted the drive and hurried toward the front of the house. A telephone company truck was parked in the driveway just behind Drew's truck.

The young man who stood on the porch smiled pleasantly when he saw her. "Hi. I'd just about decided no one was home. I came to install your telephone."

"I didn't expect you until next week," Lynn told him.

The man shrugged. "I had to come out this way to repair a line so it just seemed a good time."

"Lucky for me I was home this morning," Lynn said conversationally as she opened the front door and they entered the house.

Lucky for her in more than one way, she could not help but reflect after the man set to work and she was alone with her thoughts. Now that she was away from Drew and the magnetism of his seductive charm, she was appalled at how closely she had come to giving herself to him, to embroiling herself in a new emotional involvement with him that she had no business beginning. *That* road could lead only to trouble. She was thankful for the unexpected interruption and for the breathing space it provided her while the telephone installer was there. It gave her an opportunity to think clearly about what she had almost done and of the possible consequences and repercussions that could have resulted from so rash an act. She wanted Drew to leave, and going to bed with him would hardly further that aim.

As soon as she was alone again, she prepared a fresh breakfast to carry out to Drew. The plate she had saved in the oven had now dried into a hard, unappetizing mass. Beneath her arm she also carried an electric heating pad as she balanced a tray in her hands while crossing the yard to the garage.

Drew's eyes sparkled when she entered the room. "Ah, wonderful! Food! I'm starved!" He grinned mischievously and added, "I'd probably be dead from starvation by now if we hadn't been interrupted when we were. But we can take up where we left off after I've eaten. I remember where we were."

Lynn set the tray on the dresser with an irritable little thud, carefully avoiding his eyes. "We're not taking up again at all," she said flatly. "I must have been out of my mind!"

"Out of your mind and in my arms," Drew teased. "Now was it really such an awful place to be?"

Lynn plumped up the pillows behind his head so that he could sit up in bed and then she handed him the bed tray. "It was insanity!" she said bluntly. She gazed down at him and her lovely gray eyes were clouded and troubled. "Don't try to play with me, Drew. It's better if you just go away from here and we cut our losses. If you like, I'll file for divorce as soon as possible."

His eyes grew speculative as he studied her and a quiet gravity came to his features and he nodded.

"All right." His voice had a curious indifference. He looked down at the tray before him and picked up the fork. "I'm agreeable to that. But right now, if you'll please leave me alone, I'd like to get on with my meal and then try and get a nap. My back's bothering me and I don't feel in a very chatty mood."

Dismissed and feeling like a scolded schoolchild, Lynn returned to the house with scalding cheeks and a raging temper. She spent a fruitless half hour brooding over her anger toward Drew, her own stupidity and the unkind fate that had brought him here to severely disrupt the serenity of her life.

She very pointedly stayed away from the garage room until five that afternoon when she carried out his dinner. During this visit, they each spoke in only the curtest of monosyllables.

"Dinner," she said.

"Thanks," he responded.

"Better?"

"Somewhat." But he winced painfully as he sat up to eat and Lynn's heart sank. Soon Gwen and Cal would be bringing Joy home and there seemed to be no hope now that Drew would be off the premises by then.

It was just after dark when Cal brought Joy to the front door. Either he had not noticed the unfamiliar truck that belonged to Drew or he was simply incurious because he was in a rush. His brow was knitted above his hazel eyes when Lynn answered the door.

He handed her Joy's bag and said, "Hi, we're back. Joy'll tell you all about the trip, but I've got to run now. The freezer went out while we were gone. Nothing's spoiled, but I've got to go to town and get some dry ice to save everything until I can get it repaired." He lifted a hand to his sandy-colored hair, sketched a half-salute and ran down the porch steps and back to his station wagon.

Lynn carried Joy's small bag into the living room and then her daughter hurled herself into Lynn's arms and hugged her exuberantly.

"I missed you, Mommy!" she exclaimed with an engaging smile.

Lynn squeezed the child, then patted her on the back. "I missed you, too, sweetie pie. Did you have a good time?"

The dark head bobbed. "Grandma Jennings made us some 'vinity candy.'"

"Divinity."

"That's what I said," Joy said impatiently. "An' she let us ride her pony, too. You know, the one named Sugar. Me an' Penny an' Pat took turns."

"I'll bet that was fun," Lynn said.

"Yes. Sugar likes us. She wasn't mean to us or nothin' even though Grandma Jennings said she's getting old and 'trary."

"Contrary," Lynn corrected with a smile.

"Yes. Con-trary," Joy enunciated carefully. "What does that mean, Mommy?"

"It means the way you act sometimes when you give me trouble about your bedtime."

"When you don't want to do something?" Joy asked curiously.

"That's right. And when you're stubborn and disagreeable about it."

"Stubborn as a mule!" Joy exclaimed, giggling.

Lynn grinned appreciatively. "Now where did you hear that expression, young lady?"

"Uncle Cal said it to Kenny yesterday when he

didn't want to take his nap," Joy stated triumphant- ly, proud of her knowledge of the term.

Lynn laughed and ruffled her daughter's hair. "Okay, kiddo, I'm glad you had a good time as well as increased your vocabulary. Now, are you hun- gry?"

"Yes, ma'am! Can I have a hot dog?"

"Not tonight," Lynn replied as the two of them headed for the kitchen. "I cooked fried chicken."

"Oh, goody!" Joy approved enthusiastically. "I want a leg."

While Lynn served a plate with the stipulated chicken leg, mashed potatoes and green beans, Joy sat at the table keeping up a constant stream of chatter about her trip. Even while she ate and Lynn sat across from her, the child interspersed her bites with a few more comments about a large tree she had climbed and a visit to a dime store where Grandma Jennings had bought all of them a few trinkets.

As glad as she was to see her daughter again and to listen to her happy ramblings, Lynn was keenly aware that Drew was only scant yards away from the house. The prospect of keeping the two of them apart until he was fit to leave boggled her mind and filled her with tension. What if Drew should acciden- tally see Joy? Could she possibly get by letting him believe Joy was Gwen's child?

It seemed a cruel and hard-hearted thing to even contemplate and Lynn doubted she could even speak such a monumental lie. For a moment she was deeply ashamed of herself for even thinking it, but then she grew stern with herself. Joy *was* hers, hers alone, and Drew had no right to any claims upon her even if he wanted her. It wasn't wrong for a mother to do anything necessary to protect and preserve her child's security, was it?

Thoughtfully, she studied Joy. Bright blue eyes, fringed with thick black lashes, testified to a heritage from the father she had never known. Lynn had never told her anything about Drew except that he lived too far away to be with them. Young as she was, Joy had always accepted that explanation with equanimity. But she would not always be satisfied with that simple statement and Lynn grew cold as she realized that someday Joy would insist upon knowing more. She asked herself if she had perhaps done both Joy and Drew a terrible wrong by keeping her secret all these years, and the answer from her conscience was not a comfortable one.

Joy finished her meal and Lynn forced a smile to her lips. "Want some ice cream for dessert?"

Joy nodded eagerly. "Chocolate?"

"Chocolate," Lynn answered as she got up.

She was scooping it into a bowl at the counter when the kitchen door opened suddenly. Lynn whirled around in alarm to see Drew, fully clothed and showing a remarkable recovery, striding boldly into the room.

Instinctively, her protective gaze shifted to the child seated at the table. Joy's eyes were wide and bright with interest and curiosity.

"Hi there," Drew said with easy friendliness. He eyed the carton of ice cream and said pleasantly, "That looks good. Mind if I have a bowl of that, too?"

"C-certainly," Lynn stammered automatically, though her frozen fingers did not move nor could she drag her gaze away from the table as he sat down in the chair beside Joy.

"How're you doing, Joy?" he asked casually.

Joy looked at him with fascination. "How did you know my name?" she demanded.

"That's easy," Drew replied calmly. "I'm your daddy."

Chapter Four

*L*ynn gasped. All at once her head felt light. She gripped the edge of the counter and closed her eyes, willing away the dizzying sensation that threatened to steal away her consciousness.

Behind her, yet seeming a long way off, she dimly heard Joy ask, "Really? Are you really my daddy?"

"I sure am," Drew assured her.

Lynn opened her eyes and stared in a daze at the melting blob of ice cream that was dripping from the spoon she still held. Weakly, she put it down and turned once again toward the table.

Father and daughter were keenly enthralled with one another. There was a tender expression on Drew's face as he smiled down at the lovely child with the glowing face and shining eyes. Joy was observing him with the awed wonder she had previously reserved only for Santa Claus on her yearly visits with him. A bittersweet pain stabbed Lynn's heart. She might as well not even have been in the same room so far as the other two were concerned. She swallowed painfully over the lump that lodged in her throat.

"Are you a daddy to me just like Uncle Cal is to Penny an' Pat an' Kenny?"

"Yes, I am, princess," Drew said with the gentlest smile Lynn had ever seen. "But I'll bet no daddy in the whole wide world has a prettier, sweeter daughter than I do."

Joy beamed at him. The combined effect of her winning smile and gemlike sparkling eyes would have softened the hardest of hearts and Lynn watched in avid fascination as Drew visibly mellowed beneath its devastating charm. Then Joy suddenly thought of something and her brow puckered and her delicate face turned serious. "Mommy said you lived too far away to ever come and see us."

Drew nodded and replied in a matter-of-fact voice, "I live in California. Do you know where that is?"

Joy shook her head.

"Well, it's a very long way from here and that's why I haven't been able to come and see you before. But I wanted to meet my beautiful little girl so I came all this way. Are you glad I did?"

"Oh, yes!" Joy exclaimed. She clasped her hands together in unrestrained glee. "I can't wait to tell Penny an' Pat that I've got a daddy just like them!"

At that, Drew lifted his dark head and directed a long, level look at Lynn. There was unmistakable condemnation in his gaze and it pricked at her conscience. Briskly, she turned back to her task and a moment later carried two bowls of ice cream to the table and set them before the pair already there. Then, heavily, because her legs would no longer support her, she sat down across from them.

This time it was her daughter's accusation she faced. "Mommy, you didn't tell me my daddy was coming to see me." There was pride in the possessive pronoun she used.

"That's because she didn't know herself," Drew said. Though it was the truth, Lynn was surprised at his unexpected defense of her. Now he grinned devilishly. "I wanted to surprise her as well as you, princess."

"I like surprises," Joy stated decisively from the superior vantage point of a child who had never known any other than the most wonderful of surprises. "You liked it, too, didn't you, Mommy? Daddy's surprise?"

Lynn swallowed and, with an effort, smiled. "Of course, darling," she lied convincingly. "I was very happy to see Daddy."

"So am I!" Joy stated with strong emphasis, before lowering her head and starting on her dish of ice cream.

Drew, taking advantage of Joy's momentary distraction, looked over at Lynn again. A twinkle in his eyes told her that he was well aware of her lie but that for now, at least, he would not give her away. Then slowly, he winked, as though they were co-conspirators in some illicit scheme before saying in the blandest of voices, "Your mother was *so* glad to see me that she's asked me to stay here with you. Do you want me to stay, princess?"

"Oh, yes!" Joy said with frank pleasure.

Lynn almost choked. The audacity of the man! Her gray eyes turned to hard flint as she glared at her husband. Her lips parted with an impulsive denial, but as Drew quietly shook his head and cut his eyes toward Joy as a warning, she bit back the angry words that hovered on her tongue. His silent cautioning was well taken. If she made a scene now in front of their daughter she would only upset her child needlessly.

She knotted her hands in her lap and nibbled at her lower lip in frustrated fury. The inevitable scene that lay ahead would necessarily have to be postponed until Joy was out of hearing range and Lynn seethed impatiently as she waited for her daughter to finish eating her dessert. She shot a smoldering look at Drew that he could not fail to read as a brewing storm.

At last Joy was done. Immediately Lynn said, "You've had a long day, sweetie pie. Now I want you to go and take your bath and get ready for bed."

Obediently, Joy got to her feet, but before leaving the room, she turned to Drew and asked hopefully, "When I'm done, will you come an' hear me say my prayers tonight?"

Drew reached out to clasp one small, peach-smooth hand in his. Then he cleared his throat and said huskily, "There's nothing I'd rather do more than hear your prayers, princess. Of course I will."

"You, too, Mommy," Joy insisted, turning to glance at Lynn as though anxious that her mother not feel left out in this new set of circumstances. "Just like always?"

Lynn smiled. "Yes, darling, just like always. Now scoot!"

She sat in stony silence for a few minutes afterward until she felt certain that Joy was safely out of the way. Knowing her daughter, the next half hour would be uninterrupted, for Joy adored long baths with her large assortment of rubber toys.

"Well," Lynn's voice was sarcastic when she finally spoke, "it seems your back made a remarkable and most timely recovery."

The gibe fell wide of the mark. Drew gave her a slow smile and nodded. "Yes," he said cheerfully, "isn't it wonderful?"

Lynn's eyes narrowed and she said in a low voice filled with animosity, "I hate you for this, you know."

Drew shrugged and rose indolently to his feet. He carried the two empty dessert bowls to the sink, ran water to rinse them and then turned back to face her. "I could say the same thing to you, my dear." A sudden inflection of savagery entered his voice. "You ought to be horsewhipped for concealing my child from me all these years! It was criminal!"

His eyes blazed with a fury so black and so great that Lynn quailed before it. Drew's body was rigid and it emanated powerful waves of menacing hostility. Never had she seen him, nor indeed any other person, display such a total and consuming rage and a current of fear electrified her.

Swiftly, she, too, got to her feet and was poised to flee if he should show the least sign of physical violence. In his dark passion of anger, Lynn was unsure of what he might be capable of doing if he were further incited. She eyed him warily, scarcely even daring to breathe.

Drew laughed, a rough-edged sound of bitterness and his lips curled with scorn as he crossed his arms in front of him. "Don't worry," he growled scathingly. "I'm not going to harm you. No matter how much you deserve some form of punishment, I'm not planning to lower *myself* to the level of hitting a woman! But you certainly lowered yourself when you decided to cheat me out of my rightful knowledge of and association with my own child! In fact," he ended brutally, "I'd say you sank just about as low as it's possible to go!"

"That's not true!" she gasped in self-defense. "I had good reasons and . . ."

Without compunction, Drew cut her short. "There's not an excuse in the world that can justify what you did, Lynn, and you know it! Look me squarely in the eyes and tell me that you honestly believe that such a deceitful act was right."

Lynn lowered her head. She couldn't do it, of course. She had experienced a nagging, ever-present sense of guilt from the very day she had run away from him, despite her obstinate resolution once the decision had been made. The doubts and guilt had been intensified by Aunt Mary's and Gwen's frank disapproval and by her own uncomfortable awareness as time passed that Joy was growing up without the strong and steadying influence of a father the way most children did. The results of her action had been dear, costing her a great many sleepless nights and peace of mind, and what little happiness she had enjoyed these past few years had been tempered by a growing conviction that someday she was going to have to pay an even greater price for the spurious path she had chosen to take. Now Drew was here and he was about to call in the debt.

Nervously, she moistened her lips with her tongue before she could find enough courage to look at him once more. Then, with a tight little laugh, she said unsteadily, "Something tells me this is going to be a long discussion. I think I'd better sit down."

"Good idea," Drew said in a clipped voice. But while she moved to resume her place in the chair she had vacated a few minutes ago, he did not shift from his position. His stance was solid, his feet firmly planted on the floor with considerable space between them. He was as firm and awesome as a volcano, and Lynn still cast a watchful eye toward him lest, like a volcano, he rumbled and suddenly exploded with deadly fire.

"How long have you known?" she faltered. "A-about Joy?"

"Only a few days. Out of her entire lifetime, only a few days!" Recrimination burned in the words.

"Since you already knew, why didn't you say something before?" she asked in genuine puzzlement. "I was sure if you knew that you would have told me so last night."

Drew's mouth compressed into a grim line. "I kept waiting for *you* to tell me. Only you didn't. You had no intention of telling me, even while I was here! That's why you were in such a dither about getting me to leave. There's no limit to how far you were willing to go to keep me from my own daughter! My God, Lynn, how could you be so cruel?" His voice rasped with raw emotion.

Deep shame filled her and she dragged her eyes from his tortured expression. She had expected his anger, but somehow not this intense pain he was suffering. For the first time she squarely faced the enormity of what she had done and hot tears of remorse scalded her eyes.

"I'm sorry," she whispered hoarsely. "I'm really sorry, Drew. I never expected you would take it like this . . . be so . . . so hurt."

"Didn't expect . . ." Words failed Drew and his broken voice jerked her head up so that she was compelled to look upon his anguish.

Heedless of anything except his distress, she went to him and laid a gentle hand on his arm. Her eyes were swimming with tears and her voice was pleading and earnest as she murmured again, "I'm so sorry. I never meant to hurt you, Drew. Not in any way."

Drew took a long, shuddering breath, regaining a stern control over his emotions. Only when he was fully in command again did he speak and then his voice was biting and hard. "You never wanted to hurt me?" he asked with sharp skepticism. "You walked out of my life and carried with you the secret of my unborn child and you never meant to hurt me? Come, come, Lynn, surely you can do better than trying to feed me a fairy-tale line like that!"

Chagrined, Lynn dropped her hand away from his arm. But at the same time, her own assaulted sensibilities had had enough berating and her reasserted pride heated her voice. "I don't much care what you believe since you refuse to listen to me, but I've apologized for the last time. And now that your back's all better," she added sarcastically, "I expect you to leave here just as soon as you've said good night to Joy. In the meantime, you'll have to excuse me. I find it intolerable to stay in the same room with you anymore." She turned on her heel, about to stalk out of the kitchen, but she never managed to take the first step.

Drew's powerful fingers clasped over her slender wrist. When she turned back toward him, indignation stained her cheeks a dull red, but before she could wither him with a few pungent words that leapt instantly to mind, he snarled, "You're not going anywhere until we get a few things settled between us. And the first item on the agenda is that

I'm not leaving. Now that I've met my daughter, I fully intend to stick around and get to know her. I wasn't kidding last night when I said I'd take over the role of your hired hand. For a little while, that is." He smiled unpleasantly. "It's not a position I'm accustomed to, but I'm sure I'll get the hang of it and it'll give me something with which to occupy my time until I'm good and ready to leave."

"No!" Lynn snapped. "You will not stay here! This is *my* home," she pointed out hotly, "and you're not welcome here. If you won't go willingly, I'll get the sheriff to have you forcibly removed! You're not a part of my life anymore, Drew Marcus, and you don't dictate terms to me!"

"Don't I?" he rejoined with a hateful smile. "Fine. I'll go tonight . . . if you're prepared for a court battle over custody of our child!"

Lynn paled with alarm and she staggered back a few steps. Her heart thudded violently and she stared at him in disbelief. "You wouldn't," she whispered. "You wouldn't really do that! You're just bluffing!"

"Think so?" Drew shrugged negligently. "Then try me."

"You'd lose," she said defiantly. She lifted her chin and said with a show of spirit, "If you took me to court, you'd be sure to lose . . . a man who never wanted children in the first place!"

"You'd have to prove that," Drew stated cruelly, "which might be difficult for you to do. I, on the other hand, would have no difficulty whatsoever in proving that you not only deserted me, but that you deliberately concealed from me the fact that you were carrying my child. I've still got the letter you left for me and it mentions nothing at all about a baby. No," he shook his head, "make no mistake about it, Lynn, I'd have a case all right. I'm the wronged party in this situation and if I have to, I'll take full advantage of it. You've already cheated me out of knowing my child for almost five years and I do not intend to be cheated of the future as well."

Lynn's blood froze in her veins. Drew meant every word. She could see that by the hard, uncompromising glint in his eyes and the implacable set of his jaw. If she forced him to leave now, he would do exactly what he threatened and moreover, he had vast financial resources to back him up. He could easily afford to hire the best lawyers in the country while she, after sinking most of her money into buying this farm, could ill afford an expensive court fight. She would be whipped before it even began and she knew it.

The idea of losing Joy was wrenching. Her daughter was the only light in her entire life! To be without her was unthinkable! Lynn trembled and her shoulders sagged in defeat.

"Why are you doing this to me?" she asked at last. "She's all I have in the world, Drew." She lifted her pain-glazed eyes to his and cried out, "You can't really want her! You never wanted children at all! You told me so enough times and with such force that there could be no mistake about that! Why else do you think I did what I did? I thought you would hate me if I told you I was pregnant—that you would hate the child as well, and I couldn't face a lifetime of that, don't you see? I had no choice but to leave you! I left so you *wouldn't have to be* a father, so why this about-face now?"

"Because," Drew said flatly, "circumstances are different now. A child *does* exist and she's my

71

daughter, too." He sighed heavily and brushed a hand across his face. "I can't even begin to describe the feelings I had when I learned about her."

Lynn sighed, too, then paced restlessly across the room and back again. She shook her head. "What I can't understand is how Aunt Mary came to tell you," she said at last. "It's not like her to break a confidence and she and Gwen had both promised they would never contact you and tell you."

"Blind loyalty," Drew said with a tight smile. "I know. She explained all that to me even though she also said they had never approved of your secretiveness and had urged you to tell me yourself." He shook his head. "You can't blame your aunt for this, Lynn. I was in Atlanta on business and on an impulse, I decided to visit her to find out where you were and how you were doing. I also wanted to know the reason why you had never filed for divorce after all this time. In her living room there is a photograph of you and Joy together and I happened to notice it. After that, there was no way she could possibly deny what was so obvious—that the child was mine. She has," he added with no little pride, "my eyes."

"But for her to tell you where to locate me . . ." Lynn persisted. "I can't believe she actually gave me away."

"She didn't have much choice," Drew admitted with a hint of the ruthless strength he must have used on Aunt Mary. "I explained that if she didn't tell me, I would haul her into court as an accessory to a conspiracy to keep me from my child. But I must confess I rather expected my visit to you would be announced before I arrived. And when Joy seemed to be nowhere on the premises when I got here, I was sure of it, that the two of us were playing cat and mouse and that you intended to keep her well hidden until I either forced the issue or gave up and went away. I decided," he ended unnecessarily, "to wait you out."

"Aunt Mary couldn't have called me," Lynn mused, "because my telephone hadn't been installed yet and Gwen's was out of order. You must have really upset her over this," she chided. "I'll have to call her tomorrow and . . ."

"I'm all clean," a childish voice announced brightly.

The pair who had been deep in their private conversation turned as one toward the door. Joy stood smiling, sure of her welcome. She wore pink pajamas with enticing ruffles that matched the glowing pink hue of her skin. In her arms she carried her favorite doll, Mary Louise, and a storybook. She went straight to Drew, presented her back to him and asked, "Will you button me, Daddy?"

Lynn was startled anew at how easily Joy used the familiar address. It was as though she had been in the habit of it from birth!

"Sure, princess," Drew said smoothly. His large fingers coped with the miniscule button and buttonhole at the base of her neck just as though he performed the simple chore every evening. When Joy turned to face him again, he stooped down to her level and asked, pointing to the doll, "Who is your friend?"

"Her name's Mary Louise." Joy gave Drew a sly smile and added hopefully, "She likes somebody to read her a story every night before she goes to bed." She offered him the book.

Drew threw back his head and laughed, and there was such a sparkling ring to it that Lynn watched him with amazement. He looked like a man who had just dropped ten years of age and had discovered a buried treasure chest besides. "All right," he said with a nod. "I'll give it a try just to please Mary Louise, but I have to warn you that I'm new to this and I may not be very good at it." He scooped Joy into his arms, rose and carried her toward the living room.

Lynn remained in the kitchen for a little while. She needed to adjust herself to this new situation, the abrupt change that had entered all three of their lives. Instinctively she knew that from this point forward, none of them would ever be the same again. For better or worse, a change had come.

From the room beyond she could hear the low murmur of Drew's voice as he read, punctuated occasionally by a question or comment from Joy.

Where did they go from here? she wondered gravely. It was obvious that Drew, in but an instant, had fallen hard for the beautiful little girl who was also his daughter. It was equally apparent that Joy had felt a sudden, strong attraction to the large man who so frankly admired her. It was unrealistic to suppose that either of them would ever be willing to give up their newfound relationship with the other, even if Drew hadn't already warned her that he intended to be in his daughter's future.

But where did he intend to fit into it? The question was how all the pieces of their lives could fit together into a harmonious whole. *"All the king's horses, and all the king's men,"* Lynn thought wryly, *"couldn't put Humpty together again."* That was exactly how she felt about her own life now. It could never be put all together again. Drew had broken it into too many pieces for that.

Still, the soothing lure of his voice attracted her

against her will and she went quietly to stand in the doorway of the living room. An appealing picture that tugged at her heartstrings met her eyes. Drew sat in the easy chair beside the front window with Joy perched on his lap. Her shining head was nestled confidently against his shoulder and her face was rapt with interest as he read softly.

They looked so serenely happy and . . . Lynn searched for the correct word in her mind . . . they looked so *right* together that it brought tears to scald her eyes. Father and daughter had recognized each other at once, not just physically but as kindred spirits, and it was an utterly beautiful thing to see. In that moment Lynn was beaten and she knew it. She had been so very wrong to keep them apart. No matter what happened in the future, she would never again attempt to block or fight Drew's privileges as a father. To do so would be to harm Joy and cheat her as well.

The story ended, Drew closed the book and, looking up abruptly, he met Lynn's eyes. He gave her a warm smile that caught at her breath and left her with a feeling of confusion and uncertainty that was totally at odds with the anger and recriminations between them earlier. Then he glanced down at the heavy-lidded eyes of the child and said softly, "I think this little princess has just about had it for one day." One arm was already around Joy's shoulders and he slid the other beneath her legs and lifted her as he got to his feet.

Lynn preceded him into Joy's bedroom and went to fold back the bedcovers. Drew gently lowered Joy to her feet and she knelt beside her bed to begin her prayers.

"Now I lay me down to sleep . . ."

Lynn stole a sideways peek at the man who stood so silently beside her. There was an unearthly, tender expression on his face, warming his eyes and softening his lips as he listened to Joy. Lynn felt a rush of empathy toward him, for she knew exactly what he was experiencing. She had felt that exquisite, all-engulfing flood tide of love sweep over her many, many moments like this in the past few years.

". . . an' God bless Mommy an' Aunt Mary an' Aunt Gwen an' Uncle Cal an' Penny an' Pat an' Kenny an' my daddy who came to see me. Amen." Joy unfolded her hands, got to her feet and climbed into the bed. Lynn tucked the covers around her and kissed her, then stepped back so that Drew could have his turn.

Joy's little arms curved around his neck as he bent his dark head toward her and her voice was lilting as she said, "G'night, Daddy."

"Good night, princess," Drew said with a husky catch to his voice. "Sweet dreams."

Lynn couldn't help but realize what a perfect picture of domestic tranquility the three of them made. They looked and acted like the classic dream of a united and loving family. But the trouble was that they weren't, not really, and she was frightened and worried about the shadowy future.

Unable to watch any longer, she left the room quickly. She went back to the living room and stood at the darkened window, looking out at nothing.

An arm came across her shoulders and Drew's voice was low and gentle. "Don't worry, Lynn. I didn't come here to make trouble for you."

A sob tore from her throat and her shoulders trembled with despair and other emotions she could no longer hide. "Don't take her from me, Drew!"

she pleaded. "She's all I have, all that matters to me! I love her so!" She lifted trembling hands to cover her face.

With infinite care, Drew turned her toward him and gathered her into his arms, pressing her face into the warm crook of his neck.

He was the enemy and yet strangely enough, his embrace was comforting. With one hand, he stroked her head while he murmured again, "Don't worry, darling. It's all right."

The soothing words gradually penetrated her mind. The trembling ceased, the tears receded. Lynn lay snug against his strong chest, enveloped within the luxurious body-heat coziness of him and an unfamiliar inertia spread over her. She felt sheltered and protected and she had no desire to stir from the confines of this safe harbor.

After a time, Drew raised her tear-stained face to meet his and he smiled with gentle amusement as he took out his handkerchief and wiped away all remaining traces of her tears. Their gazes met and clung with a world of unspoken meanings and dreams and aspirations between them. Then, slowly, Drew inclined his head toward her and as though she might be frail and delicate as gossamer, his lips touched hers.

As tenuous as his kiss, Lynn's fingers brushed against Drew's neck, feather light and fleeting. Drew lifted his head to gaze down at her. His eyes were deep blue, like the ocean, questioning, recognizing the question in her own gray ones and finally, giving his answer. His arms pressed her closer to him and when he possessed her lips once more, a tremor vibrated through them both, leaving them shaken and breathless.

With an effort of will, Lynn detached herself at last from Drew's embrace. She realized that as long as he held her she could not think clearly, and there were things they must say to each other, things that must be resolved. She could only accomplish her goals by maintaining a safe distance from him.

He knew it, too. There was a slightly crooked smile on his lips as she moved away from him, but he did nothing to attempt to prevent her. He merely watched and waited patiently until she was ready to speak.

Lynn looked down at her hands and nervously clasped them together, gathering courage for what she had to say. But finally she could delay no longer and she looked toward him with earnest appeal.

"I was wrong," she began hollowly, "to keep you from knowing Joy. I could see that tonight. The two of you are a part of each other the same as she's a part of me. I beg you, Drew, don't try to take her away from me entirely. Maybe I deserve it for what I did, but I couldn't bear it if I lost her. I . . . I promise if you don't take her from me, we can work something out—a way to share her so that both of us can see her grow up. I won't try to stand in your way."

Drew was silent for so long that she began to think he would not answer her, that what she had just said had had no effect on him whatsoever. But just when she was about to acknowledge defeat, he nodded gravely. His voice was quiet. "That's all I want, Lynn. I only want the right to know and love my daughter, too. I don't want to take her from you, but I won't be kept from her any longer." He shook his head. "I don't quite know the answer to the situation," he admitted, "whether we take turns having custody of her or what, but we'll work something out. In the meantime, we'll just take things as they come, one day at a time."

His words, she knew, were meant to be reassuring, but instead Lynn was stricken with renewed doubts and anxieties.

Chapter Five

$\mathcal{F}$or the second night in a row, Lynn had trouble sleeping. Although Drew had promised that they would be able to work something out between them concerning Joy, his words provided little comfort to her during the chill hours of the night. It was going to be difficult enough to adjust to the fact that she was going to have to share her daughter, that in all likelihood there would be months at a time every year from now on when she was away visiting her father in California, but how, Lynn wondered, would that affect her own relationship with Joy?

Their life-styles were so diametrically opposed! She and Joy had always lived simply in Savannah. Their apartment had been adequate, but small; their clothes the best she could afford to buy on a teacher's salary, but hardly the sort that a designer would look at twice. Their pleasures had also been simple, an occasional dinner out, a movie now and then, a picnic at the beach. The real highlight of their lives had come on frequent weekend visits to Cal's and Gwen's farm when Lynn could enjoy the company of her sister and brother-in-law and Joy could play outdoors with her cousins.

But Drew's life was nothing like that! He lived in an elegant home and there were servants to wait upon him. There would be a swimming pool behind the house and weekend trips on his yacht. His clothes were fashionable, and there would be no scrimping when it came to buying a winter coat or lowering a hem on a little girl's outgrown dress! It would be an overwhelming change for Joy and Lynn wondered if the child, after once tasting the easily bought fruits of wealth, could ever again be satisfied living a quiet, chore-laden life in the country. Money talks its own language and to a young, impressionable mind, it would most likely shout. Seeing how her father lived would be bound to affect Joy greatly and once she began to compare it with her mother's life, Lynn was afraid she would lose her daughter completely.

And if Joy chose her father's way of life, there would be nothing Lynn could do about it. In the wee hours of the night, she was honest with herself about that. She had already been selfish enough in keeping her daughter from Drew for almost five years. Now Joy was growing up. Next fall she would be in kindergarten and time would fly. Before she even realized it, Joy would be ten, then fifteen, and Lynn recognized that if the girl then chose to live with her father so that she could enjoy all the advantages he could give her and her mother could not, she would have to let her go. In all conscience, it would be unfair of Lynn to refuse her child access to all her father—and his money—could offer.

And yet, what of a young girl's emotional needs? Lynn doubted Drew could fulfill those adequately. According to his own descriptions, his childhood had been rather cold and sterile and his father had taught him little beyond strict obedience and how to make money. That sort of education might be helpful, but it wasn't enough. A child needed more . . . much more.

But even if Drew were capable of raising their daughter alone and of giving her all the support and leadership a sensitive girl required, what about herself? Lynn had a dismal glimpse of the empty years ahead. There would be a divorce, of course, and she and Drew would both be free to marry again if they chose to. And now she was moving to the crux of what was bothering her most. Drew . . . and the intense feelings he had aroused in her ever since he had arrived so unexpectedly! In the short time since he had returned, he had forced upon her the awareness that not only was she still a woman with a woman's desires and passions, but that he alone was the only man who had ever been able to bring her to such a heightened sensuality. She had only to be in his company to be acutely aware of his potent virility. Just the sight of his face and the shape of his angular, masculine body sent tingles along all her nerve ends, and when he touched her, she melted with yielding, aching desire. He had brought to mind the memories of his expert lovemaking and the satisfying ecstasy he had once given her. It had been so long and, face it, she told herself, she was so lonely. . . .

Lynn writhed uncomfortably beneath the bedcovers. Her torturous thoughts made her body feel hot and prickly, then cold and empty. She tossed over onto her side and by the pale moonlight that filtered through the curtains, she could see the unused pillow next to hers. Its smooth neatness silently mocked her and she moaned in frustration.

When she finally dozed off, Lynn sank deeply into the rejuvenating arms of sleep. Body, mind and spirit were exhausted from the trauma of the past two days. Her subconscious understood her need for rest and Lynn slept long and heavily.

She awoke at midmorning and she was appalled when she glanced at the clock and saw that it was past ten. Bright sunlight washed over the room and its furnishings and Lynn blinked defensively against its brilliance. A heavy, unreal and suddenly ominous silence hung over the house.

With haste, she swung her legs from the bed to the floor and, not even bothering with slippers, she shoved her arms into her robe and hurried from the room.

Joy was not in her bedroom. The covers on the bed were thrown back to reveal crumpled sheets; her pink pajamas were dropped in the middle of the floor where she had left them when she dressed. Lynn hurried on past the empty bathroom and living room and into the silent kitchen.

There was evidence that the room had recently been occupied. Two plates on the table, with the remains of breakfast, gave mute testimony that both Drew and Joy had eaten. A frying pan was on the stove and the coffee pot was still half full. Lynn went immediately to the window and glanced out, but she saw no one. All was serenely still and sudden fear clutched at her heart. What if Drew had taken Joy and gone? Ice froze her veins as she hurried back to the living room where she could look out at the drive from the window there. If Drew's truck was gone . . .

But it was still in the same spot where he had parked it two nights ago. Lynn began to breathe again. Wherever the two were, they were somewhere on the property. Drew had not stolen Joy away. Slowly, the terror receded and at last she returned to her room to dress.

A half hour later, after a single cup of coffee to fortify her, Lynn went out to search for her daughter. She found them out back where they stood beside the fence that separated the front part of the property from the field. Cal, with his tractor nearby, was leaning against the fence while he and Drew carried on what appeared to be a leisurely, amiable conversation.

Joy spotted her first as she approached. "Hi, Mommy," she called cheerfully. "Daddy said you were a lazy sleepyhead today an' we had to come outside so we wouldn't wake you."

Both men swung around to face her and Lynn was excruciatingly conscious of Cal's amused assumption. The fact that her husband was here, obviously making himself at home besides being on the best of terms with his daughter, and Joy's revelation just now led him to think the most logical . . . that she was sleeping with Drew. She flushed hotly as she read his mind and his conclusion, however erroneous, combined with the still jumpy state of her nerves from when she first got up and thought Drew had carried Joy away, made her speak with a sharp edge to her voice.

"Don't you ever take off with Joy again like this

without asking me first!" she attacked Drew. "I was scared to death when I didn't find her in the house!"

A twinkle crept into Drew's eyes as he smiled at her. He knew exactly what she had feared. He moved from the fence to where she had halted a yard or so away and casually draped an arm across her shoulders. Then, heedless of the two pairs of eyes that were trained upon them, he kissed her soundly before saying in a contrite voice, "I'm sorry, darling. I didn't mean to upset you. I was just trying to be considerate. I knew how tired you were and that you needed your sleep."

Still aware of Cal's interested gaze, Lynn tried to move away from Drew in a natural, calm manner. The damage had already been done. There was no way she was going to be able to convince her brother-in-law that things were not as they seemed, and anyway, she asked herself irritably, why bother? After all, they *were* married and by the look on Cal's face, he wholeheartedly approved of the sudden turn of events that had brought Drew back into her life.

Forcing a smile to her lips, she approached the fence and said, "Gwen told me you probably wouldn't get over here to begin work until Monday or Tuesday. How come you're not in town at the shop?"

Cal shrugged. "I went in early and put in a couple of hours' work, but we weren't very busy so I headed home. Thought I'd get a jump on my start over here." His gaze veered out toward the field. "The soil's in pretty good condition, Lynn. Barring any catastrophes, I ought to be able to produce a good crop."

"I hope so," she said fervently. Now she half-turned toward Drew who joined them and she asked lightly, "What have you two been discussing? You looked like you were having a serious conversation when I got here."

"Mostly about the land," Cal replied.

Drew nodded. "Cal tells me that you should be able to realize a good amount of money from timber crops as well as leasing out the fields once you've set up a system for replanting."

"Yes. There's a mill in town that will buy it, but I don't want to be in a hurry and do things wrong. I've seen land that has been stripped without using any methods of conservation or planting for the future. I don't want to let anyone in here to start cutting down trees until I know what I'm doing."

"I've met an agricultural extension agent who's a pretty smart guy," Cal said. "I'll bring him around to look things over for you sometime soon."

"I'd like to meet him, too," Drew said.

Lynn looked up in swift surprise. She couldn't imagine why all this should matter to him one way or another. The farm wasn't his and she doubted whether he would be here long, anyway. Still, he seemed genuinely interested as the discussion moved on to other areas of farm management and of various things that faced her in the near future. They talked at length about water, fertilizers and pesticides.

After about fifteen minutes, Lynn began to fidget and when there was finally a point where she could speak without rudely interrupting them, she said, "I'd better get back to the house. There's a lot of work waiting on me." She looked down at her daughter who was turning a cartwheel in the grass. "You come with me, sweetheart. I need your help."

"Sure thing," Cal said by way of saying good-bye. "See you tonight."

Lynn paused to stare at him with a blank expression. Drew spoke up immediately. "I forgot to tell you, darling," he said smoothly, "but I invited Cal and Gwen and their family to eat with us tonight. It's been so many years since we've met, I thought it would be nice to visit again and I'm anxious to see Gwen and the children. I thought after lunch Joy and I could drive into town and pick up some steaks to grill."

Lynn was outraged. She didn't mind in the least having Gwen and Cal to dinner. They got together often. But she deeply resented Drew's high-handed tactics of inviting *her* family to dinner at *her* house without so much as a by-your-leave to her. Who did he think he was anyway, coming here and behaving as though he owned the place and had a perfect right to make decisions concerning her life! She simply wouldn't have it and as soon as they were alone she would inform him so! But meanwhile there was little she could do except acquiesce. Cal was watching her curiously as though he sensed that all was not sweetness and light in her relationship with her husband and she did not care to make a scene.

She set her teeth and mustered a semblance of a smile she hoped would pass for the real thing. "Fine. We'll see you all tonight, then, Cal." Not trusting herself to stay a second longer, Lynn whirled and added, "Come on, Joy," before striking out toward the house.

During what was left of the morning, Lynn's resentment energized her. She was like a human tornado as she flitted around the house, cleaning the kitchen, doing the laundry and finally unpacking the last of the boxes. It contained keepsakes from Joy's infancy, tiny bootees and sweaters and blankets and the like. These she tucked away in a hall closet, and the remainder of the box's contents, Christmas decorations, were hauled out to the garage room that Drew now occupied.

While there, Lynn glanced around idly. Except for the bed and dresser, the room was already a catch-all for a miscellany of storage items. Cardboard boxes were stacked at one end of the room. It was not the most pleasant place in which to sleep, she thought reflectively, and if she was able to hire someone to work for her she would have to get all this stuff out. But for now it could remain. It was a far cry from Drew's elegant surroundings at home and she felt no compunction to make the room more cheerful for him. Maybe, she laughed wryly to herself, he would soon become so sick of it that he would leave.

When she went back outside, she spotted the object of her thoughts at a fence line not far from where he had talked with Cal. With his shirt sleeves rolled above his elbows and thick work gloves on his hands, he was unwinding a coil of barbed wire.

Shock held her still as she watched. She could scarcely believe that he had willingly undertaken the job of fence repair. She doubted he had ever done such a chore before in his life and why now, she wondered, when it was for her benefit? She certainly hadn't asked him to do it. She would not have had the nerve.

A little past one o'clock, he came into the house. Lynn had prepared a simple meal of a casserole and salad and when all three of them sat down at the table, Drew ate his food with relish.

He laughed a little as he helped himself to seconds. "All this fresh air gives a man an appetite. I'd better remember to buy a couple of steaks apiece for Cal and me."

"I saw you repairing that west fence," Lynn told

him. She forced herself to add, "Thank you. I appreciate it, though I really didn't expect it of you, you know."

Drew leaned back in his chair and looked directly into her eyes. Laughter lurked in his. "You sound so polite and formal," he teased, "like a little girl telling her hostess that she had a nice time at a perfectly boring birthday party! How long did you rehearse it?"

Her cheeks flushed a hot, angry red and Lynn knotted her fists out of view beneath the table. "I was only trying to show my appreciation," she snapped. "You don't have to throw it back in my face!"

Drew actually grinned. He winked at Joy, then looked guilelessly at Lynn. "You're gorgeous when you get all excited. Your eyes flash with little shooting sparks of fire and your cheeks turn a lovely pink that's quite irresistible. And your lips," he continued innocently, "purse up like a pretty little rosebud that hasn't yet opened to the sun. Perhaps," he mused, "all they need is to be kissed often enough and then they'll open up and . . ."

"Stop it!" The stark command was issued from low in her throat. "Just stop it right now!"

Drew eyed her thoughtfully. "You know, my darling," he said with deliberation, "I think you must be sexually repressed if the mere mention of *kissing* offends you. I can remember days when you scarcely bothered even getting out of bed and saw no good purpose in putting on your clothes and now—"

"Will you hush?" Lynn begged frantically. She cut her eyes toward Joy with silent meaning.

A jovial chuckle met her ears and it was all Lynn could do to keep her knotted fists in her lap. She desperately wanted to lash out at her tormenter.

Drew sensed her anger, but he knew she would not make a scene in front of Joy, and he was enjoying himself tremendously at her expense. Even so, he turned to the child. "If you're finished eating now, princess, why don't you go get washed up? You haven't forgotten that we're going to town together, have you?"

Joy left the table with alacrity. "I'll get ready *real* fast, Daddy!" she promised before scampering from the room.

"She's not going off alone with you," Lynn stated categorically as soon as Joy was out of hearing.

Drew's smile faded. "You think I might try to kidnap her?"

Lynn met his hardening gaze without flinching. "I'm not taking any chances on it," she said coldly. "You can be sure of that!"

"That's really funny," Drew said slowly, "considering that's exactly what you did to me, in effect, when you ran away and hid, making damn sure I didn't know you were expecting my child!"

There was bitterness in Drew's retort as well as a pointed edge of truth to it and Lynn marveled anew at the intensity of it, knowing how he had never wanted children. Drew was a complete paradox and she realized that she did not really know the man at all, despite their marriage.

Joy came back, her face and hands clean and glowing with the vibrancy of youth. She brought her hairbrush to Lynn and leaned against her knee. "Brush my hair, Mommy," she requested, "an' then I'll be all ready to go."

Before Lynn could object again about the projected outing, Drew took the wind out of her sails by saying calmly, "Your mother has decided to go with us, princess. She doesn't want to be left out of the ice cream treat after we're done shopping."

Joy was agreeable to the new plan. "Can she have a banana split?" she asked. "That's her favorite."

Drew nodded. "And what's your favorite?"

"A tutti-frutti with lots of nuts on top!"

Lynn glared at Drew while merriment danced in his eyes as he caught her gaze. Once again he had outmaneuvered her. Easily surmounting her objections about his taking Joy off alone, he had included her in such a way that she would seem churlish and petulant before her daughter if she refused to play along.

That evening after her bath, Lynn dressed in a becoming cream-colored hostess gown. It went well with her coloring and her lustrous brown hair. She added a copper belt at her waist and stepped back from the mirror to take an overall survey of her appearance.

From the bathroom down the hall she could hear Drew singing at the top of his lungs above the spray of the shower. He was slightly off-key, but oddly, that only made the sound more pleasant because it was so genuinely exuberant. Lynn met her own gaze reflected from the mirror and saw with a little jolt of surprise that the gray eyes were gleaming and that a smile she was unable to repress parted her lips.

It was, she thought with honesty, *rather nice to have a man in the house singing above the noise of a waterfall.* His voice had such a homey, happy sound and it brought a new and exciting element of life into the house.

She reached into her jewelry box on the dresser and picked up a gold hooped earring. As she fastened it to her ear she thought over the afternoon. The three of them had had a wonderful time shopping for groceries. Drew had somehow managed to make a game out of what Lynn generally considered a boring job and had kept Joy giggling with fanciful stories about Abner Asparagus, Connie Cabbage, Bernie Beets and Lionel Lima. Since Joy had never been overly fond of most vegetables, it would be curious to see whether Drew had enough influence to actually induce her into eating them. Later they had all enjoyed the promised ice cream treat before returning home and though she wouldn't have admitted it for the world, Lynn had hated to see the outing end as much as her daughter.

After they had put away the groceries, Drew went out to the garage room to get ready for the evening, but he soon returned to say that if Lynn wished to have a clean husband for their guests tonight, he'd have to bathe in the house. There was something wrong with the hot-water heater in the garage.

Husband. The word seemed to halt and magnify in the forefront of her mind. Drew was her husband and yet . . . he wasn't. All afternoon they had behaved like an ideally happy couple with their daughter, but just now Lynn was not happy. She wasn't exactly unhappy either, she realized in confusion. She was just . . . The truth was she wasn't at all certain how she felt.

She picked up a bottle of cologne and sprayed it on her neck and her wrists. Replacing the bottle on the dresser, she then lifted her head and as she did, her heart skidded to a stop.

Drew stood just behind her, his black hair gleaming. His chest was bare and only a pale yellow towel covered him from the waist to about the middle of his powerful thighs. Lynn, seeing his reflection in the mirror, stood transfixed as Drew moved slowly, but deliberately toward her.

His arms circled her waist from behind and he pressed his moist cheek to hers, meeting her gaze in the mirror. For a timeless moment they merely looked at each other, saying nothing, and an intense level of emotion coursed through Lynn's body. She closed her eyes against it as though to block out the warm rush of feelings that swept over her.

With an indescribable gentleness, he turned her in his arms and she could feel his soft breath on her cheek. "You're so lovely tonight," Drew murmured huskily. "As beautiful as you were on our wedding day." His lips lightly grazed her cheek before moving downward to her vulnerable, exposed neck.

Instinctively, her head arched back, allowing him access, even as she begged in contradiction, "Don't Drew. Please stop!"

"Don't be silly, darling," he whispered as he nuzzled her. His hands were moving sensually down her back to her hips, then back again.

Tingles shivered through her as he pressed her closer to him. She was devastatingly aware of his bare chest brushing the tips of her breasts, of his naked thighs firmly rubbing against hers, of the insubstantial towel that might loosen and fall at any second.

Her hands went to his arms and traveled upward to his shoulders as Drew's mouth found hers and possessed it with a fervency that stole away her will. As his embrace became crushing, Lynn's fingers dug into his back with a responding intensity.

"Mommy!" Joy's voice pierced the intoxicating atmosphere. "They're here!" she called from the living room.

Lynn crashed back to earth, shaken and slightly

dazed. When she opened her eyes she saw that Drew's were glazed beneath heavy lids.

He smiled a bit unsteadily. "I thought I liked Cal this morning, but now . . . I'm not so sure. Let's tell them to go away."

Lynn took a deep, shuddering breath and laughed at him. "That always was one of your worst faults, Drew. Being so determined to have your own way, no matter how disruptive it might be to someone else." She shook her head and said firmly, "It's time you take the consequences for your actions. You invited them and you're going to entertain them!"

Drew grinned. "Even if it kills me, eh? That was what was always wrong with you as a wife. Orderly. Doing what you think is your duty without any consideration for me. No spontaneity at all. And now you're going to make me suffer the tortures of the damned for who knows how many hours! The least you could do," he complained petulantly, "is to pretend you're going to suffer, too."

"What?" Lynn, her equilibrium restored, openly laughed at him. "And admit I still find you sexy?" She shook her head. "No way. I have no intention of swelling your ego!"

"Get out of here now and let me dress," Drew growled in mock ferocity, "before I forget we have guests and prove to you just how sexy I *can* be!" He turned her toward the door, swatted her behind playfully and shoved her out of the room.

Lynn grinned to herself as she went down the hall and reached the living room at the same moment Cal, Gwen and their brood knocked on the front door.

Their evening together was an unqualified success. The dinner, which Lynn and Drew had prepared together, was excellent. While the children ate in the kitchen, the four adults enjoyed a leisurely meal in the dining room. Gwen had greeted Drew with her customary warmth and placidity and over dinner, after having observed his easy rapport with Joy, said bluntly, "I'll admit I was shocked when Cal told me you were here, Drew, not to mention a bit worried about how you were reacting about learning you had a daughter. But I can see you already adore Joy and it looks like you've forgiven Lynn as well. I'm glad. Glad you're here, too. I never did like the fact that you didn't know."

"Thanks, Gwen, for your support," Drew said charmingly. "Although I wish you could have had more influence on Lynn from the beginning. I've lost a lot of years with my daughter because of this girl's mixed-up thinking." He glanced meaningfully toward Lynn, but this time his smile robbed the words of any bitterness or anger.

After dinner the children went to play with the toys in Joy's bedroom. The two couples moved into the living room where Lynn served coffee and a cake she had bought in town since there hadn't been time to bake one.

Gwen, accepting her plate, glanced ruefully down at the bulk of her midsection. "I really shouldn't eat this, you know," she said to Lynn. "The doctor says I'm gaining a bit too much weight. More than I did with the others."

"Then maybe you'd better not have it," Drew said unexpectedly. "Can't it be dangerous?" he asked. "If a woman is overweight when it's time for the baby to be born?"

Gwen shrugged. "It can be if you really overdo it. Actually, I'm only about five pounds over and I have been being very strict with myself the past few days, so I don't think one piece of cake is going to hurt.

Besides," she grinned and patted her swollen middle, "Little Kicker here is hungry."

The subject was dropped then, though Lynn once or twice caught Drew observing her sister with a thoughtful frown. It seemed strange that he should display an interest and concern about her health. Once again she reminded herself of how little she really knew about this man to whom she was married.

An hour later, Cal was relating to them a funny story about a dog he had once owned when someone knocked on the door. Cal halted in midsentence as Lynn started in surprise.

"Are you expecting anyone?" Drew asked.

"No." Lynn got out of her chair. "I can't imagine who it is." She crossed the room and opened the door.

There stood John Simpson and at the sight of him, alarm signals clamored along Lynn's nerves. His smile was warm and pleasant, but it did nothing to thaw the chill that spread up her back.

"Hi," he said casually. "I decided to drive over to see you on the spur of the moment. I hated the way we parted the other night. I apologize. Am I back in your good graces now?"

"Er . . . yes, of course," she murmured in a low voice. "But I have company tonight, John, and . . ."

"Yes, I know," he said. "I saw Cal's station wagon. And someone else's truck."

A possessive hand clasped Lynn's waist and a voice near her ear said, "Invite your guest inside, darling. It's rude to keep him standing at the door." The hand drew her back against the hard, lean frame of a body.

John stepped inside, but his pleasant smile had disappeared. Drew's hand on Lynn had not escaped his notice, nor the endearment Drew had used. Hot color suffused John's face as he asked shortly, "Who is this man?"

Drew answered for her. "I'm Drew Marcus," he said nonchalantly. The easy tone of his voice was at variance with the tightening of his hand on Lynn. Now he extended his right hand toward John. "It's nice to meet a *friend* of my wife's."

"Wife?" Shock turned John rigid. He ignored Drew's outstretched hand and stared, thunderstruck, at Lynn. His voice shook as he demanded, "You're married?"

Wordlessly, she nodded. She couldn't have spoken if her life had depended on it just then.

Dark fury hardened John's eyes and he glared at her with utter contempt. "You were married all along and yet you didn't tell me! I thought you had more honor and integrity than that! No wonder you didn't want to talk about marriage. You couldn't, not with a husband hidden in the woodworks! Nice going, Lynn. If your objective was to make a fool of me, you did a good job of it!" He turned abruptly and stalked out of the house, leaving a heavy, uncomfortable silence behind him.

Chapter Six

$\mathcal{L}$ike actors in a well-rehearsed play and with each one knowing his part perfectly, movement began in the room. Cal stretched and faked a yawn. "It's been a long day," he commented idly. "Think it's about time to call it a night, honey?" He glanced at his wife.

Right on cue, Gwen nodded. "Yes, I'm tired, too, and it's way past bedtime for the children." Awkwardly, she got up from the sofa and smiled toward the couple still standing motionless beside the door. "It was a lovely dinner and we enjoyed the evening." She tossed the next line to her husband. "I'll go with you to get the children."

They left the room and when they did, Drew's hand fell at last from Lynn's waist. He crossed the room and resumed his position in the chair he had been sitting in earlier. There was a stony expression on his face and he brushed a hand across his eyes before leaning forward, hands clasped between his legs, to stare at the floor.

Lynn felt nothing. A numbness deadened all sensations. She vaguely heard Cal and Gwen talking to the children in the bedroom, she was aware, without caring, that Drew was still in the room with her, but somehow, nothing seemed to matter. It was a protection she wrapped around herself, for she knew if she allowed herself to think and feel, she would sink right through the floor with shame and horror.

Mechanically, she went to the coffee table and began gathering up cups and dessert plates and stacking them on the tray. The rattling of the dishes was the only sound in the room and it sounded unnaturally loud to her ears.

She carried the tray to the kitchen and set it on the counter with a clatter before turning away. The washing could wait until morning.

When she returned to the living room, Cal and Gwen and their sleepy children were about to leave. Drew stood beside them near the door, the cordial host to the very end.

"Glad you came tonight," he said politely. "It was lovely seeing you again, Gwen. You have a wonderful little family."

"Thank you," Gwen responded. "It was nice to see you, too. Will we see you again, Drew?" she asked pointedly. "What are your plans?"

Drew shook his head. "They're very uncertain at the moment. They depend . . ." he paused significantly, "on a number of things."

"I see." Gwen did not pretend to misunderstand and she glanced at Lynn's pale face thoughtfully before returning her attention to him. "Just promise me," she said earnestly, "that whatever you do, you won't make any hasty decisions you might regret later."

Drew smiled down at her. "You're a nice lady, Gwen," he said softly. He bent to kiss her cheek. "I can't make you that promise, but . . . we'll see." Then he shook hands with Cal and a moment later they were gone.

It was Drew who put Joy to bed that night. When Lynn made a halfhearted move toward the direction of the hall, he said sharply, "No. Sit down and relax. I'll tend to her."

Lynn obeyed because she was still too shaken to argue. She sat down and allowed him to go to Joy, but she couldn't relax. The numbness had speedily worn off and now she was as tense as some of her students at exam time.

Only she had already failed her exam. The exam of life. And she had failed it dismally. She had made a wrong choice long ago when she did not tell Drew she was pregnant; she had made another more recently by not telling John from the beginning that she was married.

What was it, she wondered now, that made her so secretive with men? Ordinarily she was a very open person. She was up-front in her dealings with friends, with Gwen and Aunt Mary and Joy, but for some reason when it came to her relationships with men she became closed and deceitful. Tonight she had angered Drew and hurt John, all because of a lack of honesty. In all her life she had never caused so much pain and turmoil for others and just now Lynn did not like herself very much at all.

She resolved to write John a letter of apology. It wouldn't help much and would solve nothing, but she knew she owed him an explanation of some sort and this time it would be the truth. A truth that came too late.

But dealing with Drew was going to be a very different matter. A well-thought-out letter was out of the question. He was here . . . and he wasn't pleased with her.

The subject of her thoughts walked into the room and he lowered himself heavily onto the opposite end of the sofa from her. Lynn's nerves tightened as she waited for the verbal lashing she knew was to come.

She did not have long to wait. Drew turned so that he could look at her. Lynn felt his movements. She also felt the piercing intensity of his gaze.

"Your friend was quite right, you know," he said with uncompromising directness. "You showed a remarkable lack of integrity to lead him on to the point of falling in love with you without bothering to tell him that you weren't free."

"I did *not* lead him on!" Lynn exclaimed indignantly.

"You went out with him!"

"Well, yes, but . . ."

"Don't you think that alone would give a man the impression that you're available?" Drew asked hotly. "That he can move in and stake out his claim to the territory?"

"You're being deliberately insulting!" Lynn grated out. "It wasn't like that!"

"Of course it was like that!" Drew shot back. "When a man continues to see a woman it's because he wants to go to bed with her!"

"We didn't—" Lynn sputtered in self-defense.

Drew cut her off. He scowled blackly and snarled, "Don't attempt to tell me that he didn't *want* to because I won't swallow that for one minute!"

Lynn nibbled at her lip and lowered her gaze to his chest. What Drew said was undeniable, of course. Sullenly, she replied, "That's besides the point. I didn't sleep with him and I did not lead him on!"

"You must have done something to encourage him if he even wanted to marry you!"

"All I did was go out with him a few times!" Lynn cried in exasperation. Her stormy gaze met his again. "Don't try to tell me *you* stayed home and lived like a monk all these years, because I certainly won't believe that!"

"Maybe not," Drew acknowledged nastily, "but if you'll recall, I was the one who was walked out on in this marriage, not the other way around! And I certainly never encouraged any woman to think I was going to marry her! You've sure been setting a fine moral example for our daughter, haven't you? Passing yourself off as a single woman and encouraging other men to be interested in you, all the while keeping her carefully hidden away from her own father! I'm not at all sure you're a fit mother!"

"That's not true!" Lynn gasped. Her face drained of color and she stared at him with the same horror she might have had at being suddenly confronted by a deadly snake. "I *am* a good mother! I swear to you, Drew, that I've never slept with another man in all the time we've been apart and I haven't set a bad example for Joy! But for heaven's sake, what do you expect out of me . . . to sit home all alone for my entire life? I get lonely, too, just like anybody else!"

"Then you should have divorced me so that you could be utterly free to do as you please!" He drew a breath, then asked in a more normal tone of voice, "How much does that man mean to you?"

Lynn shook her head. "He's just a good friend. Or was," she qualified her statement.

"Are you sure? Do you love him? Because if you want to marry him, I . . ."

"No!" Lynn interrupted him. "I don't love him and I don't want to marry him! But if you're offering a divorce, maybe it's high time we did it! That way you won't have the notion that you have a right to subject me to any more pompous lectures!" Angrily, she turned her back to him and blinked rapidly, fighting tears.

There was a long silence behind her, though Lynn was sharply conscious of Drew's eyes upon her. She caught her lower lip between her teeth and, through blurred eyes, gazed toward the bookshelves. She had no way of knowing what he was thinking or from what front he would attack next.

At last Drew spoke and when he did, his voice was thick. "Are you telling me the truth?" he asked. "You haven't slept with anyone since you left me?"

Lynn's throat was filled with tears, so she could only nod in reply.

"Why?" Drew asked gruffly. When she didn't answer, he asked again, "Why?"

Lynn shrugged her shoulders, still turned away from him. "I don't know why!" she snapped. "What difference does it make, anyway?"

"All the difference in the world," Drew told her. He pulled her around to face him, saw the glitter of tears in her eyes and laughed softly. "You act like you're ashamed of it."

"Well, I'm not!" she said with spirit. "I just don't happen to think my personal life is any of your business anymore!"

"That's where you're wrong," Drew said implacably. "You're still my wife and the mother of my child, so your life is very much my business. You used to be a very hot-blooded woman, Lynn, so if you haven't been with any man since we lived together as man and wife then maybe it's because you were subconsciously hoping I would find you."

"No!" The denial came swiftly. "It had nothing to do with you!"

"No?" The word was soft as a down feather. Drew's forefinger traced the outline of her face, gentle and light but with a powerful, tingling effect. Lynn caught her breath as the hand slid down to her throat and now edged the neckline of her dress. His fingers brushed across the swell of her breasts and she shivered from the unexpected arousal of such a fleeting contact with her skin. "No?" he asked again. "And yet you're reacting already to my caresses, and I've scarcely even touched you. How do you explain that . . . or this?" Without giving her a chance to answer, Drew cupped both hands around her face and held her still as he bent slowly toward her.

He tasted her lips gently, experimentally and his mouth was warm on hers. But soon gentleness gave way to sweet force and he parted her lips so that his tongue could begin its exploration. His hands left her face to stray to her shoulders where his thumbs rubbed in sensual circular motions.

Lynn's breath came rapidly, her heart, a staccato beat beneath her breast. She did try to resist in the beginning by holding herself rigid, but her body seemed to be ignoring the commands from her brain.

Drew's mouth released hers so that he could begin nibbling at her earlobe. Lynn sighed audibly and gave up her attempt to defy the urges that battered her senses. Her hands slid around his chest to press against his back, bringing him closer to her.

Her response stimulated him. Roughly, he crushed her to him; his lips returned to claim hers with a fervency that thrilled her. One of his hands slid down from her waist to her thigh, then up to stroke a breast. Lynn's body turned to fire every place that he touched.

At last, Drew pulled back from her a little and his eyes were dark with passion. "I ought to hate you," he said hoarsely, "for all you've done. But as God is my witness, I've never been able to get you out of my system."

"I ought to hate you, too," she whispered breathlessly, "for storming back into my life and turning it upside down. But I've never been able to forget you, either."

Drew gave her a crooked grin. "So . . . what do we do about it, I wonder?"

She laughed softly. "If you don't know the answer to that, then you're not the same man I married."

Chuckling, Drew got to his feet and pulled her up beside him. "I guess I'll just have to show you that I am, then, won't I?"

"I guess you will, at that," she said provocatively.

Hand in hand, they went down the hall together. They stopped in the doorway of Joy's room and, by the dim glow of the night-light, looked down at their sleeping daughter. Drew turned to Lynn and smiled and then, quietly, they went into Lynn's room and closed the door.

As though they were two puppets on a string following the dictates of a higher force, they moved into each other's arms. They kissed and the kiss was of such intensity, so *giving,* that it shook Lynn to her very soul. She was, she realized, back where she had always belonged. In her heart, she had never left.

Drew undressed her with leisurely pleasure. A bedside lamp softly illuminated the room and cast a golden light over her alabaster skin as Lynn's dress dropped to the floor, leaving her shoulders bare. Drew paused long enough to plant brief kisses on her shoulders and at her throat before he reached around to her back and unhooked her bra.

Shudders of exquisite sensation ran through her as he bent to take one nipple in his mouth. Her breasts hardened with desire and she reveled in the sweet torture. She threaded her fingers through his hair and whispered, "Don't torment me forever, Drew, please!" Her own hands began groping for the buttons of his shirt.

When one of the buttons popped off completely, Drew laughed at her. "Now look what you've done, you impatient woman!" He watched her with amusement as she tugged the shirt free of the waistband and finished the job by sliding it from his shoulders. Then she unbuckled his belt, but got no further as he scooped her up and tossed her on the bed.

With eyes half-closed, Lynn watched as Drew quickly shed the rest of his clothes. His physique was magnificent, strong and solidly built. His carriage was graceful and lithe, reminding her of a proud lion ruling his jungle kingdom. Certainly the arrogance and self-confidence of royalty were there, stamped on his face as he met her unflinching gaze. He was a robust, virile male and powerful passions coursed through his veins. A flame of excitement leapt in hers at the sight of him.

He joined her on the bed and made short work of removing her half-slip and pantyhose. Once those items had been tossed to the floor, he propped himself up on one elbow and looked at her. His gaze traveled the length of her from head to toe and Lynn lay silently until his eyes had looked their fill.

"If anything, you've grown more beautiful with

the years, darling," Drew said huskily. "You're still slender, but you're more rounded than you were when we married." His hand went to her bare middle and then moved slowly up to tease a breast.

Lynn's hands went to his shoulders and she pulled him forward until his firm body was covering hers completely. Their eyes met as she brought his face close to hers and something of momentous importance passed between them, though no word was spoken. It wasn't needed, for the message was clear, all the same. They were bemused by a mutual physical attraction, just as they had always been, but there was also a tenderness underscoring it that transcended and enhanced the act of lovemaking.

The hint of a smile touched both of their mouths, a signal that each had understood the other. Lynn lifted a finger and brushed it lightly across the contours of his lips. Drew kissed it before moving lower and covering her mouth with his once more. Lynn's lashes fluttered down over her eyes and she became lost, totally consumed by the searing force of her own unrestrained emotions.

Time, place, all outside conditions fell away. They came together with tumultuous hearts and feverish desires that begged, *demanded* to be placated. Only by completing and fulfilling each other could they be sated and each of them gave and touched, caressed and kissed until in one final, glorious instant, they reached the peak of ecstasy.

The most perfect sense of contentment filled Lynn afterward. It was as though somehow she was her real self again instead of merely a shadow. Drew turned over to lie on his back and he pulled her close so that her head was cradled on his arm.

"I've missed you, darling," he whispered huskily.

"I've missed a lot of things about you, but most of all this . . . making love to you, going to sleep with you in my arms."

"No more than I have," she murmured softly. "I used to lie awake nights, remembering how it felt to fall asleep with your arm across my waist, like you were protecting me after we had made love."

Drew's smile went suddenly, and it was like the sun when it goes behind a cloud and the light no longer brightens the earth below. With its absence goes its warmth and it did so now for Lynn when Drew said, "Protective, hmm? Yet you ran away because you were afraid of me, afraid to tell me that as a result of our lovemaking, you carried my child." There was genuine pain in his voice instead of anger this time and he shook his head. "Some protection," he said with self-condemnation. "You felt you had to protect yourself *against* me!"

Lynn sat up, half-turning to gaze down at him. "Drew, you were so dead set against having a family. With the attitude you had about it, I just couldn't talk to you, couldn't tell you."

"I know." For the first time he admitted that his own attitude was at least partially to blame. "I backed you into a corner and gave you no room to escape. I can see now that you felt you couldn't be open and honest with me."

Slowly, she nodded. "Yes." Her answer came in a tiny thread of her normal voice.

He tugged on her arm and pulled her back down beside him. "I'm sorry." His words shook unsteadily. "I'm really sorry, Lynn. I fell a long way short of the sort of husband you needed. I guess the truth is that I just didn't know how to go about it."

"Marriage is sharing, Drew," she said softly. "And talking. Communicating. Discussing things together and then making decisions together. We didn't have that. You only told me what you wanted or didn't want and then expected me to abide by your decision whether it was about having a family or my going out to work."

He nodded. "I can see that now. I made a lot of mistakes along the way, Lynn. My only excuse, and it's a poor one, is that I just didn't know better. I was taught to be hard and decisive. Dad never considered a single opinion of mine in his life. He just told me and expected me to abide by his wishes. In business, it works well. I did the same thing after he died and I took over his concerns. I guess I just thought that was how a marriage worked, too. I never gave you a chance."

They were both silent at this admission until finally Lynn asked, "If I hadn't run away, if I had told you I was pregnant, what would have happened between us, Drew?" She paused and then asked the pertinent question. "You wouldn't have been pleased, would you?"

He was quiet for a long time and Lynn felt him stiffen beside her. She held her breath as she waited for his reply and her heart sank when he finally said in a stark statement, "No. I wouldn't have been happy about it." He turned his head to look at her then and again, there was pain in his gaze. "I know that disappoints you, Lynn, but I'm trying to be honest with you. I would," he finished gruffly, "have hated it!"

"But . . ." She ached to understand, but failed miserably. "But now she's here, you act like you adore Joy!"

"I do," he responded quickly.

"You're not making sense!" Lynn protested in exasperation.

"I know." Drew managed a weak grin. "It's just something that I can't explain, darling. Something I've never told anyone in my life."

"But I was your wife!"

He bent to graze her forehead with a tender kiss. "You *are* my wife," he corrected. "And a wonderfully sexy gal in bed!" He smiled. "Let's just enjoy the present and drop the past for now, all right?"

With instantaneous intuition, Lynn realized that Drew suffered from a devil within him, that he was tortured by some inexplicable, demonic hang-up that she could not even begin to understand. It was something stronger than the love he had once had for her, an unseen enemy that she had been helpless from the beginning to fight.

Compassion swept over her. Drew was chained within the prison of himself and she could only speculate about the agonies of punishment he endured. She had no wish to compound his distress. Maybe in time, with understanding and support, he would be able to liberate himself—and her as well.

Now she returned his smile, nodded and slid her arms around his neck. "Show me again," she said mischievously, "how to enjoy the present."

"Forgotten already, teacher?" A glimmer of humor lit his eyes.

"I'm a slow learner," she said. "I have to be taught through repetition."

Drew's hand moved silkily down the length of her, from her throat, over her breasts, across her stomach and onto her thighs. A ripple of pleasurable anticipation went through her as the lesson began.

When morning came, it felt strangely satisfying to awaken to the toasty warmth of a man's body close beside her. Lynn gazed tenderly down at Drew's sleeping face and emotion clogged her throat. He looked so peaceful, happy even, for an unconscious smile touched his mouth and seeing him this way, without defense or attack, she encountered a fact she had not allowed herself to face since his arrival. She was still very much in love with him in spite of the years of separation, in spite of the reasons why she had left him. Last night had not brought a return of that love, for it had always been there, just beneath the surface, just below conscious acknowledgment. Rather, their lovemaking had merely compelled her to face reality.

Softly, so that she would not disturb Drew's rest, Lynn slipped out of bed. She covered her nakedness with her robe, thrust her feet into scuffs and stole quietly from the room.

A half hour later, from the kitchen where she sat enjoying the early morning stillness along with a cup of coffee, Lynn heard stirrings from the back of the house. Either Joy or Drew or both were awake. She got up and went toward the refrigerator. It was time to begin breakfast.

The two of them came in laughing as Joy rode piggyback on Drew's shoulders. Joy's face was flushed with sleep and excitement, her hair a dark, fluffy cloud against the angelic white of her ruffled nightgown. Drew wore a blue robe that increased the deep blue pools of his eyes. Shadowy bristles stubbled his jaw, chin and upper lip and seeing him like that, needing a shave and casually attired, did something to Lynn. This intimate early morning glimpse of him, besides the heartwarming sight of him enjoying his daughter's company, pulverized any lingering resistance to him that she might have had.

He caught her gaze and grinned. Once he had put

Joy on her feet, he ran a hand across his chin, making a raspy sound. "I know. It has to go, but not before my coffee." He crossed the room to where she stood beside the stove. "And not before my good-morning kiss." He inclined his head and his twinkling eyes laughed at her dilemma, for he was as well aware of their daughter's wide-eyed presence as she was. Then, gently, he kissed her before patting her bottom and saying, "Better rescue whatever that is you're cooking."

With a startled cry, Lynn turned back to the stove and lifted a pancake with the spatula. She now had one nicely charred, black, inedible blob.

By the time she had her cooking under control once more and could spare an instant to turn around, Drew was seated at the table and Joy was perched contentedly on his lap.

"Do you like to kiss Mommy?" she asked guilelessly.

Drew lifted his gaze to Lynn's face and grinned before answering, "Sure I do. She's nice and soft and she tastes good, too."

Joy took the statement as a matter of course. "Uncle Cal kisses Aunt Gwen a lot. He says it's more fun than hugging the puppies!" She wrinkled her nose as though she could not quite swallow such a whopper and asked, "Is it, Daddy?"

Drew tossed back his head and roared heartily. Finally, he shook his head. "I don't know, princess. I don't kiss your Aunt Gwen."

"Daddy!" Joy giggled. "I know that! Daddys are only supposed to kiss the mommys," she said wisely.

"That's right," Drew replied. "And their little princesses," he added as he planted a kiss on Joy's upturned cheek.

Joy returned the kiss, but after a moment she squirmed off his lap and went to Lynn with an entirely different subject than kisses absorbing her interest. "Mommy, are you sure the Easter bunny will know where I live now?"

Lynn smiled. "Of course, darling. While we're at church, he's going to come to Aunt Gwen's house, remember? He'll hide your eggs there so that you can hunt for them with Penny and Pat and Kenny. And after that, we'll all have a picnic down by the creek."

"Daddy, too?"

"If he wants to come along," Lynn said non-comittally.

"Sure, I'm coming, too," Drew said with enthusiasm. "I wouldn't want to miss seeing how good an egg hunter you are!"

"I'm *real* good!" Joy boasted. "Last year only Pat found more eggs than me." She paused, then asked, "Are you coming to church with us, too?" She climbed into her own chair at the table as Lynn set her plate of pancakes and sausage before her.

Drew again lifted his gaze to meet Lynn's and there was an odd look in his eyes that she couldn't decipher before he nodded at Joy and said in a thoughtful tone, "Yes, I think I will. I'd like that very much."

Lynn was taken aback, but she carefully concealed her surprise as she turned back to the stove to scoop another pancake onto the platter.

While they ate, Drew surprised her again. "To-morrow," he said idly, as though it were the most natural thing on earth, "I'll go into town and see about hiring some men to start the barn. Cal promised to lend me his tractor so that I can plow the garden. It'll depend on when he doesn't need to use it himself, of course, but it shouldn't take me too long once I get started."

"I can't afford the barn just yet," Lynn said flatly. "I plan to buy the materials and then try to get a man to work part . . ."

"It would take forever that way," Drew interrupted. "Don't worry about the cost. I'm footing it."

"But why?" she asked bluntly. "After all, this isn't your property. It's mine. Why should you be out any money on it?"

Drew shrugged indifferently, then bit into a piece of sausage. It was several minutes before he finally said, "You're still my wife, Lynn. If a man can't help out his wife and child, then who should he help?"

"Yes, but . . ."

"No 'buts,'" he said shortly. "I want to do it, so I'm going to. Okay?"

Lynn fell silent, but not because his answer satisfied her. A multitude of questions skipped around in her mind. Drew's response was just a bit too pat, just a little too vague, meant to conceal his real motivation. And what about their own relationship now? she wondered. Where did they go from here? Last night they had made love; this morning nothing could seem more like a normal family life than a discussion over breakfast about going to church, enjoying an Easter outing and plans for improvements to one's home. It was almost as though they were back together for good, with a shared future ahead.

Lynn did not attempt to kid herself. She wanted it to be like that. Last night had proven that. She wanted Drew in her life again, not temporarily, but every day, every night, for the rest of her life. She wanted him to fill her nights with love; to wake up each morning to his smile, to the cosy family discussions of a day's work ahead, to share the pleasures and trials of raising their child, to grow old together after satisfying years and blended memories behind them. Her desires were exactly the same as they had been when she first fell in love with him and married him.

But Drew had said nothing about permanence. He was still physically attracted to her enough to make love to her, true. Equally true was the fact that he cared for Joy. He could even sit and casually talk about building her a barn and plowing her a garden, but none of that spelled forever. He still had a life, a home, a business in California and it could only be a matter of time before he returned to it.

Lynn ached to ask him how long he planned to stay, how much time this renewed closeness between them would last, what the future held for them all, but she was afraid of the answers. She had just glimpsed real happiness, but she was unable to grasp it and hold it to her. It was like the sunbeam that danced across the kitchen floor, eluding possession, coming and going as it willed.

Chapter Seven

The town of Williamsboro had a peaceful, settled atmosphere. Graceful old whitewashed houses of an earlier, less mass-produced era with stately oaks shading their lawns fronted the main street on either end of the town. Some yards boasted rose gardens; others featured flowering dogwood trees or camellia bushes.

The center of town, the business district, consisted of mostly brick storefronts with the look of weathered time and permanence on their faces. Normally a busy and thriving community, on Easter morning the downtown area was deserted except for an occasional parked car.

The church, which Lynn and Joy had attended numerous times with Gwen's family, was located on a side street two blocks from Main Street. Here there were signs of life, for cars filled the parking lot beside it and lined the sides of the streets skirting it.

Families, men in conservative suits, women and children in colorful spring outfits, spilled from the automobiles and made their way to the church doors.

Drew found a place to park Lynn's car, which they had decided to use instead of the truck, and the three of them were soon following the other worshipers toward the church.

Joy skipped ahead, as pretty as a rosebud in her pink dotted-swiss dress with a matching pink linen coat. Lynn and Drew followed at a more decorous pace.

When the child reached the foot of the steps, the pastor's wife, who had been chatting with another lady, saw her and smiled. "Good morning, Joy. It's so nice to see you again. You look very pretty today."

"Thank you, Mrs. Hamilton," Joy responded with an angelic smile and a dash of panache. "So do you. I like your dress. It's the same color as the sky."

Mrs. Hamilton laughed and brushed a finger lightly down Joy's cheek. "Well, thank you very much." She lifted her head to glance at Lynn. "With such flattering compliments as that, I predict this child will go far in the world!"

Lynn smiled. "You're probably right."

"How are you, my dear?" Mrs. Hamilton asked now. "Are you all settled into your home?"

Lynn nodded. "Yes, I am. It's nice to know that I'm actually a part of this community now."

"We're glad to have you," Mrs. Hamilton said warmly. "I think you'll like it here. Most people are very friendly and helpful to newcomers. You must certainly call on me if you need anything."

"Thank you, I'll remember that," Lynn said. Now the pastor's wife turned her enquiring gaze and welcoming smile toward Drew and Lynn suddenly tensed, knowing there was no way out of introducing him. With an effort, she forced out the words. "Mrs. Hamilton, I'd like to introduce you to Andrew Marcus. Drew, Mrs. Hamilton is the pastor's wife."

"Marcus?" A puzzled look came to the lady's eyes even as she extended her hand to Drew. "Are you related to Lynn, then?"

Drew clasped her hand in his as he gave her a dazzling smile that Lynn knew was calculated to charm. "In a manner of speaking," he said with a twinkle in his eyes. "I'm her husband."

Mrs. Hamilton was clearly taken aback. *And no wonder,* Lynn thought grimly. Until this minute she had never given any hint to the residents she had met in town that she even possessed such a thing.

"Oh. How nice to meet you," Mrs. Hamilton said after she recovered from her surprise. "It's lovely that you could join us for services today."

"Thank you," Drew answered. "I'm happy to be here. I haven't been able to join my family before because I had business commitments in California."

"I see. Well, now that you're here, let me introduce you to some of our members." Mrs. Hamilton turned toward a couple who was approaching up the walk and beckoned them to join their little group.

Before they were finally able to go inside, Mrs. Hamilton had introduced Drew to at least a dozen people. Lynn had to endure it all with a tight, set smile and the odd casual comment or two. She was well aware of the curious speculation they received, for most of the people had met her many times over the past year or so, during which she had never been accompanied by the man they now met as her husband. For Drew's part, though, he seemed not to notice the unvoiced question in people's eyes as he smiled and shook hands with them. He appeared to be thoroughly enjoying his welcome to both Williamsboro and the church and was not in the least self-conscious.

Lynn, though, was suffering the most acute discomfort and embarrassment of her life and when they at last entered the sanctuary and slipped into a pew, she was far from feeling pious. Her one overriding emotion was relief at getting away from the necessity of talking with anyone else.

Soft organ music filled the room as the congregation entered and took their seats. The gentle sound was meant to soothe, to put one in a receptive, worshipful mood, but within Lynn a storm churned and raged. Drew had no business coming here with her today, she thought rebelliously, meeting people, smiling, placing his hand intimately at her waist for all to see, giving one and all the deliberate impression that they were a happy, devoted couple. Now those same people would expect to see him with her always and she would only have to endure their curiosity all over again once he was gone.

The church service began and Lynn struggled to center her attention on it instead of on the disturbing man who sat on the other side of Joy. She was glad he wasn't sitting next to her. His nearness affected her too much as it was and if their bodies were close enough to make even the most casual contact, she would really have been hard put to focus her mind on the sermon.

Gradually, though, the lovely, age-old story of resurrection and glory gripped her and Lynn felt a strange peace flow over her like warm, gentle water. Springtime was reborn within her heart as she stole a sideways peek at Drew and Joy and she thought suddenly that perhaps, after all, the love that had once been between Drew and herself could, in truth, be renewed. After all, he *was* here. He had come to find her, he was enthralled by his daughter and last night he had proved that he did not completely despise her any longer. Perhaps there was hope for their marriage, just as the pastor told the tale of an even greater hope.

Outside after church, a few more people introduced themselves to Drew, but this time, with her new serenity, Lynn did not allow it to upset her. Gwen, Cal and their children joined them for a few moments and if they were surprised at seeing Drew with her today after the tense scene of the previous evening, they did not show it.

"You're coming over with Lynn for the kids' egg hunt and our picnic, aren't you?" Cal asked.

"I'll be there," Drew promised.

Cal nodded. "Good. When you come, I'll show you where I keep the tractor and the fuel for it. You can use it Tuesday if you want. I'll be tied up all that day at the shop in town." He called to Penny and Pat, "Come on, twins. Time to get home." He glanced down at Joy and added, "Want to ride home with us?"

Joy nodded. "Can I, Mommy?" she pleaded.

"Sure," Lynn agreed. "But try not to get your dress dirty. I'll bring some play clothes for you when I come. Oh, and don't you dare start hunting eggs until we get there. I want to take pictures."

"Don't worry." Gwen grinned conspiratorially, then whispered, "Cal got up early and hid them all down by the creek instead of around the yard. We figured it would increase the suspense for them because this time they won't be able to search in familiar spots."

"Good idea." Lynn laughed.

Before turning away to follow her brood toward the station wagon, Gwen added, "You don't have to rush about coming over. I've got to make my potato salad and ice my cake before we can go to the creek, so it'll be at least an hour or so before we're ready."

Lynn nodded and they parted, Joy dancing along with Penny toward the Jennings' station wagon, Lynn and Drew heading in the opposite direction.

When they reached the car and got inside, Drew turned to smile at Lynn before he put the key in the ignition. His gaze slid from her face downward to the soft green dress that fitted flatteringly over her breasts, tucked in at her waist and skimmed her rounded hips. The curling brown mass of her hair had been pinned up in an artful design with a few stray ringlets falling softly to frame her face. Drew reached out to tug lightly at one of them. His fingers brushed against her earlobe, and even that fleeting touch immobilized her.

"Did I tell you how lovely I think you are today, Mrs. Marcus?" he asked huskily.

Lynn's quick, indrawn breath was barely audible. A rush of warmth spread through her, erasing the doubts that had tormented her earlier. When Drew smiled at her like that, with that special, intimate expression in his eyes that had always been reserved just for her, it was easy to forget everything except the moment at hand.

She found an answering smile and shook her head. Her voice was slightly unsteady as she replied, "I don't recall your saying anything on that subject to me, as a matter of fact. Only to Joy."

Drew's eyes laughed at her. "Know why? If I had told you, I would have had to kiss you and if I had kissed you, it's highly doubtful that we would ever have made it to church at all."

"I . . . see." Her own eyes sparkled and her face flushed softly with pleasure. "And now?"

Drew shook his head and scowled at her with ferociousness. "Don't tempt me, woman! This is a public place. But just you wait until I get you home!" He turned from her, put the key in the ignition and switched it on.

"Threats, threats," Lynn taunted. "All talk, no action!"

Drew glared at her through narrowed eyes. "You'll pay for that, you little devil!"

And pay she did. As soon as they entered the house, Drew lunged for her. Lynn squealed and darted behind a sturdy chair. Drew merely lifted it and set it out of the way as though it weighed no more than a piece of paper. "You may as well stay put, woman!" he thundered as she whirled and dashed toward the kitchen. "No woman taunts me like that and gets away with it!"

"You have to catch me first!" she jeered over her shoulder. In the kitchen, she jerked out a chair from beneath the table and thrust it behind her before she made for the back door. A moment later she heard a crash, then a muttered oath and she giggled helplessly as she turned the doorknob.

She never got through the door. A large hand covered hers and a low rumble at her ear said, *"Now* you'll pay for those words . . . and for the bruise I just got tripping over that chair!" He scooped her squirming body into his arms as easily as if she had offered no resistance at all and his eyes blazed with mischief and something else that caused her heart to skip erratically.

All at once the laughter was gone from them both. Their faces were close and their gazes became intent as they looked at each other with wonder. Lynn lifted her hand to entwine her fingers in his thick hair and the action brought his face, his irresistible lips closer. She bent her head just enough to meet his lips with her own.

When they lifted their heads to look at each other again, Lynn saw that his eyes had darkened with desire. Wordlessly, Drew carried her into the bedroom.

As they had done the night before, they undressed each other. Lynn removed Drew's suit coat, his tie and began unbuttoning his shirt.

"Try not to pop one off this time," he teased.

"If I do," she said and laughed, "I promise I'll sew it back on for you."

She finally had it unbuttoned without mishap and ran her hands across his strong shoulders, his furry chest and the flatness of his belly. She liked the firmness of his skin against her fingertips, the tantalizing crispness of the dark hair that was centered on his chest and tapered downward to his waist. She planted a kiss at his collarbone and when she did, Drew's arms encircled her and he said hoarsely, "My turn."

Her dress and undergarments were tossed recklessly to a chair and soon she stood completely naked before his sultry gaze. Then he pulled the hairpins from her hair so that it fell in a dark wave against her back. A blaze flared in those eyes and her bones turned to jelly as he pulled her to him and his teeth began nibbling at her lips.

His hand slipped between them to cup one full breast and as his head lowered to it, hers went back and her body arched forward, seeking the moist warmth of his mouth.

She trembled as he teased first one breast, then abandoned it in favor of the other. She quivered as

123

an aching, hungering sensation weakened her. Her dusky nipples hardened beneath the torment of his love play and she clung tightly to him, never wanting it to end.

But at last she realized she had not completely undressed him. His belt buckle pressed into her tender flesh. She groped for and found it, undid it and then watched Drew's amusement as she slid his trousers down around his feet.

He helped her then, kicking free of them, ridding himself of shoes, socks and shorts and then he laughed, low in his throat, as he looked at her once more.

"Satisfied now?" he asked.

"Not quite," she retorted quickly.

He chuckled. "I'll see what I can do to remedy the situation." He scooped her into his arms again and carried her to the bed. As he began to lower her, she pulled him with her so that they landed in a tangled heap of arms and legs.

The tone of their lovemaking today made that of the night seem a tame thing of comparison. Perhaps then it had been borne of too much urgency. This time it was slower paced and infinitely more satisfying. There seemed not a place on her entire body that Drew did not touch and kiss. Lynn glowed from his murmured words of her beauty and shivered with exquisite, sensual delight as he drugged her with his kisses and brought her to a wild, frenzied level of excitement. In turn, she enjoyed the pleasure of stimulating him to the same high-pitched arousal by running her hands teasingly down the length of him. Each was as intent on pleasing as being pleased and it brought about total abandonment as they prolonged the inevitable finale.

But at last, just when Lynn knew she could not

hold back any longer, Drew's body moved over hers. Eagerly, she received him and her hands slid around his chest to his back to hold him close.

Slowly, rhythmically, they began to move together in unison. Drew clasped her tightly against his chest and buried his face in the crook of her neck. Their breathing became rapid until finally it became labored gasps for air.

They reached a precipice, trembled and hung there, precariously balanced and then a shower of stars exploded, so hot they were melded together. Very gradually, the cliff broke apart and like tiny stones rolling and falling, they tumbled back to earth.

For a long time afterward they lay unmoving and silent, their moist bodies still as one. Their breathing became more normal and at last Drew lifted his head so that he could look down at her.

"Hello, darling," he whispered.

Lynn smiled. "Hello, darling," she echoed.

"I can't tell you how wonderful it is to have you back in my arms like this, to be making love to you again."

Lynn smoothed a lock of hair from his glistening forehead. "You just did." She laughed softly. "I've missed you, Drew. Desperately."

"No more than I've missed you," he said thickly. He became aware that his full weight was still upon her and he levered himself up and rolled away. "I'm about to suffocate you," he said and laughed. Then he pulled her over on top of him and smiled as he wrapped his arms around her, lightly trailing one hand over her back while the other lovingly caressed her rounded bottom. "Must we get dressed and go to Cal's?" he asked in a petulant voice. "I'd much rather spend the afternoon in bed with you."

Lynn quirked an eyebrow at him. "And not watch Joy hunting for her Easter eggs? Don't be silly. She would be outraged if we missed such an important event."

Drew laughed. "You're right, of course. I guess I'm just not used to thinking like a father yet."

"It takes a little practice," she said grinning, "but you'll soon get the hang of it." She enjoyed her breathtakingly close view of his face and bent and deposited a quick kiss on his lips before escaping from his arms and scooting to the edge of the bed. "Come on, lazy," she told him. "It's getting late and we've already wasted enough of the afternoon as it is."

"Wasted, is it now, hmm?" Drew swatted her bare behind and then, leaping to his feet, beat her to the bathroom by an inch.

The afternoon was perfect for a picnic. The sky was clear, the sun bright and warming to the skin. The stream that ran through Lynn's property and formed the back boundary of Cal's and Gwen's, gurgled merrily just below the slope where a cloth had been laid for the food. It was still far too early in the spring to take a dip, but when summer came the children would enjoy happy hours splashing in its shallow waters.

The egg hunt had been an unqualified success. Joy and the twins had shouted with glee or squabbled amicably over a particular searching place as they quickly loaded their baskets with their finds. Even little Kenny had found his share of the booty with a bit of help and encouragement from his mother. Lynn had snapped pictures of them all as the children darted from bush to tree to a clump of woods that might conceal one of the treasured colored eggs.

126

Afterward they had eaten their meal and now the children played in a nearby clearing while their parents remained beside the picnic paraphernalia.

Cal had thoughtfully brought along a folding lawn chair for Gwen and she sat there like a queen on her throne while the others cleared away the clutter from the meal and stowed things back into baskets.

"I feel like a cheat," she said as she watched their activity. "I'm not pulling my weight today."

"Weight is the word, honey," Cal teased. He paused to reach out and lovingly pat her belly before he sank down on the grass beside her.

Gwen stuck out her tongue at him. "It's mean of you to remind me that I look like a blimp," she complained. She turned toward Lynn and said, "This morning when we were dressing for church, he told me I waddled like a duck."

"A sweet, lovable, fat duck," Cal said.

"A pregnant duck," Gwen grumbled sourly.

Cal grinned. "Don't worry, honey," he soothed. "I like lovable, pregnant ducks."

"You'd better," Gwen told him, giving him a threatening look. "If I so much as catch you even looking at a *skinny* duck, I'll . . ."

They all laughed, drowning out whatever dire fate she had been about to pronounce for him and Gwen joined in with them.

Lynn and Drew had both sat down in front of her and when the laughter died away, Drew said, "I know you're just joking around, Gwen, but does it really bother you, being pregnant?"

Gwen sobered and looked at him in vague surprise. "Bother me?" She shook her head. "Of course not. Why should it?"

Drew shrugged and plucked at a blade of grass near his right foot. "Well, being big, as you said, and knowing you have to face the pain of labor and delivery. Doesn't that frighten you?"

Gwen laughed and it was a gay sound, like a tinkling bell. "I'll admit it's not exactly ego boosting to look down at yourself and realize you're big as an elephant, but it's a temporary condition, after all. But that part is balanced by the thrill of knowing you're carrying a new life inside of you and there's just nothing like the feeling of it moving, stretching its little arms and legs. It's wonderful!" Her face glowed and there was no mistaking the sincerity in her voice.

"But the labor and delivery part," Drew pursued, "doesn't it hurt a lot? Doesn't it scare you to have to go through it?"

Lynn looked at Drew with a thoughtful frown. She was astounded that he was so interested in her sister's pregnancy and yet he clearly wanted to know Gwen's feelings about it. *What made him so curious?* she wondered. It puzzled her and when she glanced up at Gwen, she could tell that she was equally mystified.

Gwen answered slowly as though she were carefully searching for the right words to answer the questions instead of just rushing on with a flip response. "It's painful, Drew, I won't deny that. More so for some women than others. But I can't say it scares me. It's the least pleasant aspect of the entire process, naturally, but again, it's only temporary. It doesn't last and when it's over, you have a new baby placed in your arms and that makes up for everything else." She reached for her husband's hand and smiled as she added, "I love Cal and our children very much and I wouldn't *not* have them even if I had to go through ten times the pain involved."

"I see," Drew said quietly. He shifted his position where he sat on the ground and his eyes met Lynn's briefly. There was something strange in the depths of them and Lynn wondered anew what was really in his mind. He seemed to be honestly concerned about the pain connected with childbirth and yet it seemed incredible. Why should he care about Gwen's sufferings when he had not even wanted his own wife to have his child?

It hit her then. Something to do with such pain must be why he hadn't wanted her to have children. It frightened him in some way, and yet he had never admitted it to her. He had just coldly and arrogantly laid down his command that she was not to bear children and expected her to honor his wishes.

Lynn faced the fact again that she had known little about Drew when they had married. She had only been aware of her love for him and his for her and how happy she had been to be with him. She got to her feet abruptly and walked down to the edge of the stream, feeling a sudden need to be away from him, from Gwen and Cal and their conversation that had turned to politics.

She stared down into the gently running water and tried to remember the few things Drew had told her about his life. She knew he had never been close to his father, an autocratic figure who had demanded complete, unquestioning obedience and who had offered in return little, if any, love to his son. Maybe Drew's strange aversion to having children had been because he had been so unhappy as a child. Perhaps he had been afraid that all children's lives were equally miserable. But he could see that Joy was a happy, well-adjusted child, as were Gwen's and Cal's children. Besides, he adored Joy and lavished upon her all the affection he himself had been denied as a youngster, so it couldn't be that . . . not entirely, anyway. No, it had to do with pregnancy and childbirth itself. It was all a mystery to him, one that bothered him a great deal. She supposed it all stemmed again from his lack of knowledge of women when he had been growing up. He couldn't accept the idea of pregnancy and childbirth as the natural conditions they were.

But suddenly, for the first time she considered an idea that had never before crossed her mind. Maybe Drew had had another woman in the past, before he even met her, and something had happened between them. Maybe she had become pregnant and had resented it and took it out on Drew, hurting him badly because of her own frustrations. Maybe even now Drew had another child somewhere that she, Lynn, knew nothing about!

The thought shook her and yet the more she considered it, the more logical it all seemed and a cold chill layered her heart with ice. It was the most reasonable explanation there could be and it also explained why he had not confided in her. He hadn't wanted her to know there had been someone else first, someone who perhaps resented and hated him, someone who was also the mother of his child! Maybe, her thoughts went on relentlessly, the child had even died at birth. That would explain even more his inner torment and unvoiced fears.

Deep resentment now spread, freezing the blood in Lynn's veins. Drew had deliberately deceived her before they were married. There was something he had carefully hidden from her, if not what she had just guessed, then something close. She was certain of it! Drew had wanted to marry her, he had cared enough for her for that, but he had never loved her enough to be honest with her. He had correctly assumed that she would have had grave doubts about marrying him had she known beforehand of his objections to having a family and because of it, she had been denied the shared happiness of expecting a baby with her own husband!

She half-turned to glance back toward the others. Drew had left Cal and Gwen and was in the clearing tossing a ball with Pat. An hour ago the sight might have warmed her heart, but now it did nothing to thaw the cold anger that paralyzed her. He could show concern for Gwen's welfare, he had apparently had it for some other woman he had once loved, but it had not been there for her! For her had been the necessity of running away to hide, suffering through the long months of pregnancy and finally giving birth, all alone, without the support of a loving husband!

In that moment, Lynn believed she actually hated him.

For the remainder of the afternoon, Lynn took care to mask her emotions. Everyone else seemed to be having such a good time and she did not wish to spoil it for them. But for her, all pleasure had vanished and she had a desperate struggle pretending that nothing was wrong, especially whenever Drew touched her, smiled or engaged her in conversation. Once or twice she thought she detected a glimmer of questioning in his eyes, as though he guessed that something was bothering her, but to her relief he did not probe.

It was after nine that evening when they finally returned home. They had remained at the creek until the air grew too cool and then they all went back to Gwen's house where they made sandwiches with the remainder of the ham. Later, while the children played together, the four adults indulged in a game of gin.

Once they were back home, Lynn busied herself overseeing Joy's bath and checking what clothes she would lay out for morning. Easter vacation was over. Tomorrow she would return to work and Joy to the day-care center. They would have to make an early start for the long drive to Savannah and she did not want to make last minute preparations concerning what they would wear.

Drew made himself comfortable in the living room with the Sunday paper while Lynn flitted about doing her various chores, but when Joy was ready for bed, he joined them in her room to hear her prayers and to give her a good-night kiss.

When the two of them returned to the living room and Lynn went to lock the front door, Drew came up behind her and slid his arms around her. He pressed his face against her cheek and murmured softly, "You seem tired, darling. Go on to bed. I'll finish locking up and then join you."

"No!" Lynn unclasped his hands from her waist and moved away from him before turning to look back at him. Her gray eyes were dark and somber as she shook her head. "No, Drew. I'm not sleeping with you tonight."

Drew's brows snapped down over his eyes. "I think you'd better explain that," he said in a granite-like voice.

"It's self-explanatory," she said brusquely. "You'll sleep in the garage room tonight."

"What's the meaning of this?" Drew took a firm step toward her and his jaw jutted out as he glared at her. "Everything was just fine between us earlier.

132

What brought on this change of heart? I thought we had a wonderful day together."

"Well, you thought wrong," she replied. In a rush, she said, "You've come along and turned my life completely upside down, Drew. Because you went to church with us this morning, now all the locals will be gossiping about the sudden appearance of my husband. You've got Joy all excited about having a daddy. You've even conned Gwen and Cal into accepting your presence here just as though you belong, just as though everything's as it should be between us. But it isn't! All you've managed to do is to insure that when you leave, I'll be left in an awkward position."

"And is that all you care about?" Drew asked with a dangerous stillness about him. "Appearances? I thought after last night and again this afternoon that our lovemaking meant something important to us both . . . that maybe we could work things out between us after all and consider some kind of a future together, for our sakes as well as Joy's."

She fought a battle with herself to resist the pull of what he was saying. She didn't want to hear him say things like that, she didn't want to think it anymore. "There's nothing to work out," she said dully. "You'll be leaving soon and then I'll be left with the same life I had before you came."

"Including Simpson?" The tone of his voice was steely.

"Leave John out of this discussion, please!" she said swiftly.

Drew raised a hand and pointed an accusing finger at her. "No," he rasped, "*you* had better leave him out—out of your life. You're still married to me and don't you forget it! I'll not have my wife, the mother of my child, involved with another man! Do I make myself clear?"

"And I'll not have you back in my life!" Lynn stormed. "Is that clear?"

"Perfectly," Drew said coldly. "But remember this, you stole my child from me all these years and because of it, you have a lot to answer for. I'd watch my step if I were you!"

There was such a black fury in his eyes that Lynn trembled beneath the impact of his gaze. Before she could recover, Drew pivoted, went through the house and slammed the back door with such violence that even the living room windows vibrated.

Chapter Eight

$\mathcal{T}$here was a definite chill early Monday morning that had nothing at all to do with the temperature of the air. Shortly after Lynn rose and put on the coffee, a soft knock fell on the back door. It was Drew, dressed in denim jeans, a dark brown shirt and looking tired, as though he had not had any more of a restful night than she had. Neither of them spoke as he came in and helped himself to a cup of coffee.

Lynn ignored him and turned to the cupboard where she took out a box of oatmeal. A moment later she heard the scrape of a chair leg, which informed her that he had seated himself at the table.

When the saucepan of water began to boil, Lynn poured the oatmeal into it, stirred it and then lowered the flame. She felt Drew's gaze burning into her back. He was watching her every move and it was not a pleasant sensation.

She dropped a couple of slices of bread into the toaster and then she left the room. She went down the hall to Joy's bedroom and gently woke the child before returning with reluctance to the kitchen to pour the hot cereal into bowls.

Drew broke the tense silence then. "There's no sense in hauling Joy off at this hour all the way to Savannah, you know. Let her stay here with me."

"No." The word came out flat, uncompromising. "She's going with me."

"You still don't trust me. You're still afraid I'll skip with her."

Lynn whirled to face him. "Maybe I am," she admitted impatiently. "After all, I hardly know you."

"Hardly know me?" he echoed in amazement. "What kind of nonsense is that? I'm your husband, damn it!"

"So you are. But you very carefully kept from me before we married the fact that you had no intentions of ever having a family. And I'd say that was a very important omission on your part, wouldn't you?" She shrugged her shoulders lightly. "I didn't know that, so there's no telling what else I don't know about you."

"Like what?"

"Like *why* you didn't want children. Like what you intend to do next."

"I intend to be a father to my daughter," Drew said emphatically. "I've told you that before. As for the other, all that's ancient history and has no bearing on the situation now. But if you want my promise that I won't run off with Joy, you've got it. Now why don't you be sensible and let her stay home with me? Having to drive all the way to Savannah and back every day is going to make terribly long days for a little girl."

"Maybe so, but all the same, she's going with me."

Renewed hostility flared between them and they glared angrily at each other. Only when Joy entered the room did they both attempt to conceal their feelings and put on pleasant faces for her.

When she finally drove away from the house an hour later, Lynn was glad to leave the heavy tension behind. She felt her tight nerves beginning to relax. The Easter holiday had been overwhelming with all the work involved in moving, the two bad scenes with John and the emotion-charged dealings with Drew. It had all been too much for her and now she looked forward to returning to her job as a much needed escape from her personal life. She felt like she had been on a seesaw for days, rising high, then falling low with the accompanying sinking sensation in the pit of her stomach. She needed desperately to get back on to an even keel.

The familiar routine at school was exactly the prescription she had needed. Lynn immersed herself in the lessons and her young students' constant demands. By the end of the day she felt better able to cope with life in general. And one of the things she knew she had to cope with immediately was John Simpson. She had hurt him badly and while she couldn't alter what had already happened, she did owe him an explanation and an apology.

She drove directly to his office after school. She had thought of calling first, but she was afraid if she did, he would refuse to even see her.

His office was in the older section of the city in a renovated building on Broughton Street. Lynn was always captivated by the graceful beauty of Savannah's historic district. Its lovely squares, first laid out by James Oglethorpe, who founded the city in 1733, invited strollers to linger beneath the shade of magnificent oaks, and stately homes demanded appreciation of their fine architectural features. Being there was like stepping back into the past, a time when southern ladies adorned the city in their elegant, flowing dresses and gallant gentlemen courted them with flowery manners.

A black, lacy wrought-iron fence bordered the tiny front garden of the brick office building. Azaleas and cherokee roses bloomed within it and ivy and jasmine vines poked through the open spaces of the fence.

Lynn went through the gate and up the steps to enter the reception area that was tastefully decorated with pieces of Chippendale and other valuable antiques.

The young receptionist recognized her at once and smiled in welcome. "Hello, Mrs. Marcus," she said.

"Hello, Sue. Is Mr. Simpson busy?"

"He's busy, but he doesn't have any clients with him. I'll just tell him you're here."

"Don't bother," Lynn said quickly. "I'll surprise him." Before the girl could object, she went to the door of John's office and opened it.

She entered the room quietly and closed the door behind her. John was at his desk, head bent as he worked over some papers, but at the sound of the door he glanced up, an expression of impatience on his face that quickly turned into a frown.

"How did you get in here without Sue announcing you first?" he asked ungraciously.

"I didn't give her the chance," Lynn said frankly.

"I thought you might not see me if she told you I was here."

"You thought right." John tossed down his pencil to the deck, then leaned back in his chair. "Okay, you're here now, so say whatever it is you came to say. I'm very busy." He glanced pointedly at his wristwatch.

Lynn swallowed, then said softly, "I came to say I'm sorry."

"It's a bit late for that, Lynn," John said in a flat, emotionless voice. "You already made a fool of me. What more do you want now? To twist the knife?"

"Stop it!" she exclaimed. "I came to apologize and to explain. I figured I owed you that, at least!" John glared forbiddingly at her, but at least he didn't say anything, so she rushed on, the words tumbling out in her haste to get it over. "Until a few days ago, I hadn't seen my husband in over five years. He showed up unexpectedly and though I tried to get him to leave, he wouldn't go."

John's face was skeptical. "If you hadn't seen him in all those years, why weren't you already divorced from him?"

Lynn nibbled at her lower lip. "It's hard to explain."

"Try."

She looked down at her hands. "I . . . left him while I was expecting Joy. I won't go into the reasons why, because it isn't necessary. But I was afraid if I filed for divorce he would find me and try to take her away from me. So I . . . did nothing. I . . . it was never meant to hurt anyone, John, believe me, and the night you asked me to marry you I knew I was going to have to tell you the truth about myself. But then Drew came and you saw him when you came back. I'm really sorry you had to find out that way. I know it was a shock and that it hurt you, but I honestly didn't mean for you to learn about my marriage that way."

John was silent for a long time. "Is he still there?" he asked finally.

Lynn nodded.

"Have you reconciled, then?"

"Not exactly."

"What does that mean?" he demanded. "Either you have or you haven't."

"Well, we haven't," she snapped defensively.

John's gaze narrowed. "Have you slept with him?" he asked bluntly.

Lynn felt her face warm. "That's a rather personal question and I don't think it's any of your business."

"That answers it for me, anyway," John said dryly. He stood up. "So . . . that being the case, exactly why are you here?"

"I told you, I came to apologize. I'm sorry I wasn't honest with you from the beginning, John."

"Yes," he replied. "So am I. Now, if you'll excuse me," he said with formality, "I really am busy."

Lynn's confidence in her ability to cope was shattered by the time she was back outside on the walk. John had made himself quite clear. He was far from forgiving her and now she realized she had been naive in hoping that he would. As far as she could determine, she had only made a worse muddle of things all the way around. She had just made him angry all over again. Yesterday she had done the same thing to Drew.

She sighed wearily as she returned to the car. She made a hopeless mess out of everything these days! She seemed to curse all the lives she touched, she thought disparagingly.

It didn't help, either, after she picked Joy up, to have a cranky, tired child for the long drive home. It only emphasized again her shortcomings. Drew had tried to convince her to let Joy stay home with him because he had known such early risings would be hard on her, but would she listen to him? Not a chance! Know-it-all Lynn wasn't about to allow anyone to tell her a thing!

She was so thoroughly disheartened by the time she neared home that she was close to tears as Joy complained about the unfairness of the day-care center workers and the selfishness of her playmates there. Lynn knew that it was only because the child was out of sorts that made her talk that way and that it would blow over by the morning, but she was tired, too, and Joy's list of grievances was getting to her. On top of that, just the thought of a fresh confrontation with Drew tonight after her scrape with John was enough to send her into hysterics. Impulsively, she drove straight past her own driveway and on toward Gwen's house. Not once since Drew had arrived and everything had gone haywire had she spent a moment alone in private conversation with her twin. Just now, she felt a desperate need for it.

"We're not going home to Daddy?" Joy asked plaintively as the car whisked by the familiar turnoff.

Lynn swallowed down her irritation at the question and answered as calmly as she could. "In a little while, sweetie. Right now I need to talk to Aunt Gwen. Anyway, it'll give you another chance to see how the puppies are doing."

"Okay." For the first time since they had gotten into the car, Joy smiled her old, cheerful smile and, as soon as they arrived, she clambered from the car and dashed toward the house.

Lynn found her sister in the kitchen preparing dinner. The scent of baking chicken filled the room and she sniffed with appreciation. "Smells good," she said by way of greeting. "I may just invite myself to stay instead of going home and having to cook when I get there."

Gwen turned from the counter and laughed at her. "Sorry," she said with a rueful grin, "but as hungry as Cal says he is this evening, I doubt there'd be enough to go around. Besides, I can't be expected to feed the Marcus family *every* meal, can I?"

There was a teasing quality to the question, but Lynn ignored that and raised her eyebrows in surprise. "Every meal?"

"Gwen's eyes twinkled as she nodded. "Drew had lunch with us."

"He *did?*" Lynn was astonished. "What brought that about?"

"Cal called him this morning and asked him to pick up some fertilizer for him while he was in town. Drew brought it over around one and since he hadn't already eaten, he had lunch with us." She paused and looked thoughtfully at Lynn. "He didn't seem very happy today, somehow. Not at all like he was yesterday at our picnic. Anything wrong?"

Lynn grimaced and sat down at the table while she watched Gwen cut up some potatoes and toss them into a pan of water. "You name it, it's wrong!" She sniffed, then sucked in a deep breath. "I don't know what's the matter with me anymore, Gwen. One part of me is so glad he's here—and that part of me responds to him just as eagerly as I ever did. But the other part of me is still hurt and angry with him and because he deceived me in the past, I still can't really bring myself to trust him."

"I think you must have been completely wrong

about his not wanting children, Lynn. Any fool can see he dotes on Joy and yesterday he seemed to be doting on you, too!"

Lynn shook her head. "I'm not mistaken, believe me. He didn't want a family and I think I've finally realized why. I think he must have gotten some other woman pregnant before he ever met me and something happened between them. She either resented it and keeps the child from him or maybe she even lost the baby. You can see for yourself how obsessed he is over your pregnancy! All those questions about pain and fear! Don't you see . . . something had to have happened to scare him."

Gwen nodded. "I've guessed the same thing myself. But if that's the case, Lynn, why can't you have some compassion for the man? Surely you can't believe he enjoys having this abnormal fear about childbirth!"

"Of course not!" Lynn exclaimed. "But that's not the point. The point is that he won't confide in me, that he hid his feelings about it until after we were married! And he was so adamantly against it. He didn't play fair with me, Gwen! You don't have any idea how much I've envied your relationship with Cal! Why, he's always been so thrilled at the news that you're going to have a baby and wild horses couldn't keep him away from you at the time of birth! But I never had any of that." Her voice trembled with strong emotion. "I had to go through it all without a husband and it just isn't fair! Drew says I've been cruel and that I've cheated him out of Joy's early years, but he cheated me, too!"

Gwen stopped her dinner preparations and joined Lynn at the table. "Face it, sis," she said quietly, "both of you have been at fault and until there is forgiveness on both sides, there will be bitterness instead. Am I right in assuming you're still in love with Drew?"

Lynn nodded, then pushed her hair away from her hot face. "Unfortunately, yes," she answered dully.

"Why unfortunately?"

Lynn shifted restlessly in her chair. "What good does it do me?" she demanded. "He's here for now, but he won't stay indefinitely. And he hasn't once mentioned resuming our marriage on a permanent basis. Only that we'll work out some fair arrangement about sharing Joy."

"You're sleeping together, aren't you?"

Lynn grimaced. "That's the second time today somebody has asked me that!" she said in exasperation. "Maybe I should just announce it on the radio and be done with it! Yes, we've slept together—when we weren't fighting, that is! What does that prove, anyway?"

Gwen laughed. "Well, it *is* a form of communication, you know! And if you still care enough about each other to make love, there's always hope!"

"Sex isn't the panacea for all the woes in the world," Lynn grumbled.

"Maybe not, but it does solve a lot of problems between a man and a woman. Who," she asked curiously, "was the other person who asked you about your sex life today?"

"John. I went to his office to apologize about the way he found out I was married. He wasn't very friendly."

Gwen shrugged. "I can't say that I blame him," she replied with honesty. "No man exactly likes to be duped by a woman. His pride is hurt as much as anything else, I imagine."

"I know," Lynn said. "That's why I went over to apologize, for all the good it accomplished." She got wearily to her feet. "It's getting late. I'd better go on home. Joy's bound to be starving by now."

Gwen stood, too. "Lynn," she said gently, "try not to be so hard on Drew. I think he must still really love you and that he's been hurt badly by everything that's happened. Hurt badly by something else in his past, too. Maybe it's such a deep scar that he simply can't talk about it with anyone, even with you. Just give him a fair chance to work things out. Love's too precious a thing to throw away just because a person's too proud to forgive. Think about that, will you?"

Lynn smiled wanly. "Why is it that for identical twins, I've made such a complete mess of my life while you're the wise one?"

Gwen laughed. "Don't ever think that. I've just been more fortunate than you up until now, maybe. It's always easier to stand back and see where others make mistakes with their lives, but never your own. When I'm tested, I'll probably foul things up worse than you ever did. Until we experience something, we never really know how we'll act.

When Lynn reached home, it was nearly dark, but she could easily see Drew's dark silhouette against the sky as he worked in the back, well beyond the house. Joy saw him, too, and once they were out of the car, she ran toward his bent form, crying, "Hi, Daddy! We're home!"

Drew stopped what he was doing and opened his arms wide to receive his daughter's small body as she threw herself against him in an exuberant embrace. Lynn watched them with a heavy heart and a lump in her throat before, at last, her leaden legs carried her toward them.

Drew released Joy slowly and then brought himself up to his full height. In the semidarkness of early evening, his eyes appeared to be almost black as he met Lynn's gaze. For a long moment they studied each other in complete silence, the tension and strain still palpable between them.

"Good evening," he said at last.

"Evening." Lynn nodded briefly, then flickered her gaze over the pile of wood and wire that littered the ground. "What are you doing?"

"You said you wanted chickens," he said. "I'm going to build you a hen house."

"I . . . well, thank you," she said stiltedly.

"You're welcome," he replied just as tightly. Then his voice relaxed. "You're awfully late getting home, aren't you?" he asked. "I was just about to start worrying about whether you'd had an accident."

Lynn shrugged. "I decided to stop by and visit Gwen for a few minutes."

She could see his quick frown, before he asked, "Didn't it even occur to you that I might worry? Why didn't you call me from her place?"

She didn't like the accusation in his voice and a spurt of anger erupted. "It never dawned on me to do so," she answered. "I've lived a single life for a long time now. I don't have to report to anyone about what I do or when I come home."

"You're wrong about that," Drew snapped. "As long as I'm here, I at least expect the common courtesy of a little consideration. I have no desire to be left here to worry about my daughter's safety and well-being just because you feel like gallivanting around without bothering to tell me you'll be late."

"You can't order me around!" Lynn sputtered furiously. "I won't have it and I . . ."

"And I won't have such a blatant disregard for my feelings, either!" Drew said ruthlessly. "I've told

146

you before and I'm telling you again, Lynn. Don't push me too far!"

For a moment, it was an impasse as they stood glaring at each other. Lynn felt like screaming with vexation over his arrogant demands, but she thought better of it in time. Drew meant what he said. If she didn't treat him with the proper regard that he considered his due, he would make trouble for her. Trouble in a courtroom. Trouble she could ill afford.

She swallowed hard over the angry retorts that rose in her throat and forced herself to back down for prudence's sake. But she was darned if she would apologize, either. She had been forced to endure a lot from this man, but she wasn't about to humble herself before him. At last, in as calm a tone as she could manage, she said, "I'll go start supper." Without waiting for any reply, she turned on her heel and left him.

She was trembling with fury as she crossed the lawn to the house. She saw Joy closing the door to the car, where she had returned to fetch a drawing she had done at the day-care center and she was glad the child had not heard the hostile scene between her parents. It was bad enough that Joy would spend the rest of her youth being bounced back and forth between them like a yo-yo; she shouldn't have to witness the harsh conflicts as well.

When Drew came into the house for supper, he had already showered and changed from his work clothes into neat black slacks and a casual white shirt. His black hair had bluish highlights and the scent of his aftershave cologne wafted in the air, compelling Lynn's awareness of his vibrant masculinity whether she wished to acknowledge it or not.

For Joy's sake, she did her best to be pleasant over the meal, and so did Drew. He asked Joy questions about her day at "school" and with his friendly encouragement, she chatted happily about the things she had done. Already forgotten, seemingly, were the complaints she had favored her mother with on the drive home.

Drew complimented Lynn on the meal as they all left the table and while suspiciousness over his sincerity leapt to her mind, she responded with deliberate equanimity.

Joy went to take her evening bath and Lynn began clearing the dishes from the table. When Drew started to help her, she looked up in surprise. "You don't have to help me do this," she said quickly.

"I don't mind," came the calm reply. "You've had a long day and I'm sure you're tired. If I help, it'll give you more time to relax."

For a little while, they worked in silence. Drew stored away the food while Lynn stacked the dishes onto the counter and ran her dish water. Once she began washing them, he picked up a towel and started to dry them.

"You need an automatic dishwasher," he commented idly.

Lynn shrugged and her lips parted with a tiny smile. "I know. I already miss the one I had in my apartment. It's on my list of 'someday,' but for now there are too many other things I need more." With a friendlier attitude than she had displayed when he had first told her, she added, "I really do appreciate what you've been doing around here for me. I need that hen house and I was wondering whether I'd be up to building it by myself. You did save the receipt for the supplies you bought, didn't you? I intend to pay you back, of course."

"Forget it," Drew said. "I just added it to the bill

for the barn materials and I already told you I'm paying for it."

Lynn resisted the easy smoothness in his voice. She knew Drew could afford to pay for those things without giving the matter a second thought, but she didn't want to be beholden to him.

She shook her head firmly and met his eyes with determination. "No, Drew. I intend to pay my own way. I don't need your charity. I've managed just fine all these years on my own."

"Maybe you have," he said coolly, "but whether you like it or not, I'm in the picture now and I'll do whatever I see fit where my daughter's welfare and support is concerned."

"That's fine." Lynn matched his coldness. "But I fail to see what her welfare has to do with a barn. I'll build it as I can afford it."

"Wrong," Drew said implacably. "I hired some men to start on it tomorrow. I want it built as soon as possible so that there will be a shelter for her pony."

"*What* pony?" Lynn gasped.

"The one I bought today from a man near town. He'll keep it until I'm ready to have it delivered."

"Drew, don't you think you should have consulted me before you bought her something like that?" she demanded in outrage. "How dare you come to my home and just . . . just take over and do as you please without so much as even discussing it with me first?"

He shrugged carelessly, picked up a plate and wiped it dry. "It just seemed like the easiest way to avoid an argument," he told her calmly. "What's done is done."

"No!" she snapped hotly. "You can undo every bit of it. Tell the men you hired to build the barn not to come after all and then get your money back from the man who sold you the pony!"

"Sorry," he said in a maddeningly steady voice. "The barn will be built and Joy will get her pony."

They finished the job of cleaning the kitchen in stony silence. Lynn was so angry at his high-handed tactics that she no longer trusted herself to speak. Drew probably felt he had no need to say more since he had already made it plain that he fully intended to have his way.

They both visited Joy's bedroom to bid her good night and once they left her room, Drew said mildly, "It's far too early to go to sleep, yet. Mind if I stay here and watch some television?"

"Suit yourself," she replied with tight-lipped control. "I'm going to take a bath and go to bed. Just be sure you lock up before you go out to your room, okay?"

Drew nodded. "Sure. Good night." Without bothering to look at her again or giving any hint that he minded being left alone, he went toward the living room.

A few minutes later, Lynn ran her bath water and slowly undressed. Tiredness from the long day and the strain of dealing with both John and Drew had taken their toll. Exhaustion rolled over her in numbing waves. She ached, mentally as well as physically, and she wondered whether her life would ever again run smoothly. Tonight it seemed like a very remote possibility.

The bathtub filled with hot, steamy water. Lynn poured some perfumed bath oil into it, then pinned her hair atop her head. She stepped into the tub and slowly eased her body down. The water slid over her feet, her long, slender legs, finally across her hips and stomach and at last swirled over her breasts as she lay back in a reclining position.

She sighed heavily as the warmth of the water immediately went to work loosening tense muscles and she closed her eyes in order to savor the pleasure. She felt her entire body yield its stiffness to the soft heat that radiated through her. The silky water caressed her and the perfume gave a sensual touch of exquisite luxuriousness. Gradually, she reached a state of complete relaxation.

Her mind floated listlessly as though it, too, was being gently stroked by the soothing water. Now the arguments with Drew this evening appeared as nothing more than foolishness. She had been angry because first he had been concerned over why she was late and second, because he had taken upon himself to do a kindness for both herself and Joy. Both times her, and Joy's, welfare had been at the core of what he had said and done. Instead of appreciating it, she had resented it. She had allowed herself to become so upset over everything that at this point she seemed to lash out at Drew at every opportunity! Somehow she had lost all sense of proportion, all rationality.

She would, she decided sleepily, apologize to him when she got out of the bath, if he happened to still be in the house by then. Her efforts at apology had already been spurned once today, she thought wryly, but perhaps she would have better luck this time. After all, Gwen was right. Love *was* too precious to throw away because of pride. She didn't know whether she and Drew could ever work things out satisfactorily, but one thing was certain. It would never happen if they didn't try . . . if there wasn't some giving on both sides.

But did Drew still wish to try? He had said something along those lines last night, but since then they had done nothing except quarrel. It was entirely possible that he was no longer interested in trying now.

The bathroom door swept open abruptly. Lynn's eyelashes flew upward and her pupils dilated with surprise as Drew strode boldly into the room, his hands filled with flaming camellia blossoms.

From her reclining position, Lynn could only watch in helpless astonishment as he came directly toward her to stand at the edge of the bathtub. His blue eyes darkened and flared with unmistakable passion as he gazed down at her nakedness. A nerve twitched at the corner of his mouth.

Then, slowly, he held out his hands until they were above her and let the flower petals shower down to light upon the water's surface.

A gentle smile relaxed his lips then as his eyes met hers. "That's my peace offering," he said in a low, husky voice. "I don't want to continue fighting with you, darling. I'd much rather be making love to you instead."

Chapter Nine

$\mathcal{L}$ynn did not even realize that she had caught her breath until a rippling sigh caused her to quiver. Drew's face was tense and held an odd vulnerability as he looked down at her. There was entreaty mingling with the passion in his eyes as their gazes met and clung in an ageless message. Wordlessly, the softening in Lynn's own gray ones answered him. Her lips parted in a tiny smile, slowly stretching wider and wider until the sound of her laughter came, gently bubbling up from somewhere deep inside her.

Lynn sat up and held out both arms invitingly. Something akin to both relief and happiness sparkled in the depths of Drew's blue eyes and he knelt quickly beside the tub so that he could slide his arms around her.

Their lips met, hers moist and yielding, his warm

and firm. It was a long, deep kiss that robbed them both of any lingering vestiges of resentment. Drew's lips moved over hers with hungry urgency, his tongue darting in and out of her mouth like leaping fire. Lynn felt a fervency rising within herself to match his. Her flesh came tinglingly alive to his touch. When his hand moved down to stroke the tip of her breast, a quickening desire pulsated through her entire being.

She wrapped her arms around his neck, pulling him as close as she could with the barrier of the rim of the tub between them. Her heart raced as the fire of his lips scorched her tender skin every place they touched on her face, her golden shoulders, her delicate throat, and when his hand left her breast to travel downward, flitting lightly over her hips and thighs that were still submerged by the water, she gasped with excitement.

Drew lifted his head to smile at her. A heavy ardor darkened his gaze and gave him a slumberous look.

Lynn saw that his shirt was now splotched with water. "I'm getting you all wet," she murmured as she rubbed a finger against his damp neck.

A flashing light gave an iridescent glow to his eyes. "So what?" he whispered in a low, languorous voice. "What mortal man can mind a little wetness if the arms of Aphrodite are around him and he can taste the sweet wine of her lips?"

Lynn drew back to gaze at him in delightful amazement. "Drew, you poetic man! What a surprise you are!" She started to laugh, but then something about the intensity of his expression choked it off. An instant later, like Venus rising from the sea, she rose gracefully to her feet. Moisture beads adorned the smooth silk of her skin as she stood quietly before his fascinated gaze. Then slowly she lifted her hands to the thickness of her hair, removed the hairpins and allowed the rich, dark mane to tumble to her shoulders. All the while, her eyes never left his face.

Drew was utterly still for a long moment as his eyes swept over her gleaming skin. Then a strange sound came from his throat, a cross between a groan of pain and a whoop of glee. His arms closed around her and Lynn was lifted from the bathtub and her wet body was crushed tightly against the long, hard length of him.

Her heart pounded at the strength of his embrace and she trembled at the savage intensity with which he kissed her once more. It was almost as though Drew would merge their bodies into one from head to toe. His lips on hers were bruising, suffocating, as if he drew life from her very breath; his hands molded her back and hips to fit his body as though he were bonding them together for all eternity. The power of his emotions swept through her like a strong current of electricity and Lynn went limp as her own senses capitulated beneath the force of his.

At last, his hold slackened a bit and his mouth relaxed against the soft corner of hers. "I'm sorry," he murmured. His breath gently caressed her cheek. "You ignite my blood into a raging fire. But I'm afraid I'm hurting you." He laughed unsteadily. "You bring out the fierce beast in me, darling!"

Lynn's voice was no firmer than his. "I must, at that." She smiled. "Tomorrow I'll probably be all black and blue and then I'll have you charged with wife abuse."

A quiver of a smile tugged at his lips. "Why not tonight?" he asked hoarsely.

"Because tonight," she admitted shakily, "I seem

to have no resistance to you whatsoever. I only want you to go on and on holding me and to put out this fire you started in me!"

Drew lifted her into his arms and carried her, still wet, into the bedroom.

He shed his clothes quickly and came to her on the bed with an eagerness that gave her a thrilling sense of a woman's power. But that sense was soon relinquished beneath the dominance of his power over her. Her nostrils were filled with the masculine scent of him. Her hands splayed across his chest and the feel of him seduced her mind and enticed her body until all thoughts other than the needs he awoke in her were driven away.

Despite Drew's own keen desire, he deliberately took his time. With torturous slowness, his hands explored her body, every inch, every curve, every secret place. He tantalized her with kisses, he nibbled teasingly at her ears and shoulders; he brought her nipples to hard peaks of arousal with his tongue and he stroked her thighs until they throbbed with aching desperation.

Only when her body had been brought to the point where every cell screamed for release, when every nerve was taut with strain, when she burned with a fever of passion that threatened to completely consume her did Drew at last fill her with himself. Lynn cried out with relief and her fingernails dug into his back as she held him closely pressed to her breasts.

At last the wondrous moment of fulfillment came, bursting over them both like scintillating fireworks. Lynn felt a shudder rumble through Drew as he held her and a gasp of satisfaction escaped from her lips. Pure rapture held her at the zenith for a long, long moment before a blissful peace gradually stole over her.

Drew rolled away to lie beside her and for a little while they were both silent, sated, recouping strength as their pulses slowed.

But after a few minutes, Drew left the bed. Lynn's admiring gaze followed him as he padded toward her closet. His shoulders and the powerful muscles in his back gleamed in the dim glow of the lamplight and her eyes traveled down to the firm, narrow hips and long, tapered legs. Even just after lovemaking, the sight of him increased the tempo of her heartbeat. He was so perfectly built, so splendidly proportioned, so vigorously masculine in every possible way! No other man could ever measure up to him and she supposed subconsciously she had always realized that. Perhaps that had been partly the reason she had never sought a divorce. She had known all along that no other man could ever do for her.

He extracted his robe from the closet, shrugged into it, then turned to flash her a quick smile.

"Where are you going?" she asked lazily.

"I'll be back in just a minute," he said. "Don't go away. I've got a little surprise."

She half-smiled as he left the room, not really curious. She was too content just now to think about anything at all. She closed her eyes dreamily. Drew had already done what only he could do—set her world right.

He returned in a few short minutes and his eyes laughed at her as he held something behind his back.

"What have you got?" she asked with the beginnings of a smile.

"Guess."

"Does it bite?"

Drew grinned and produced his surprise. It was a bottle of California wine and two wineglasses.

Lynn sat up abruptly. "Oh, Drew, how lovely!" she exclaimed. Immediately, she plumped up both their pillows against the headboard so that they could sit comfortably in bed. When they had first been married, they had soon established the custom of often enjoying a glass or two of wine after they had made love. Drew had called it their celebration of love.

Now he poured them each a glass, handed her one and slid back into bed beside her. His face was tender as he turned toward her and held out his glass for a toast.

She touched her glass to his and her throat tightened with sudden emotion as he said, "To us."

Lynn swallowed, then whispered huskily, "To us."

They both drank and then Drew leaned back against his pillow, his mood turning pensive. He stared down at the roseate liquid in his glass. "Darling?"

"Hmm?"

"I have to tell you something."

Lynn lifted her gaze to his face, for the first time realizing the full extent of his mood swing. She tensed automatically. "What is it?"

"I've got to go back to L.A." The words dropped like hailstones between them.

Lynn squeezed her eyes shut as a wave of desolation swept over her so that she actually felt ill. She had known all along that the day would come when he would leave her to resume the life that was separate from hers. It had always been a matter of time. She should have been ready for it, but she wasn't.

Still, Drew was waiting for her response and she couldn't let him see how much she was hurting, how dead she felt inside. She gripped the wineglass tightly and opened her eyes again. "I see," she said quietly. "When?"

"Friday."

Lynn nodded and smiled and she was proud of herself for being able to manage it so well. "It's been fun," she said lightly. Again, she raised her glass in salute, then bent her head to take a sip, needing the fraction of a minute when he could not see her face to compose herself.

When she lifted her head again her eyes were glazed and she blinked to keep the tears from falling. She could not . . . *would* not . . . disgrace herself by crying.

Strong, bronzed fingers came to raise her chin and slowly turned her face until Drew could look into her eyes. What he saw in them made him swear softly before he leaned forward and gently brushed his lips across hers.

"I'm not leaving for good, my silly darling."

Lynn blinked again. "You're not?"

Drew smiled, shook his head slightly, then wiped away a tear that clung to her lashes. "No," he said flatly. "I'm not. Did you really believe for one minute that I could walk away as easily as that now I've found you again? Now that I've met my daughter as well?"

"I . . . how could I know?" she countered. "How long will you be away?"

Drew frowned in thought. "I'm not sure. Maybe a couple of weeks. Three at most. Whatever," he added as a warm smile creased his face, "you can be certain I'll return just as soon as I possibly can. I've been doing a pretty good job of running things by phone, but I can't conduct all my business at long distance. I've got a number of things to do . . . look over new building sites, meet with architects and the like. Now tell me," he added teasingly, "did that long face and those tears mean what I think they did . . . that you're going to miss me?"

She could be honest now that she knew he was coming back to her. "Yes," she said with a husky catch to her voice. "I guess they did. Joy," she ended musingly, "is going to miss you, too."

Drew smiled with satisfaction. "My little princess," he said tenderly. "You named her well, Lynn. I've been meaning to tell you that. She *is* a joy."

"I know." Lynn gave him an answering smile. "It was how I felt about her from the minute she was born, even though at the time I was still so unhappy about ending our marriage because I thought you wouldn't love her or want her." She fell silent and took another sip of her wine for courage before pleading, "Won't you please tell me why, Drew? Why you didn't want me to have a baby?" She turned toward him, saw that his face had tensed, and rushed on earnestly, "If there was another woman you loved before me, another child before Joy, I can accept that, honestly."

The strangest look Lynn had ever seen before flickered across his face, and then was gone. And then he answered her in a choked voice. "Don't think that!" he said quickly. "Never think that! Joy is my only child and while I won't pretend there haven't been other women in my life, both before I met you and after you deserted me, I never loved them. I never loved any woman except you, Lynn.

The sincerity in his voice was genuine. It had the clear ring of truth to it. The words warmed Lynn, gave a flare of hope to her heart, but the feeling was fleeting. Drew looked anything but happy and her own small pleasure at his words drained away.

"Then what?" she prompted softly.

Drew shook his head as though to dispense with the cobwebs in his mind. "It's something that happened so far back in my life that it shouldn't even matter now—and it doesn't bother me as much as it once did." His eyes were dark with that private pain of his that shut her out. Then, changing the subject, he asked abruptly, "What do you think of me as a father to Joy?"

Lynn stared at him in surprise and for a moment, disappointment swept over her because she thought he was making a little joke only to distract her. But all at once she realized that the question had not been asked lightly. It was of immense importance to Drew and there was a strained whiteness about his mouth as he waited to hear her answer. She was sure that it had something to do with his own relationship with his father, with the way he had been treated as a child, with the past that was still wrapped up in a concealing fog.

Instinct told her that Drew hoped she did not discern just how vital her response was to him, so when she did answer at last, she strove to make her voice casual and teasing. "As a matter of fact, I've been meaning to discuss that very subject with you. For the most part, I think your being here has been marvelous for her. As you know, she's quite thrilled over having her daddy here. You're a fairly good bedtime storyteller, you're not too bad at buttoning a child's dress and you're terrific at getting her to at least taste the vegetables on her plate. However, while I could overlook such indulgences as ice cream treats and piggyback rides on your shoulders, the pony is something else again. Now, if you're going to spoil her so rotten that she becomes unbearable to live with, I may have to revise my first opin . . ."

The flow of words was abruptly silenced by the simple expedience of a kiss. It was a brief one, but Lynn decided she liked it so much that when Drew would have moved away, she threaded her free hand through his hair and held him close so that this time she could force a kiss on him.

When they did part, only an inch or so in order to see each other's eyes, Drew was smiling again and the tension that had been there on his face a few minutes ago was gone. "Did I tell you yet," he asked thickly, "how much I'm going to miss you . . . as well as my little princess?"

Lynn shook her head and her own voice cracked as she replied, "Then hurry back to us both. And Drew?"

"Yes?" he murmured as his lips now nuzzled her neck.

She pushed him back so that she could look at him fully. Her eyes were dark and serious as she told him, "I've been very wrong, and cruel, not to trust you alone with Joy since you've been here. If you want, I'll let her stay home with you all this week until you have to leave."

Drew gave her a dazzling smile. "Thank you, darling," he said simply. "That proves beyond a doubt that we've already come a long way from where we were the night I arrived. That . . . and us, here in bed together." He nibbled at her shoulder and one hand went up to cover a rounded breast, sending delicious shivers to race through her.

And then Lynn gasped at what he did next and

shrieked, "Drew, your glass! Watch your wine! Drew, you're going to spill . . . !"

After that, the days sped past on wings. On Tuesday, when Lynn arrived home from work, it was to discover that the groundwork had indeed been laid for the new barn. Progress on the hen house had come to a standstill, however, for Drew had made use of the loan of Cal's tractor and spent most of the day plowing a large garden plot.

On Wednesday, the hen house was complete with roosts, nesting boxes and a mixture of fresh sawdust and hay spread on the floor. By Thursday afternoon, a heat lamp had been installed and Lynn came home to find a batch of twenty-five baby chicks in a round cardboard nursery.

Joy had been happy all week. Every evening she had proudly shown Lynn what she and Daddy had accomplished that day, but this time she was absolutely ecstatic. Not only were there the baby chicks to ooh and aah over, but she had also brought her puppy home at last from Uncle Cal's. He was a cute little bundle of brown and white fluff and he waddled as he followed her every step.

"Watch him chase me, Mommy!" Joy shouted as she darted across the space between where the barn was rising and the fenced garden area. The puppy bounded along in hot pursuit and when Joy sank to the ground to wait for him, he jumped into her lap and started nipping with enthusiasm at her fingers.

Lynn laughed as she watched the play and thought that she had never seen her daughter looking quite so disheveled—or satisfied—before. Her hair was a nightmare tangled mercilessly by the wind that had tossed it for hours. She wore a cotton tee shirt, jeans and tennis shoes, all of which were soiled by freshly turned earth. A reddish brown smudge was streaked down one cheek, but beneath all the dirt, the small face was glowing from the pleasure of both her new pet and her active day spent outdoors.

She turned to Drew with a smile. "It's been good for her, staying home with you these last few days. Look at her! I think she's already beginning to get a little tan."

Drew nodded. "She's been enjoying every minute of the day. And so have I. She's a daughter to be proud of," he added quietly, and there was a husky break to his voice. Then he shook off the emotional moment and said, "Now come with me to the house. I have another surprise for you."

Lynn lifted her eyebrows. "Something more than the baby chicks and the puppy?"

Drew nodded again and his fingers closed around her arm, urging her toward the house while Joy stayed behind to continue rolling on the ground with her puppy.

They entered the kitchen and Lynn spotted it immediately. Exactly as though it had been made to fit there, standing in a small corner of the room next to the counter, was a brand-new dishwasher.

Lynn whirled around toward Drew, her eyes sparkling with delight. "You couldn't have pleased me more!" she exclaimed. "Oh, the thrill of knowing I don't have to stand here washing dishes for hours anymore!" She sighed deeply just at the thought.

Drew chuckled, but then he quickly frowned. "Is that," he asked pointedly, "the only thanks I'm going to get?"

Lynn laughed, shook her head and went readily into his arms. She lifted her face to kiss him, loving the warm glow that lit his eyes. Her arms encircled his neck and then she closed her own eyes as their lips met.

Drew's arms went around her, bringing her close until her breasts rubbed against the fabric of his shirt. What began as a light and fleeting kiss turned quickly into one of passion. Longing flared within them both and their hands began a sensual exploration of the other's body.

Only the sound of Joy's voice outside, coming ever closer to the house as she talked to her dog, drew them apart. Drew released her with obvious reluctance and Lynn laughed softly at the frustrated expression on his face. "Did I thank you nicely enough?" she teased.

"Not *nearly* enough," he growled.

"Then remind me later tonight," she whispered, "and I'll say it again."

"I'll remind you, all right," Drew said gruffly. Their gazes met with strong intensity. Each of them was acutely conscious of the fact that this would be their last night together for weeks.

Joy came into the house then and the magical moment between them was broken. "Daddy," she asked, "can we take a walk down to the creek? I want to show it to Fluffy."

"Is that what you named him?" Lynn asked in a rather bemused fashion. She was struggling to get her emotions back under rigid control and it wasn't easily done with Drew still standing so close beside her.

Joy nodded, then returned to the matter of her request. "Can we, Daddy?"

Drew glanced toward Lynn, his face inscrutable. Lynn couldn't tell what he was thinking—or feeling.

If he was suffering from the same devil she was, it was not apparent.

"Go ahead if you want," she told him. "I'll start supper."

"No," Drew said decisively. "If we go, we all go together. Besides, the exercise will do you good. You're the one who's been cooped inside a building all day. Go change your clothes and then we'll leave."

"But what about supper?"

Drew shrugged carelessly. "We can make do with sandwiches tonight." His eyes were dark, his voice low as he added, "I just want your company this evening, darling, so go change your clothes like a good girl and come enjoy what's left of the afternoon with us."

Lynn obeyed with alacrity. It was what she wanted to do, after all. The past few days had been so wonderful, for there had been such a spirit of togetherness, of family about them. Even though she had gone off to her job each morning, whenever she returned, Drew and Joy had been there waiting for her, glad to share the evenings with her. And the nights spent in Drew's arms had been incomparable. She could not bear to think of how empty the bed was going to be without him.

Once Lynn was attired in jeans, a light sweater and sturdy walking shoes, they set out across the back of the property. For a time Fluffy made a stab at keeping up with his young mistress, but before they reached the creek he simply stopped, wagged his tail and refused to budge.

"You'll have to carry him, princess," Drew advised. "He's tired already. His little legs can't keep up with you."

Joy scooped him into her arms and trudged along, not seeming to mind her burden at all. But by the time they arrived at the creek's edge, Fluffy had regained his second wind and once again bounced around happily in eager play.

A thick stand of pines grew up to the very edge of the creek. It was much more densely wooded than the section that ran behind the Jenning's property.

While Joy and her pet darted among the trees in a frisky game of hide-and-seek, Lynn and Drew sat down on a bed of pine needles and looked out over the water. To the left was a bend in the stream and the previous owner had told Lynn that the water was very deep there, just behind a natural dam of fallen tree trunks and a tangle of logs and branches. The water swirled across the snarl of debris, trickled down and once more ran shallow and free just in front of where they sat.

For a time, they sat in companionable silence, taking quiet pleasure in their surroundings and listening contentedly to Joy's ringing laughter as she romped with Fluffy.

Drew had just begun to tell her about a business telephone call he had received that morning from his office when a sudden shriek and then a loud splash rent the air.

They both leapt instantaneously to their feet. Lynn's searching gaze swept past Drew and what she saw filled her heart with cold terror.

Joy had somehow gotten too close to the deep pool in the creek and had tumbled in. She was thrashing about wildly and one leg seemed to be caught in the tangle of debris. It imprisoned her like wooden tentacles and all at once, her head vanished beneath the water's surface.

"There!" Lynn gasped at Drew even as she had begun to run. "She fell into the deep end and something's got her pinned down! Oh, God, she's gone under!" Every nerve in her body was taut with fear and her throat was dry and tight. If only she could get to her in time! she prayed silently. She did not even pause to consider the fact that she herself was a very poor swimmer. All that mattered was that her child was in grave danger.

"Get out of the way!" Drew's strong voice ordered curtly. Just as Lynn reached the edge of the slope, he shot past her and, heedless of dangerous debris that might also be lurking beneath the water's surface to entrap yet another victim, he plunged in head first.

Lynn's breath had literally stopped, but even as Drew dove, she saw Joy's head bob above the water again. She was sputtering and gasping for air. Although Lynn had thought her throat was paralyzed from fear, she managed to shout, "Hang on, baby! Hang on!" A frantic sob broke from her as the dark head submerged once more.

Drew came up from his dive and glanced around him in panic. "Where is she?" he shouted. "Where the hell *is* she?"

"There! There! Near that big trunk!" Lynn pointed toward the litter of tree branches that thrust up above the water. "Hurry!" she begged. "She just went under again!"

Drew immediately sank and for a long moment that seemed to Lynn like the whole of eternity, the surface of the dark, treacherous water remained calm, deathly calm.

A fresh sob assailed her and she felt icy cold with dread. "Oh, God!" she moaned. "Oh, God, please!" Before the words were completely uttered for the second time, the water gave a warning ripple and then two heads came into view.

Lynn clambered down to the muddy, slippery bank and looked around wildly for a long, stout branch while Drew struggled laboriously toward her, not an easy task because both arms were filled with the still form of their child.

But just as she was about to give up in tearful frustration, Lynn found what she needed. She grabbed one end of the long stick and then bracing one foot against a partially submerged log, extended the pole out over the water.

Drew grabbed it with one hand while he cradled Joy's head in the crook of his other arm. With every ounce of strength she possessed, and a lot she never dreamed she had, Lynn pulled man and child to the bank.

When he could rise to his feet, Drew handed Joy to Lynn so that he could lift himself from the water. Hot tears of the most agonizing grief she had ever experienced spilled over, spattering the little white face.

Once he was out of the water, Drew grabbed Joy back into his arms and started climbing up toward level ground. "Don't think it!" he ground out harshly. "She's not gone!"

He laid the child gently onto the ground and then began the process of mouth-to-mouth resuscitation. An instant later, due to the pressure he had exerted on the small chest, water ran freely from Joy's mouth. She coughed, opened her eyes and coughed again.

Lynn, who had followed close behind and then stood gazing in frozen horror as Drew had begun the life-saving efforts, cried out and fell to her knees, gathering Joy up against her breast. Tears of relief rolled down her face and yet she was gasping with laughter at the same time.

"Thank God!" she exclaimed fervently. "Oh, thank God, you're all right, sweetheart! You'll be okay now. Your daddy took good care of you!"

Joy sputtered, coughed once more, then pulled back from her mother's uncomfortably tight embrace. "Where's Fluffy?" she asked with concern.

Lynn's eyes met Drew's. He was hunched on his knees, sucking in great gulps of air, but he gave her a weary smile, one of mutual understanding. They both knew then that Joy was going to be just fine.

The tiny dog came out from behind a tree and Joy held out her arms to him. Lynn brushed her daughter's wet hair back from her face, then glanced back at Drew. "Are you all right?" she asked anxiously.

He nodded. "Just had to catch my breath, that's all." He got to his feet and gave a slight shiver as his drenched body chilled in the evening coolness. "Let's get home. I need some dry clothes and so does Joy."

They made a far more solemn and slower procession going back to the house than when they had first left it. Drew carried Joy in his arms, and really tired now and trembling with cold, she wrapped her arms around his neck and burrowed her head against his shoulder. Lynn carried the puppy, who seemed as exhausted by all the excitement as the humans.

As soon as they reached home, Lynn immediately gave Joy a hot bath while Drew took a shower in the garage. Afterward, they all opted for bowls of steaming soup for their supper instead of cold sandwiches.

While they ate, Lynn marveled over how normal Joy seemed after having gone through such a near brush with death. Her color was good, her appetite was enormous and it was as though she hadn't been affected in the least by what had happened. *Or maybe,* she thought, *she simply hadn't realized just how dire her predicament had been.* Which was just as well, Lynn decided, even though she made a point of emphasizing the danger of ever playing so near the water again and so did Drew.

"This summer we're going to get you some swimming lessons," he told Joy in a voice that defied anyone to argue with him. "But even after that, when you're a very good swimmer, I want you to promise me that you'll never go near any water when you're alone."

Joy promised and then her big blue eyes grew larger as she seemed to realize the seriousness in her father's voice. Her lower lip began to tremble and she asked in a small voice, "Are you mad at me, Daddy?"

Drew's face suddenly thawed into a smile. He shook his head and reached across the table to place his hand on Joy's shoulder. "No, princess," he said gently. "I'm not angry. I just love you very much and I never want anything bad to happen to you, that's all."

Joy's winsome smile came. "I love you, too, Daddy." Then her eyes clouded and she frowned. "Do you have to go far away to California tomorrow?"

"Yes, I do, sweetheart," Drew said. "But I'm coming back to you real soon."

Later, after Joy was asleep and Drew and Lynn lay close together in bed, arms draped across each other, the horror of what had almost happened returned to haunt Lynn. She trembled and Drew, immediately aware of it, asked, "What's the matter, darling?"

She shook her head and chewed at her lower lip. "She could have died!" she said in a low, unsteady voice.

Drew's hand, on her bare hip, moved up to rub soothingly across her back. "Hush, darling," he murmured. "It's over now. Don't think about it anymore."

"I can't help it," she insisted. She looked him fully in the face. The bedside lamp cast a soft gold glow across his features and she raised a hand to caress his forehead. "She almost did die! Drew, if it hadn't been for you, she very likely would have! You know I can't swim very well and besides, even if I could, I doubt whether I'd have had the strength necessary to pull her free of those branches and then get her all the way to the bank!" She shuddered again. "What if you hadn't been there?"

"Darling." Drew's eyes were dark and compelling. "I know you don't want me to go tomorrow, but honestly, you can't be afraid something else like that will . . ."

Lynn shook her head urgently and cut off his words. "No! That's not what I'm trying to say!"

Drew's hand on her back stilled. His eyes were questioning. "Then what *are* you trying to say?"

She nibbled at her lip again, searching for the right words. At last, in a burst, she said, "I guess what I'm trying to do is to apologize to you all over again for running away like I did, for hiding Joy from you all these years. I appeased my conscience all along by convincing myself that since you didn't want any children you could never love her as much as I do. But if I needed any more proof than I already have had since you've been here that you love her, too, it was today. When you dove into that pond, I was afraid . . ." She choked before she was able to go on. "I was afraid I was about to lose both of you! You saved her life and if you hadn't found us when you did, been here these past couple of weeks over my objections, she would have drowned!" She lowered her gaze to his furry chest, sucked in a ragged breath and forced herself to add, "What I'm really trying to say, Drew, is that no matter what happens after this, if you change your mind after all and decide not to come back, I . . . I will never fight your right to have Joy part of the time in your life, too. She's your daughter as much as mine and I won't stand in the way of what is best for her or for you."

Drew placed a finger beneath her chin and raised her face until she was forced to meet his eyes. "I'm coming back," he said firmly. "And when I do, we're going to have a long discussion, fully clothed and away from this room so that we can both think logically and dispassionately about exactly what the future does hold for us. For all of us. But right now it's getting late, darling, and I'm tired. Playing farmer all day, not to mention taking an impromptu swim, has worn me out and I've got that plane to catch in the morning. Let's get some sleep, hmm?"

"All right." But then Lynn couldn't resist asking, "Have you liked playing farmer?"

Drew grinned and closed his eyes. "It hasn't been half bad, at that," he admitted sleepily. "I'm developing a feel for it. I kind of enjoy this countrified style of living."

"Enough to stay here for good?" she asked, catching her breath.

Drew opened his eyes and looked directly at her. "No," he said bluntly. "Not that well."

Chapter Ten

On Friday morning they awoke to a gray, gloomy day and soft rain. Lynn's mood was equally gray as she dressed in beige slacks, a printed silk blouse and a brown jacket to top it. Drew was leaving today and the knowledge had her spirits as low as the ground. The fact that he had told both her and Joy that he would come back helped little. So quickly had she become dependent on his presence again in her life, dependent on his judgment and decisions concerning her new farm, even dependent on the shared responsibility of their daughter. But more than all of those things, she had become used to the delights of living with him again as husband and wife. That aspect of her life had been dead for so many years that she had thought she had completely adjusted but now, in only a couple of short weeks, Drew had brought her tinglingly alive again to a man's touch, to thrilling nights of love and the delightful satisfaction of awakening each morning close beside him. And now she had to adjust all over again to doing without him.

She did her best to conceal her depression, though, as the morning routine got under way. She helped Joy into her clothes, prepared a quick breakfast and helped Drew to locate a couple of last-minute items he needed to pack. Every minute counted and there was no time to indulge in self-pity even if she had been willing to let him see how unhappy she felt.

And anyway, she wasn't willing. Now that the hour came nearer for his departure, Drew was completely brisk and businesslike and he seemed eager to be on his way. If he had any qualms, any reluctance about their imminent separation, he did not show it. Thus, Lynn was also careful to maintain a stiff upper lip. She had been an independent woman standing on her own two feet for a good many years and pride demanded that she be strong now, that she show not the slightest evidence of weakness.

Because Lynn was to accompany Drew to the airport in Savannah before going on to school for the day, time was of the essence this morning. She wouldn't have any to spare to take Joy to the day-care center as well, so the night before she had arranged with Gwen to allow her to spend the day at her house.

At Gwen's, there was a touching parting scene between Drew and Joy that only intensified Lynn's melancholy. Drew's invasion into their lives had made as tremendous an impact on Joy's life as on her own and the child clung to him, teary-eyed, as she begged him not to leave her. Lynn's throat choked up and she had to turn away to keep tears from springing to her own eyes. Until this moment she had never fully understood the depths of Joy's need for a father figure.

When they left Gwen's, Drew drove Lynn's car and for a time they were both silent. Rain splattered the windshield, the motor hummed and the tires swished over the wet pavement, but though they were physically cocooned together within the confines of the car, their minds were isolated, each of them engrossed in separate thoughts.

At last, Drew roused from his musings. "I never expected her to react like that to my leaving," he said huskily. "I didn't intend to upset her."

Lynn's smile was wan. "You gave her a daddy," she said simply. "She doesn't want to lose that."

Drew laughed gruffly. "And she's given me a sense of responsibility I never felt before in my life." He fell silent again for a time and when he spoke once more, it was in a normal, even voice, and concerned only mundane matters. "I gave you the keys to the truck, didn't I?"

Lynn nodded.

"The men won't be out today to work on the barn. Not in this weather."

"No," she agreed.

"When they do get back to it, get Cal to come over every day or two and check on things. He'll know whether they're doing the job right or not. And if you need any new supplies either one of you can order them from the lumberyard in town and charge it to the account I established."

"All right."

All too soon they were nearing the airport where Drew would catch a flight for Atlanta and from there on to Los Angeles.

When they arrived, Drew parked the car, handed Lynn the keys and then they went inside the terminal. There were a few minutes to spare after he picked up his tickets and Lynn waited with him until it was time to board.

They stood close together, a little isolated from the other arriving passengers. Drew's expression was somber as he looked down into her eyes.

"We both have some major decisions to make, Lynn," he told her in a soft voice that would not carry to anyone else. "We've been thrown off balance a little, seeing each other again. Our bodies have been drawn like magnets to each other and we've been existing on a constantly emotional level. I think we need this time apart from each other so that we can both think clearly about the future—and about where we go from this point. You know as well as I do that we can't continue indefinitely in this marital limbo state. It's just no good in the long run." But he didn't say what he thought would be best.

Lynn was chilled to the marrow by his words. Drew really did want to be away from her in order to think things over, to decide whether he wanted to continue their marriage! Except for the short while they had been together when they first married, he'd had a lifetime of completely masculine living, having things all his own way, doing exactly as he pleased without having to consider a woman's wishes or desires. While he was still physically attracted to her and had even told her he'd never loved another woman, a decision to resume their marriage would mean a radical change in his life. Drew was used to a bachelor's existence and the total freedom that went with it. To take on a wife and child permanently was a major change and perhaps he wasn't sure it was what he wanted for himself. All morning she had sensed his withdrawal from her. Already his thoughts had reverted to the life he was returning to, a life unconnected with her or Joy.

Yet for herself, she needed no time to think. From the moment she had first lain in his arms again, she had realized she was still in love with him, would always and forever love him and she had waited hopefully for him to say he loved her too, that he wanted to spend the rest of his life with her.

But it hadn't happened and Lynn struggled to keep her face impassive. Pride kept her from revealing the hurt and uncertainty that gripped her. She would not do a single thing to influence him. If Drew needed to be away from her to arrive at a decision, then she would have to let him go freely, without any sort of pressure concerning her own feelings.

Now, wordlessly, she nodded agreement to what he had just said, for she didn't trust herself to speak.

The announcement for passengers to begin boarding the plane was made. A general shuffle ensued by groups of people surrounding them. But Drew did not move. He gazed down at Lynn as though he were storing up memories of her, just as she was doing. Then his arms went around her and he crushed her to him in a fierce embrace as his lips sought and found hers. Lynn, betraying herself more than she realized, clung to him and returned his kiss with urgent fervency.

When they separated, Drew reached out to touch her hair with a tender gesture and a tiny, intimate smile played across his lips. "Take care of yourself . . . and Joy," he said softly. "I'll call you tomorrow night."

Lynn nodded. Her throat was dry and scratchy. "Take care of yourself, too," she whispered. And silently, she added, "And please, come back to me."

It was amazing how long each day seemed, even though Lynn packed as much work into every one as she possibly could. On Saturday she cleaned the house and did the laundry, then drove into town for groceries and stopped off at a nursery for vegetable seeds and small tomato plants. By Sunday afternoon the ground had dried enough so that she could work in the garden, setting out the plants and spreading the seeds along the rows. It was more strenuous work than she had supposed, with all the bending and stooping and hoeing and by the time she finished in the late afternoon, her entire body screamed in protest from the unaccustomed exertion.

Although every muscle was stiff and sore the following morning, Lynn was still glad to have a busy day ahead. Time passed faster whenever she was busy and then she did not think of Drew quite so often as she did during the solitude of night.

Joy missed him, too, and that first week that he was gone, she was cranky and out of sorts much of the time. Nothing pleased her. She didn't like the clothes Lynn laid out for her in the morning; she refused to touch the vegetables on her dinner plate at night; she resented bath time and she protested bedtime. It was all very disheartening and Joy's attitude tried Lynn's patience to the limit.

The only thing that saved her sanity was Drew's nightly telephone call. Although his voice sounded far away and only emphasized the miles between them, still his tone was warm and caring. He always spoke a little while with Joy and then when Lynn came on the line, he would tell her that he missed her before launching into a recital of what his day had been like and then listening to a recount of her day. Every night Lynn wanted to ask him whether he had come to any final decision, but she always refrained from doing so out of fear of the possible answer. And Drew himself never once mentioned it.

During that week, Lynn only stopped by to visit with Gwen once, though they usually spoke briefly each evening on the telephone. But the following Saturday, instead of driving into the multitude of chores awaiting her at home, Lynn completed only those of absolute necessity. She fed and watered the chicks, put a load of clothes into the washer and quickly ran the vacuum cleaner over the floors before telling Joy that they were going to Penny's house.

Joy, who had been pouting because they were out of her favorite breakfast cereal, brightened at the prospect of visiting her cousin, and Lynn was glad to see it. She had been afraid her daughter would grumble about going out so early and the last thing she felt her twin needed at this point was an extra child in her house who was in a querulous mood.

Gwen was now about a month away from her delivery date and her movements had grown increasingly slower and more awkward. She tired easily and Lynn knew her sister could use a bit of a helping hand with her own housework.

Lynn noticed that Cal's truck was gone as they walked around to the back of the house to enter through the kitchen. Joy dashed ahead of her and, opening the door, went in, exclaiming in singsong fashion, "Hi, Aunt Gwen! I came to play with Penny!"

"Well, hi, honey," Gwen responded. "What are you doing here so early this morning?"

Lynn followed Joy into the kitchen and Gwen's questioning gaze went to her face.

"I thought I'd come over and let you play lady of the manor today," she said.

Gwen frowned. "What do you mean?"

Lynn's gaze surveyed the kitchen that silently testified that a family had just finished a meal. "I came to be your maid today." She laughed and turned back to her sister who was still regarding her in confusion.

"But . . . why?" Gwen demanded. "I'm not sick or anything!"

"No," Lynn agreed with a twinkle in her eyes. "But all the same, the house isn't up to its usual sparkling par, either. I'm going to give it a good going-over and watch the kids while you do something just for yourself for a change."

"Like what?" Gwen looked completely baffled as though she had never heard of the wild notion of having free time to devote only to herself.

Lynn waved a hand and said airily, "Like anything at all." She eyed Gwen's bulky form, still clad in her nightgown and robe. "Go back to bed if you like," she suggested. "Or take a long bath or read a book. Whatever you prefer. I'm going to clean the house and do the laundry and then this afternoon I'm going to pack up all your little chicks and take them home with me for the night. Besides a rest from housework, it wouldn't hurt if you and Cal had an evening all to yourselves for a change."

Gwen wavered for a moment. Conflicting emotions flitted across her face. It was obvious that she felt she should object to the plan, but it was equally obvious that it greatly appealed to her. Lynn almost laughed at her expression.

At last Gwen acquiesced. "You're the best sister

a girl ever had," she declared. "And I promise I'll pay you back somehow one of these days!"

"Don't be silly!" Lynn exclaimed. "You helped me when I was moving, didn't you? Besides taking Joy with you to visit Cal's mother." She began rolling her shirt-sleeves above her elbows, then added, "Now tell me where the kids are and then scoot!"

"They're watching Saturday morning cartoons right now," Gwen said. "That ought to occupy them for at least an hour."

Lynn nodded, then went to the table and started gathering dishes.

Three hours later she felt well satisfied with her morning's work. The last load of laundry was in the dryer, the house was clean and neat, all the beds had been changed and the bathroom scoured and mopped. She had more or less bribed help from all the children with the promise of a hamburger and ice cream treat in town this evening and they had willingly fetched and carried for her and stored away toys and clothes.

Gwen had utilized her free morning by sitting placidly in a lounge chair outside in the warm sun, knitting an afghan. The children had been unexpectedly good about keeping away from her after Lynn explained to them that they should give her the "present" of a little time all to herself to do exactly what she wanted.

With the chores done, Lynn put on a pot of coffee and while it brewed, began mixing a tuna salad for lunch. Once the coffee was ready, she sent Pat outside to invite his mother in for refreshments. She had made sandwiches, some tuna, some peanut butter and jelly, for the children to carry out to the backyard for their own private picnic.

When the children were settled at the picnic table with their food and tumblers of fruit juice, Lynn and Gwen enjoyed their coffee in the kitchen.

"Are you hungry yet?" Lynn asked. "I'll fix your plate if you want to eat now."

Gwen shook her head. "Cal should be home in another half hour or so. I'll wait until he gets here. Lynn, this morning has been heavenly, and you've done so much! The house looks marvelous. I can't thank you enough!"

"You're welcome," Lynn said easily. "Everybody needs a break now and then."

Gwen stirred her coffee and sipped at it. Then, very casually, she asked, "What do you hear from Drew? Has he said when he's coming back?"

Lynn shook her head. "Not so far. He just says he's working hard, getting a lot accomplished and that he'll be back as soon as he gets things squared away."

"Then why the long face?" Gwen asked pointedly. "Don't you believe him . . . that he has business to attend to?"

"It's not that," Lynn answered. "Of course he does and I realize he can't very well neglect it forever. I guess what I don't believe is the part about his coming back."

"Why not?"

Lynn shrugged. "He said we needed to be apart to think things over before we make any major decisions."

"What's wrong with that?" Gwen asked. "Maybe you do."

Lynn shook her head. "He's already told me he wouldn't be satisfied living here and he knows how unhappy I was living his kind of life-style. What hope is there for us at all, Gwen? I still love Drew and I know he has some feelings left for me, but I'm not sure they're strong enough for us to overcome the differences between us. Always supposing he even wants that, of course."

"Maybe," Gwen said sagely, "you're just borrowing trouble."

Lynn grimaced. "I wish I could believe that, but I think the trouble hasn't even started yet. The trouble of dividing our custody time with Joy." She couldn't even begin to express the deep pain that accompanied that thought, the feeling of absolute helplessness it brought or the bleak emptiness that dulled her mind and left her cold with dread. As close as she was to her twin in a multitude of ways, this desolation inside of her was something that could never be shared. While sympathetic, Gwen could not possibly understand what it was like to face the threat of separation from her child, knowing that while the absences would be brief in the beginning that with time they would lengthen and stretch into permanence. No, Gwen, secure in her husband's love and confident that her precious children would always surround her, was utterly incapable of truly understanding Lynn's fears.

The back door opened. Kenny came inside to beg for an apple. While Lynn pared and sectioned one for him, Cal arrived home. The intimate little talk between the two sisters was at an end.

The following week seemed even longer and emptier than the first since Drew had gone away, and Lynn's apprehension grew. She didn't hear from him at all for three straight days and nights, and his sudden, inexplicable silence seemed ominous.

She could have tried calling herself, of course, but something held her back. If Drew wanted to talk to her, she reasoned, he would call. She was reluctant to press him in any way.

By Friday night her depression was so great that she could scarcely even think straight. It took all the effort she possessed to complete her various jobs around the house and then to devote the attention that Joy required. She only wanted to hide away, to be allowed to come to terms with her new pain without the necessity of wearing a false facade of normalcy.

When she went to bed late that night she ached all over, as though she were ill. Her throat was tight and her eyes burned, yet there was no easy release. The unhappiness went too deep for tears.

Finally, she fell into a restless sleep, but her dreams were as troubled as her waking state. There was Drew saying, "You'll pay! You'll pay! I'm taking Joy away from you!" and then there was Joy, a grown-up teenaged stranger who looked at her and asked politely, "Who are you?"

She awoke abruptly to an unpleasant, insistent noise. Lynn groaned, rolled over and groped for the alarm clock, but the sound continued even after she thought she had pressed in the button. Frowning, she opened her eyes, glanced around disoriented, and finally realized that the telephone was ringing.

She grabbed the receiver and after fumbling a moment or two, carried it to her ear. "Hello," she mumbled sleepily.

"Good morning," a deep, familiar voice said cheerfully.

The simple words, the familiar voice, brought her fully awake. Lynn sat up in bed, glanced toward the clock and saw that it was just after seven. "Drew!" she exclaimed. "Why are you calling at this hour?"

She heard him chuckle. "What? No 'it's wonderful

to hear your voice' or even a 'why in the hell haven't you called me the past three days'?"

Suddenly everything was right again in Lynn's world. Sunlight filtered through the bedroom window, warming her face, but it was no warmer than the smile that curved her lips. "Why the hell haven't you called me the past three days?" she demanded.

Drew laughed. "I figured that would be the one you'd choose. I've been working night and day trying to get a lot of things squared away so that I could get back to you sooner. By the time I got home every night I couldn't even keep awake long enough to call you. You'll have to forgive me, darling. It really is the truth. And now I'm calling to ask if you can meet me in Savannah at about, um, ten forty-five?"

"This morning?" She gazed in surprise. "Where are you?"

"Atlanta. Just got in. Well," he asked impatiently, "will you meet me?"

"Of course I will!" she said happily. "See you soon."

"Not soon enough," Drew said. "It's downright strange how much I've missed my two best girls!"

An hour and a half later, with Joy beside her, Lynn drove away from the house and set off for the long drive. But unlike school mornings, when she counted the weeks until she was done with the lengthy, daily round trip, the miles seemed to fly past. Her heart was singing with anticipation.

When they met Drew, Lynn felt a surge of possessive pride. He came toward them, dressed in dark slacks, a casual shirt and a tan sports jacket, and she couldn't help but think that he was the best-looking man in the crowd. His tall form and jet black hair were commanding, his face was chiseled and firm, yet even from a distance, she spotted the definite sparkle in his piercing blue eyes and noted the laugh lines that crinkled about them.

Joy dashed from Lynn's side and ran toward him. Her hair bounced and billowed behind her and Lynn smiled indulgently as she watched her daughter fling herself into Drew's waiting arms.

"Hi, princess," Drew said as he hugged the child to him. He kissed her forehead, then lifted her up so that he could carry her back to where Lynn waited. "Did you miss me?"

"Yes," Joy assured him. Her smile beamed like warm sunshine.

"And did your mother miss me, too?" Drew asked. They had reached Lynn by then and the two of them looked at her expectantly.

Lynn laughed and nodded. "Yes," she admitted softly. "I missed you, too."

Drew put Joy down to her feet and then his arms went around Lynn and he bent his head to kiss her. They were in a public place and besides, their daughter was avidly watching, so it was a brief kiss of greeting.

Drew released her slowly and his eyes were laughing. "Not in any way a remarkable kiss," he observed dryly. "We have too much of an audience for me to kiss you the way I really want to, but," his eyes darkened and a huskiness coated his next words, "I *am* glad to see you. Very glad."

"So am I," Lynn whispered. Her heart thudded with a thrill of happiness. "Welcome back."

They collected his bags and once they were in the car, with Drew behind the wheel, he said, "You know, I've never even seen this city. I've only been to the airport and that's it. Why don't we find some place to have lunch and then you can show me some of the sights today?" He grinned at Lynn with an expression of infectious friendliness. "I go first class or not at all, and I figure there can't be a more beautiful tour guide in all of Savannah."

"Thank you very much, sir," Lynn said demurely, though a hint of laughter lurked in her voice. "I'll do my very best to make your visit to the city most enjoyable."

Drew had suddenly turned an ordinary Saturday into a holiday for them all. While Drew drove the car, Lynn directed him where to go and she took him first to the riverfront, a favorite haunt of hers. They walked across Factor's Walk to the old Cotton Exchange and glanced down from the rails to the picturesque cobblestone lanes below, where once a flourishing cotton market had thrived. The old warehouses had been converted into quaint shops and restaurants, but Lynn could still imagine what it must have been like filled with bales of cotton to be loaded from wagon carts to warehouses to ships.

They descended the stairs and strolled along River Street, pausing occasionally to browse inside an interesting-looking shop and Drew seemed to enjoy the diversity of businesses and the high-quality merchandise to be found in a number of them.

They had lunch at one of the waterfront restaurants and were served a meal of delicious seafood and yellow rice. The food was excellent, the atmosphere nautical and appealing, but best of all was the company. They were together again, a family.

When they had finished their meal, Drew pulled from his pocket two long, slender boxes. One he placed in front of Joy; the other, he put before Lynn.

"Is it a present, Daddy?" Joy asked eagerly.

Drew smiled. "Open it and find out," he instructed.

Joy obeyed. Inside was a gold, heart-shaped locket with her name inscribed on it. She clasped her hands together with glee and then demanded that he put it on for her. Drew complied and after they had all duly admired how pretty the necklace looked on her neck, Drew turned back to Lynn.

"You haven't opened yours yet," he said quietly.

Lynn opened it to find a magnificent watch fashioned in delicate strands of gold with the face outlined with diamonds. She gasped softly. "It's gorgeous!" she exclaimed. "My goodness, Drew, this must have cost you an absolute fortune!" She lifted her eyes to his face. "But why? What's the occasion?"

Her breath caught in her throat at the tender light in his gaze. "The occasion?" he echoed so low that only she could hear. "To tell you how much I love you. To tell you how glad I am to be with you again. To tell you that life has no meaning without you. Are those good enough reasons to give my wife a gift?"

Lynn glanced down once again at the glittering watch and her eyes were shining as she met his gaze once more. "The best of reasons," she said emphatically. "Oh, Drew, I really didn't need a present, though. The words themselves are gift enough."

There was a long, intense silence between them. "Stop looking at me like that," Drew growled at last. "Or I'll forget propriety and take you into my arms right here and now!"

"Would you care to order dessert, sir?"

It took Drew the space of a heartbeat to become aware of the voice behind him, yet another moment to collect himself and pull on the mask of civility. Slowly, he straightened in his chair, then looked across at Joy. "I'm almost certain," he said finally, "that this young lady will require something."

When they left the restaurant, a ship was passing on the river, bound for the open sea. It sounded its horn and Lynn touched Drew's arm and pointed toward a statue that faced the river. "That's the Waving Girl," she explained. "At one time there was a girl here who for years came and waved to all the ships entering or leaving this harbor. The horn just now was the captain's way of saluting her."

"Can I wave, too, Mommy?" Joy asked. "Just like her?"

"Sure."

Joy waved, then squealed with delight when a young crewman on board returned her wave.

The remainder of the afternoon sped by quickly. Lynn took Drew on a driving tour through the historic district. She pointed out some of the places she knew such as the Pirate's House, an old seaman's tavern that was now a restaurant, the house that was used as General Sherman's headquarters during the occupation of Savannah during the Civil War, the birthplace of Juliette Gordon Low, the founder of the Girl Scouts, and also some of the wonderful old churches that still stood with inspiring grandeur. Drew laughed with her when she pointed out the unique fish rainspouts on some of the homes they passed, but like her, he was filled with admiration of the graceful beauty of most of the homes with their wrought-iron balconies and lush gardens.

"No wonder they call Savannah a lady," he said. "She is one, indeed, full of graceful charm and dignified beauty."

"I think so," Lynn agreed. "It has a genteel atmosphere that I've never seen anywhere else, except maybe Charleston. But for myself, I prefer Savannah."

"And yet you wanted to move away," Drew said.

Lynn shrugged. "Well, I didn't have the money to live in this part of the city," she pointed out. "I certainly couldn't buy a renovated town house and if I bought one that needed restoration, I wouldn't have been able to do it justice. I thought the money I did have would serve Joy and me better with the farm, and it's nice to live so close to Gwen."

She fell abruptly silent. Drew had come back, just like he said, and he had told her he loved her. He sounded as though he wanted to make their marriage work after all. And yet, the fact remained that they did lead two separate lives: hers with the farm and her teaching, his with all his business interests in Los Angeles.

A golden brown hand left the steering wheel and stretched across the car seat to cover her hand. Lynn glanced up in faint surprise to find Drew's eyes, dark and serious, upon her. "We'll work it out," he told her, obviously having read her mind. "We'll work it out."

Lynn hoped they would. With all her heart, she hoped.

Chapter Eleven

Lynn awoke to the marvelous sensation of being toasty warm and cozy. And yet, there was something that had brought her out of the deep state of sleep and after a moment, she realized what it was. Her neck was being nuzzled and a hand was gently sliding up and down her back, over the swell of her hips and back again.

She opened her eyes and met a pair of clear blue ones as Drew lifted his head from her neck. He smiled, almost wickedly, and then had the audacity to ask in an innocent voice, "Did I wake you?"

"Of course you woke me," she answered, trying to sound severe, yet failing because her lips were stretching into a smile at the same time. "Wasn't it what you meant to do?"

Drew grinned. "Guilty," he admitted. "I've been awake for at least a half hour and I was beginning to feel very lonely. And jealous."

Lynn quirked an eyebrow at him. "Jealous?"

He nodded. "Jealous. The satisfied expression on your face looked like you were having a very good time in your dream and I felt left out. What were you dreaming about?"

"You."

"Really?"

Lynn smiled reminiscently. "Ummhmm," she drawled. "You were kissing me, among other things."

There was a quick flash of Drew's teeth as he grinned. "What other things?"

She gave him a provocative look, then shook her head. "I'm not the sort of girl who kisses and tells," she teased.

Drew growled in displeasure. His hand left her back and slid around to her breast and began teasing it into a hard peak. "Was I doing this?" he asked. The hand went lower, tracing a tantalizing circle over the flat of her stomach. "This?" It inched lower still, until suddenly she shivered in automatic reaction to what he was doing. "Maybe this?"

Lynn laughed. "All that and more!" she gasped, suddenly breathless from the little thrills that were racing through her. Her arms went out to encircle his chest, drawing him closer to her.

But all at once, Drew swatted her bare bottom and sat up in bed, heedless of the sheet that fell to his knees, leaving his naked body completely exposed to her fascinated gaze. "Not now," he said sternly. "I just heard Joy moving around in her room." He got to his feet, padded across the room to a chair where both their robes were tossed and taking hers, threw it to her. "Cover up," he said in an urgent undertone. "I have a feeling we'll have company any minute now."

He was right. They had both scarcely knotted the belts of their robes when the door opened and a sleepy-eyed Joy came in, cradling Mary Louise in her arms.

"I'm hungry," she announced.

"So am I," Drew seconded. But when his eyes met Lynn's for a brief instant, the devilish twinkle in them told her that his appetite was a far different one than the child's.

In spite of herself, Lynn felt her face heat beneath his lecherous gaze. Her heart thudded, still with the lingering excitement he had only recently aroused in her and from the unmistakable teasing desire with which he looked at her now. *He was an impossible man,* she thought. Fun . . . but impossible!

She got off the bed and went toward the door. "Since it's a unanimous decision that everyone's starved, I guess I'd better get breakfast started."

Joy and Drew trailed behind her as she went to the kitchen and put the coffee on to brew. Then she opened the refrigerator and took out several eggs for an omelet.

"What dress should I wear to Sunday school this morning, Mommy?" Joy asked.

"How about the red one?" Lynn suggested. "You look very pretty in it."

"Do *we* have to go to church this morning, too?" Drew asked.

Lynn turned to look at him with mild surprise. "Don't you want to?" she asked.

He shook his head and his face was serious as he joined her at the counter and said in a low voice, "I really don't this morning. Last night I was too tired to talk and the truth is that except for when we went to bed, we haven't had a moment alone to talk. And I really would like to talk. About us. About everything." He paused, then added, "Couldn't Joy go to church today with Gwen and Cal? It would give us the time we need."

Lynn searched his face, trying to read it, trying to find some sign of what was bothering him, but it was impossible. His expression, though somber, gave away nothing of what he was thinking or feeling. A prickle of apprehension crawled up her neck and tightened her shoulders. Suddenly the pleasure and fun and lightheartedness that had been there ever since she had met him yesterday at the airport, was gone.

Slowly, she nodded, her own face as serious as his. "All right," she agreed. "I'll call Gwen and ask."

"I'll call," Drew offered, "while you're cooking breakfast."

Two hours later the Jennings' station wagon pulled into the driveway and Cal tooted the horn. Lynn kissed Joy briefly on the top of her head and sent her outside to meet them. Then she turned back toward Drew, who stood in the doorway between the dining room and the living room, and said almost lifelessly, "She's gone. Now we can talk."

"Right." His voice was flat.

It was as though during the past two hours, reality had returned, cruelly jolting them out of the magical fantasy land in which they had existed for the past twenty-four hours. Time had been suspended, problems and doubts and conflicts had been chased away by the temporary sunlight of happiness. But now the dark cloud of truth and reckoning had returned to weigh them down again.

They took separate seats, Drew in a chair, Lynn on the sofa, as if to further emphasize the distance that was between them, emotionally as well as physically. Lynn's mouth dried with fear and she clasped her hands tightly in a desperate effort to keep them from shaking.

Drew leaned forward in his chair and propped his elbows on his knees, raising his hands to rub across his face. He had dressed casually in a pair of Levis and a plaid shirt, but there was nothing casual about his demeanor. The tension within him was as palpable as a heartbeat.

At last, hands locked together, he dropped his arms between his legs and he looked at her. "Yesterday," he began, "was a little unreal. It was great, we all had fun and it felt like a family. Like we really belonged together and to each other, forever." He sucked in a deep breath, then added, "I know family life and marriage isn't always wonderful, that there are problems and adjustments to make, but all the same, Lynn, I've discovered that it's exactly what I want in my life—for good."

Lynn licked her lips. "Drew," she began hesitantly, "are you saying . . . ?"

"I'm saying that I still love you, dammit!" he snapped. "That despite everything that happened, I still want you for my wife, that I want the three of us to be a real family!" He was actually glowering at her.

Lynn gazed at him in wonder. Whatever she had expected him to say, this was definitely not it. "Why," she asked meekly, trying not to infuriate him further, "are you so angry?"

"Because I don't know if it'll work," he practically shouted. "And I don't know how you feel about things! I wasn't the best husband in the world the first time around, as you've pointed out, so I'm sure you've got a lot of doubts about us. I know I do. I've been used to making all my decisions alone, of having things my own way. I still am. The truth is I honestly don't know how to live with a woman—to compromise the way two people have to do to make a marriage succeed. I can try, I *will* try, but Lynn, I can't guarantee how things will work out. I nurtured an awful lot of hatred for you all these years since you left me and I'm not very thrilled about the fact that I never got you out of my system!" He shook his head and grimaced, but continued with a lowered voice. "I can't possibly explain how bitter I was when your aunt told me about Joy. I came here hating you even more than ever and I fully intended to make your life a living hell for what you did! I wanted to make you suffer as much as you'd made me and if you had left me alone with Joy those first few days, I might have kidnapped her just as you feared."

"Why . . . why are you telling me this now? Today?" Lynn asked so quietly that the words were scarcely audible.

Drew's gaze was unwavering as he looked at her. "Because I want you to know the truth of how I really felt—and how much it's changed." His voice softened. "I love you," he said for the second time. "I've been confused these last few weeks about how I really felt. We were sleeping together and that part was as wonderful as ever. We seemed to be getting along pretty well in other ways, too, drawing closer, but I wasn't sure if the feeling would last once we were no longer together."

He got to his feet and moved restlessly across the room to look out the window. But abruptly, he turned around and gazed at her with a brooding expression. "When I went back to L.A., I realized that while I absolutely adore Joy, she was only a part of what I missed. All of a sudden I felt deprived and lonely and very angry . . . all the things I had felt when you first left me years ago. I missed *you*, Lynn . . . not just our sexual relationship, but you . . . your face and all the different expressions on it depending on your mood; your voice, your ideas and hopes and dreams. I missed everything about you, like the way you hug Joy and then give her an affectionate swat on the bottom; the way your eyes lit up when we showed you the baby chicks; the way you put special effort into frying an egg so that the yolk doesn't break and the edges don't brown; the close, easygoing companionship you have with your twin. I missed all the things that go into making you who and what you are and I want to spend the rest of my life with you."

Lynn got swiftly to her feet and went to join him. Her eyes were brilliant with unshed tears, but her lips were smiling. She reached out to press a hand to his chest, just over his heart.

"I love you, too," she said unsteadily. "And I want exactly what you do—to be able to spend the rest of my life with you. It's only that . . ."

Drew captured the hand that fluttered against his chest and carried it up to his lips. The action brought her eyes to meet his.

"Only what?" he prompted gently. But there was a sudden wary tension about him that had not been there a moment before.

Lynn tugged her hand away, knowing she could express herself better if he weren't touching her. Now it was her turn to gaze blindly out the window while she tried to sort out her thoughts.

"It's just that I can't go back to the sort of useless, idle life I had before when we were together." Slowly, she turned, forcing herself to face him again, for she had to know his reaction. "I really did try to be content then, Drew. But I hated it. There's more to life than bridge games and spending money on clothes!"

A sudden smile twitched Drew's lips. "Obviously," he said with dry amusement while his gaze slid down to take in the tee shirt and faded cutoff jeans she wore.

"Be serious!" she sputtered in exasperation. "Having a purpose in life is very important to me and . . ."

Drew's arms slid around her until he held her close. The tips of her breasts rested lightly against his chest. "I know, darling," he said. The amusement had gone and he was serious again. "I was wrong back then to ask you to give up your career. It was selfish and unreasonable of me. Just seeing you with Joy and Gwen's children makes me realize what a wonderful teacher you must be because you're so good with them. To ask you to abandon teaching is not only depriving you, but also the children who could benefit as your pupils. But I wouldn't stand in your way about that again, I swear!"

"You wouldn't?" she asked, amazed.

Drew shook his head. "I know you're not exactly crazy about Los Angeles, but it is where my business is located, darling. If we're going to be together, we'd have to live there, you realize that. But there's no reason you can't teach there as well as you did here."

Lynn nodded. "I know," she said thoughtfully. "I'd have to go back to college to become accredited to teach in California, but that wouldn't really be a problem. But what about the farm?" There was real pain in her eyes at the thought. "I just bought it! Joy's just settling in here!"

Drew bent to lightly brush his lips across hers, then with his arm around her shoulder, he guided her back to the sofa where they sat down together. He sighed heavily and nodded. "I know. The farm. I realized that would be a sticky part, that you wouldn't want to leave it or your sister." He looked down at her and grimaced. "I've given it some thought and I think maybe I've come up with a solution of sorts, but I'm not sure it'll be good enough to suit you."

Lynn stiffened. "Sell it?"

Drew placed both his hands on her shoulders and began to massage away the tautness there. "No," he replied evenly. "We could keep it, hire Cal, if he's willing, or someone else if he's not, to run the entire place for us. We could come out on holidays and plan to spend our summers here when Joy is out of school."

"But you couldn't stay here three solid months at a time!" she protested. And the idea of being separated from Drew for that much time every year was entirely unappealing and unacceptable.

Drew smiled at her. "I think airlines will continue to have a pretty regular service between L.A. and Savannah," he teased. "I'll just do a bit of commuting in the summer while you and Joy stay on here and enjoy your family. Come on, darling," he urged, "look at the bright side of things. We'd have the best of both worlds, our business and professional lives in the city where Joy can grow up exposed to cultural opportunities she couldn't possibly have here, and then the simple life and good fresh air of wide open spaces in the country for our vacations. What do you say?" For the first time his face gave a hint of anxiety and uncertainty.

"I think," Lynn began slowly, with a grave expression. Abruptly, the gravity vanished, to be replaced by a look of sheer delight as she threw her arms around Drew's neck and exclaimed, "I think I married a genius!"

Drew chuckled. "It's about time you realized that," he joked back. But all the same, there was blatant relief in his eyes just before he closed them and bent forward to kiss her.

His lips moved warmly over hers, searching, probing, seeking out every little crevice and corner and finally the liquid, soft interior of her mouth. Lynn snuggled closer to him, winding her arms around his neck.

Drew's hands were at her waist and now one of them slid underneath the shirt she wore and up to cover a breast. "Damn!" he muttered against her mouth.

"What's wrong?" Lynn's fingers were threading through the hair at the nape of his neck and already her senses were becoming bemused.

"You're wearing a bra!"

Lynn giggled. "It's a thin shirt. If I didn't, you'd be able to see straight through it."

"And feel right through it, too," he grumbled. "Why do you think I'm complaining?" He gave a firm tug at the garment that offended him. "This . . . contraption was only invented to give a man a hard time! I'm surprised they don't still sell chastity belts as well!"

Lynn choked with laughter. "I'll write the manufacturers first thing tomorrow morning suggesting it and . . ." Her words were smothered as the tee shirt was suddenly pulled over her face, then tugged off and tossed to the floor. Drew's hands reached behind her where he unhooked the bra and it, too, went sailing to the floor.

"Now!" Drew said with satisfaction as he eyed her pear-shaped breasts. "Never let it be said that Andrew Marcus will allow himself to be defeated by women's wear!"

Very shortly, all joking came to an end. Drew bent his head to a breast and that wonderful agony of desire began stirring anew within Lynn. Her hands raked through his hair as she quivered beneath his expert touch.

Drew pressed her back against the pillows of the sofa and made quick work of removing her shorts and bikini panties. Shedding his own clothes, he stretched out beside her. "This is closer quarters than the bed," he whispered with the faintest suggestion of a twinkle in his eyes, "but then again, here, you're not going to escape from me."

"So who's trying?" she retorted. "Oh, Drew," she whispered in an entirely different tone of voice, "I'm so glad you're back!"

His mouth trailed across her cheek, toward her lips. "Shut up and kiss me," he ordered huskily. "We're both doing far too much talking."

Lynn agreed with him and willingly offered him her lips while their hands stroked each other with fine appreciation. She loved to run her fingers through the dark mat of hair on his chest and to locate his heart and feel it pounding. It was peculiarly satisfying to trace the rocky curves of his shoulders, to allow her hands to roam across the broad span of his back and downward to lean hips and muscular thighs. She reveled in the touch of him, the clean male scent of him, the warmth of his body heat as he lay pressed close to her.

And what he was doing to *her* sent exquisite

tremors rippling through her! Drew was a superb lover, as bent on giving satisfaction as in being gratified himself. His kisses, wherever they landed, were fiery; his caresses, silky and tantalizing; his timing drawn out, calculated to drive her slowly mad.

He nibbled and stroked, teasing her body into wild desperation. Her breasts became hard peaks of craving. Her lower limbs became leaden with the pain of urgency. He was tormenting her by fanning the torrid flames of desire that licked mercilessly at her veins.

A storm of passion broke over Lynn, and with it came a fog of sensations that clouded her mind and obscured all awareness except for her excessive need. She was weak with longing and tormented by the sea of emotions that tossed her.

But just when she could endure no more, when the relentless storm was about to submerge her, Drew shifted his position and moved over her. With glad abandon, she gave herself to him. In the precious oneness of both spirit and flesh, they merged, moving together, reaching the intoxicating heights of loving together.

Savage release came at last, lifting them both from unquenched craving to rapturous culmination. Sharp, panting breaths mingled and gradually slowed to soft, velvety sighs. The mellowness of contentment came last and as Drew moved to lie at her side once more, smiles of deep happiness glowed on both their faces and gave an incandescent light to their eyes.

They were quiet and still for a time, regaining strength after the fierce assault on their energies. Lynn's head lay on Drew's arm; turned toward her, he rested his free arm over her stomach.

"After that," Drew murmured, "I doubt if anything will ever come between us again. If that doesn't prove how much we belong together, nothing can."

Lynn hoped he was right, but now she remembered something she had forgotten, no, actually shoved to the back of her mind ever since his return and a small, nagging whisper of apprehension came to disturb her. But quickly, she pushed the thought away. This was a happy, joyous day and she wasn't going to spoil it by unnecessary anxiety. Not yet. There was time enough later on, if she must.

A little while later, they took a shower together. They took turns soaping each other and their laughter was carefree and contagious as their hands roamed over slippery skin. It was an exciting departure from the norm, since they had not done such a thing since Drew had located her. But it brought back pleasant memories of the past. When they had first married, showering together had been the rule rather than the exception.

Drew's large hands slid over Lynn's breasts and glided across her ribs in a smooth, sensual motion. His eyes sparkled as he smiled at her through the spray of water that fell over them. "Remember," he asked huskily, "how it used to be? How we'd shower and then make love, sometimes on the bed, sometimes on the rug?"

Lynn laughed and nodded. "And then we'd raid the refrigerator," she said, "and the next day, poor Mrs. Watson would find that the ham or whatever she planned to use for a meal was gone. I'm afraid we gave her a hard time." Her gaze took on a faraway look of remembrance.

"And after the assault on her food supply and maybe a glass of wine, we'd make love all over again before we finally fell asleep out of sheer exhaustion." He chuckled. "You were such a gluttonous woman! Kept me tired all the time! You were making an old man out of me, wearing me down!"

"Liar!" She smiled. "It was me who stayed worn out! I spent a fortune of your money on vitamins just to keep up with you!"

"So *that's* where all my money went!" His arms tightened around her waist as he pressed her slick body to his. "Tomorrow," he teased, "I'll go out and buy a new supply for you."

Lynn's eyes widened as though she were surprised. "Do you think I'm going to need them?" she asked with deceptive innocence.

"I'm positive of it," Drew replied.

Proving his point, they made love again after their bath, this time in bed, and afterward, as they lay in total collapse, Drew grinned wryly. "I'd better double that supply of vitamins," he observed. "We're both going to need a lot of them at this rate!"

"Health foods, too," Lynn mused. "I can see we're going to need all the help we can get. Let's see now, we'll need yogurt, alfalfa sprouts, soybeans, brewer's yeast, lots of liver and . . ."

Drew roughly clamped a hand over her mouth. "No sense in getting carried away," he said fiercely. "I draw the line at liver, even for you!"

Lynn giggled. She had expected that reaction, knowing Drew's strong aversion to liver. She affected a pout. "If you really loved me, you would eat it," she told him.

Drew shook his head. "I never heard of liver breaking up a marriage before, but I suppose there's always a first time for anything. If I have to take you *and* liver, my love, the deal's off."

Lynn looked at him with sorrow. "I'm finding out that there are limits to your love, after all. However, I suppose if I must compromise, I must."

He looked at her suspiciously. "Compromise?"

She nodded. "Certainly. Instead of liver, I'll just have to serve you oysters." That was another food he detested and knowing it, Lynn was ready. Before he could lunge in attack, she was already off the bed and running.

By the time the others returned from church, Lynn and Drew were fully clothed once more. Lynn had put a large roast in the oven and as they had planned, when the station wagon entered the driveway, Drew went outside to invite the Jennings to stay for Sunday dinner.

The invitation was accepted and after Cal and Gwen went home to change their clothes and the children's, they returned. The house was suddenly filled with noisy, convivial chatter. The children went to Joy's room to play with her toys and the two men settled into the living room while Gwen joined Lynn in the kitchen.

An hour later, Lynn had everything ready. Gwen had set both tables for her and poured glasses of iced tea for the adults and milk for the children. While Lynn placed dishes of mashed potatoes, green beans and salad on the table, Drew sliced the roast.

Lynn and Gwen served the children at the kitchen table before they and the men sat down at last in the dining room.

After they began eating, Lynn glanced up to find Drew, at the head of the table, giving her a quizzical look. She understood its message perfectly and with the tiniest inclination of her head, she silently told him to go ahead. They had decided earlier to break their news to Cal and Gwen together over dinner and now the time had come.

"I have an announcement to make," Drew began, looking first toward Gwen, then at Cal. A little smile accompanied the words as he added, "May I have your complete, undivided attention, please?"

Gwen straightened in her chair. She looked quickly at Lynn, then at her husband before finally turning to Drew. "That sounds very important," she told him.

"It is." Drew favored her with a wide smile. "Mrs. Marcus and I have arrived at a momentous decision," he said with grandiloquence.

A delighted smile flashed across Gwen's face. "You're getting back together permanently!" she exclaimed.

Drew scowled at her. "Did you have to steal my thunder, woman?"

Gwen only laughed at him and reached out to touch his hand. "I'm so happy you've both come to your senses at last! It's about time!"

"You don't act very surprised," Drew grumbled.

"Neither am I," Cal said. "Gwen's been telling me for weeks that you two would settle your differences and straighten everything out." He offered his hand to Drew and grinned. "I'm glad for you both, too."

The two men shook hands while Gwen got out of her chair long enough to hug Lynn and whisper, "This is wonderful news! I'm thrilled for you."

Lynn hugged her back. "I know you are." She smiled, then added in a low whisper, "Oh, Gwen, you can't imagine how happy I am!"

Next, Lynn received a kiss on her cheek from her brother-in-law while Drew and Gwen lightly embraced. It took a little time, but finally they all settled down to their meal again.

"I'm glad for you both, really I am," Gwen said, but her voice suddenly became a little wistful as she looked at Drew and continued, "but I suppose this means you're going to take Lynn and Joy away from us."

Drew gave her an apologetic look. "'Fraid so, Gwen."

She sighed despondently. "I knew it."

"When will you go?" Cal asked.

"Not for quite a while," Drew answered. "Gwen, dear, don't be too upset. I'm not planning to steal Lynn away from you just yet and even when we go, it won't be forever. There's only about three weeks left until school is out. Lynn will naturally finish out the term. And she and Joy will stay here this summer. You're going to need a bit of sisterly help for a while after the baby comes, and I'm not such a heartless monster as to take her away just when you need her most."

Gwen caught her lower lip between her teeth. "Thanks," she said huskily, though she shook her head. "But much as I'd like her to be here then, I'm not about to jeopardize things between the two of you by asking you to be separated all summer."

"We won't," Drew assured her. "I'll commute between here and L.A. during the summer, and then in the fall we'll all go back there together so we can get Joy into kindergarten and Lynn into college. She is going to take the courses she needs to teach in California."

"That's mighty considerate of you, Drew," Cal

said, "but I agree with Gwen. We can't impose on the two of you to that extent!"

"It's what we want, isn't it, darling?" Drew appealed to Lynn for confirmation.

She nodded. "Our minds are made up," she said firmly. "Drew will be here with us as often as he can. But besides my wanting to be here to help you, we both want Joy to have a nice summer in the country."

"What happens in the fall?" Cal asked. "I suppose you'll put the farm up for sale?" There was a thoughtful frown crinkling his brow and Lynn and Drew both knew he was already worrying about losing the lease of her fields when a new owner took possession.

Drew winked at Lynn, then said, "That's partly up to you."

"To me?" Cal was clearly taken aback.

Drew grinned. "Well, I have a proposal to make to you, although if you don't want to do it, just say so and I'll try to find someone else for the job."

"What job?"

"Lynn and I want to keep the farm," Drew explained. "We plan to come out as often as we can, long weekends, holidays, the summers. So what the place is going to require is someone to manage it full time for us, to harvest the lumber crops, tend to the chickens and the pony I bought for Joy, to keep the house and barn in good repair—in short, the whole works. Still, it shouldn't require a great amount of your time and it would leave you with plenty of free time for running your own place." He named a figure he was willing to pay and added, "Would you be interested in taking it on?"

Cal threw a swift look of excited surprise toward

his wife and then he burst out laughing. "Damn it, Drew, need you ask? You know how much I want to farm full time and that much extra income every month would put me over the top so that I could quit that mechanics job in town! Of course I want it!"

"Then it's a deal," Drew said with a grin. "Later, we can discuss how to work out the leasing arrangement you've already got for the fields. You can continue with it as is or farm it for us for a percentage of the profits."

They finished the meal in high spirits and then Lynn served strawberry shortcake with whipped cream.

"Just a tiny piece for me," Gwen said resolutely. "I've got to go to Savannah tomorrow for a checkup and I don't want the doctor yelling at me like he did last month."

"I thought you told me you'd been doing well at keeping your weight down the last few weeks," Lynn said.

"I have," Gwen laughed, "but I don't want to blow it today."

"How much longer do you have to go, Gwen?" Drew asked.

"Probably three weeks. Maybe a little longer," she replied.

"Now that you two are back together for good," Cal teased, "you need to get busy and see about providing Joy with a little brother or sister. She's going to be lonely, you know, when you move her away from all her cousins."

Drew grinned in response, but Lynn noted that the smile never reached his eyes. A moment later he completely changed the subject and she knew instinctively that he had done it with cold deliberation.

A chill crept up her spine. Drew obviously still did not want her to bear him children, even though he frankly loved Joy. So now she was back to square one. It was far too early to be sure, to dare say anything yet, but for the past few days, Lynn had begun to suspect that she might be pregnant again.

Chapter Twelve

$\mathcal{T}$he days fell into a predictable pattern. Lynn went to Savannah each weekday to finish out the school year. Her pupils had been bitten hard by the spring bug and every day it was more difficult to maintain discipline in the classroom or to hold their attention. Lynn couldn't blame them in her heart, however much she struggled to keep up some semblance of routine. She was competing against warm days, bright sunshine, daydreams of kite flying and the long summer vacation. In all honesty, she was having as hard a time as the children in keeping her mind on the work at hand.

Now that Drew was back, they had worked out a fair and pleasant schedule concerning Joy. There were days when Drew needed to concentrate fully on work around the farm, or paperwork to mail to Los Angeles and didn't need or want the distraction of watching after a small child. Also, they had decided that a certain amount of "school" was good for her, so she finished out the term by attending three days a week, spending Tuesdays and Thursdays and the weekends at home. Joy herself was happy with the arrangement, for it gave her ample time to enjoy the freedom of her life outdoors, yet still having the opportunity to be with her playmates at the day-care center and participate in the learning activities there.

The barn had been completed over a week ago and when Joy had arrived home with Lynn from the city that afternoon, Drew had blindfolded his daughter and surprised her with a pony.

Joy took to riding as though she had been born to it. Seeing how much the child loved it, Lynn couldn't have possibly held on to her grudge against Drew for buying the pony, even if she was still angry with him, though he had fun teasing her about it.

Every afternoon while the daylight held, Lynn and Drew would explore their private little world together. Hand in hand, they would go to check on the growing chicks, making certain they had enough food and fresh water; they would visit the vegetable garden and marvel over how much plants could grow in just a single day beneath the life-giving warmth of the sun; they watched their daughter ride her pony around the yard before helping her bed him down in the barn for the night; and they all took turns frolicking with Fluffy, who was also growing by leaps and bounds.

To Lynn, this springtime was a season of wonder. Everything grew so vigorously . . . plants, animals, even their daughter. But most satisfying was the love that continued to grow between herself and Drew. It was a glowing, exciting thing by night as they lay in each other's arms, but by day it came as the quiet commitment of two people who want to spend a lifetime together. It showed in their plans for Joy, such as swimming lessons in the summer, ballet classes in the fall; it was revealed in discussions of the life they would share again in California, redecorating the house there, Lynn's return to college, business decisions Drew must make. It also showed in the little things they did for each other.

The only shadow that lay over Lynn's happiness was the anxiety of whether or not she was pregnant. She wished she could believe that if she was, Drew would be pleased, but she was too much of a realist to deceive herself that way. Now that they had Joy, he might be happy to have another child, but then again he could be as much against it as he had been from the beginning. He had certainly not appeared to favor the idea when Cal had teased them about adding to the family.

No matter what happened, though, Lynn assured herself of one thing. If she was expecting a child, this time she would not keep it from Drew. If they were ever going to make it together, they had to be done with secrets. They would have to face the issue together.

Still, she remained silent. There was no sense yet in broaching such a sensitive subject and disrupting their current harmony on the strength of a maybe. She would wait until school was out, which was only a couple of weeks away, and then visit the doctor if she still wasn't sure by that time. Once he confirmed or denied her suspicions, she would confront Drew with the facts.

The possibility haunted her one night as they were in bed. Joy was already asleep and they were spending a companionable evening together even though they were both occupied with something more than each other. Drew, propped up against a mountain of pillows, was going over some legal papers he had received in the day's mail. Lynn was busy grading students' test papers.

For almost two hours, the only sound in the room was the occasional crackle of papers. But around ten, Drew sighed heavily, shoved his papers into the briefcase that rested at the foot of the bed, then tossed his extra pillows to the nearby chair and finally turned to Lynn. "I'm calling it a day," he said. He yawned, then tapped a finger on the papers that still littered her lap and asked, "How much more do you have to go?"

"This is the last one," she said with an air of relief. Swiftly, she went down the page, marking with a red pen. When she had finished, she put the grade at the top of the page and drew a caricature of a smiling, happy face. Then she gathered them all into a neat stack, replaced the cap on her pen and laid it all aside on the bedside table. She switched off her light, smoothed out her pillow and scooting down, stretched out full length beneath the covers. "Ah, this feels heavenly," she murmured in appreciation.

Drew snapped off the lamp on his side of the bed as well and the room was plunged into darkness. A moment later he pulled her close to him and one of his hands strayed up to lightly caress her shoulder.

"Tired?"

"Umm."

"Me, too. Darling?"

"Umm?"

"Next week I may have to go back to L.A. for a few days."

"Again?" The thought didn't dismay her this time as much as it surprised her. "I thought you had squared things away so that you wouldn't have to rush back so soon."

Drew sighed. "So did I, and believe me, it's the last thing I want to do. But we're having some trouble over the title to a piece of property we bought and it's turning into a real pain."

"Can't your lawyers handle it?"

"I hope. But unless there's some kind of break-through in the next few days I need to be there. We're trying to settle it before it gets into court. We've sunk a lot of money into that land and we can't see it going down the drain. Still," now his arms tightened around her and he dropped a brief kiss onto her forehead, "I shouldn't be away as long as the last time. A week at tops." A hint of laughter shook his voice. "You won't miss me, anyway. You'll be so busy with school and test scores and all the chores to do around here that you probably won't even realize I'm gone."

"Think not?"

"No," he declared. He stirred beside her and then she felt his lips grazing her throat.

Her heart fluttered when his hand came up to cup a breast, but she struggled to keep her voice solemn. "Of course I won't miss you, at all," she agreed. "Most of the time I'm hardly even aware you're around. *Particularly* in bed. So . . . what's to miss?"

"I'll show you!" he growled low against her ear as he stroked her hair. Lynn giggled, but soon her laughter died away as Drew showed her indeed . . . and in a most satisfactory manner.

After his soft breathing told her he was asleep, Lynn lay awake, thinking of how wonderful the present was, yet how nebulous the future. They had agreed to resume their marriage, but now it might include yet another child and she tensed with anxiety. There was nothing she would like more than to have a baby, if only she could be sure that Drew would welcome it. But what would such news do to him? Would it anger him, terrify him, annoy him or somehow miraculously delight him? If only she knew.

On Friday morning, Drew cooked their breakfast while Lynn and Joy dressed and added a few last-minute items to a small overnight bag. Joy's best friend in Savannah, a little girl who also attended the same day-care center, was having a birthday party the following day. The child's mother, whom Lynn had known for two years, had invited Joy to spend the entire weekend with them. The two little girls had taken turns spending the night with each other a few times during this past year, so Lynn had no hesitations about allowing her to stay over for a weekend. She wouldn't get homesick in the middle of the night and cry, and she liked the family she would be staying with.

Mornings, like this one, were still rather fresh, though usually by midday the temperature was almost like summer. Drew had already been outside to tend to the chicks and to feed the pony. When Lynn and Joy entered the kitchen and sat down to eat, he frowned and asked, "Are you sure it's wise for Joy to go to the beach on Sunday?"

Lynn nodded as she buttered a piece of toast for Joy. "Kathleen told me they aren't going swimming. Just for a picnic."

"An' anyway, Daddy," Joy assured Drew, "I wouldn't go swimmin' by myself." She was remembering the evening down at the creek and her promise to him afterward.

218

Drew smiled. "I know you wouldn't, princess," he said. "I was talking about the weather, anyway. It's pretty cool out. I just thought it might be a bit too cold yet for a swim at the beach."

"Will you take me to the beach this summer?" Joy asked hopefully. "When it's hot an' I can swim?"

"Sure, I will," Drew assured her. "We'll pack a huge lunch and invite Penny, Pat and Kenny to go with us. How does that sound?"

Joy grinned at him. "Like fun! An' will you build a sand castle with me?"

"You bet! We'll build the biggest and the best one in the whole, wide world!"

"A *great* big one!" Joy declared.

Lynn quietly enjoyed the easy repartee between her husband and daughter. The close relationship they had developed was the only hope she had to cling to that Drew would take a second child in his stride. How could he not love his own child from its infancy, as much as this daughter he had only met so recently? A peaceful calm stole over her. Of course he would accept and love another child. It was not children that bothered him—it was something to do with the pregnancy and delivery. And surely she would be able to reassure him about that aspect of it, especially since she had already gone through it once.

They finished breakfast and Joy went outside for a quick good-bye visit with Fluffy and her pony. Lynn and Drew lingered over their coffee.

"Are you coming straight home from school today?" he asked.

She shook her head. "Since I don't have to pick up Joy this afternoon, I thought I'd do a little shopping. I need a new pair of sandals for summer and then I thought I'd go ahead and do my week's grocery shopping there, too. That way I won't have to take time out to go into town tomorrow. What about your plans for the day?"

"I'm going to do a little hoeing in the garden before it gets too warm, then go into town for a few supplies after I've called the office. Later this afternoon I thought I might go over to Cal's and borrow his lawn mower. The grass around the yard is starting to get high."

Lynn finished her coffee and got up with reluctance. "It's getting late. I guess I'd better be leaving."

Drew stood, too, and his blue eyes were soft and warm as the spring sky as he looked at her. "We'll have the entire weekend to ourselves," he reminded her. "Much as I love Joy, I confess I'm looking forward to it."

Lynn smiled. "So am I," she answered in a lighthearted vein. "It means we can get a lot of work done around this place without constant interruptions and . . ."

Drew stopped this nonsense with a long, suggestive kiss. His hands made a fondling journey across her back, down over the curve of her hips and slowly up again, and he didn't release her until she was breathless.

"Believe me," he warned with a mischievious grin, "you're going to be far too tired to even want to get out of bed, much less to spend your weekend working. I'm going to make love to you and make love to you and then . . ."

Her eyes danced. "And then?"

"And then I'll make love to you all over again," he stated wickedly. He patted her behind. "Get going, girl. You're liable to be late as it is and if you continue standing here looking at me like that, I won't be responsible for the consequences."

Lynn laughed at him, taking deep pleasure in her woman's power over him and the happy feeling that his passionate gaze instilled in her carried over throughout the day.

In the end, she got home sooner that afternoon than she had planned. After school she decided against shopping for shoes and went straight to the supermarket, where she sailed through her grocery list in record time. Joy would soon be needing some new summer clothes, so she might as well wait until she took her some Saturday and do all personal-type shopping at the same time.

Drew's truck was missing when she pulled into the driveway. *He was probably in town picking up the supplies he had mentioned that morning,* Lynn thought, as she carried two bags of groceries toward the back door. Either that or he was over at Cal's. The yard, she noticed, hadn't yet been mowed.

Lynn busied herself storing away the groceries and when that was done she went to the bedroom to change from the dress she had worn to school into a comfortable pair of jeans.

She was tugging a beige knit shirt over her head when the telephone rang. Lynn finished pulling the shirt into place, then moved around the bed to pick up the receiver.

"Hello."

"Thank God!" Drew's voice exclaimed.

Lynn tensed instinctively. "What's wrong?"

"I'm at Gwen's. Get over here right away. I need you." He sounded frantic.

Lynn's fingers tightened around the receiver. "Drew, what's the *matter?*" she insisted.

"No time. Just get here!" He hung up on her.

Panic dried her mouth like cotton. Something was wrong—terribly wrong! Something had happened to Gwen or Cal or one of the children. Adrenaline surged through her veins. She shoved her feet into a pair of shoes and ran from the room, snatching up her purse and car keys from the kitchen table without even breaking her stride as she headed toward the back door.

Five minutes later her car squealed to a noisy halt in front of Gwen's house. She leapt from the car and raced toward the house and into it.

The door slammed behind her and she paused momentarily in the empty living room. "Drew?" Her voice was a shrill shout.

"In here," he yelled back. "In the bedroom!"

When she reached the room and entered it, she stopped short near the door, scarcely believing the evidence before her eyes. She sucked in a deep, shuddering breath.

"My God!" she whispered softly.

Gwen, limp with exhaustion and wet with perspiration, lay on the bed. A tiny, wrinkled red face lay snuggled in the crook of her arm. Crumpled bedcovers were mounded over Gwen's legs and pulled up to her breasts.

Drew stood beside the bed, paler than death, his eyes dark and sunken as though he had just passed through a debilitating illness.

Gwen managed a weak ghost of a smile. "We did it, sis. Drew and I did it together. Come see my little daughter."

Lynn moved forward slowly and bent over to peer down at the tiny creature. The baby's eyes were tightly shut, for she was sleeping, peacefully oblivious of the excitement she had caused. Her tiny lips were puckered as though she were dreaming of her first meal and one little hand was balled into a fist, pressed against a fat cheek.

"She's beautiful," Lynn declared softly. She straightened, then looked across the bed to her husband. "But I don't understand. Where's Cal . . . and why didn't you get her to the hospital, or at least get the local doctor out here?"

Drew sighed raggedly and gave her a dark look. "You think I wanted it like this?" he asked shortly. "Or that Gwen did?" He shook his head. "Cal's off working the field over at our place. I came by to pick up the lawn mower and found Gwen in labor. She'd already tried to call the doctor in Williamsboro, but he's away on vacation. There was no one to drive her to the hospital in Savannah and by the time I got here, it was too late to move her. So I . . ." His voice shook and broke off.

"So he took over," Gwen said in a tired, sleepy voice. "And I can tell you, Lynn, he was magnificent. But even so, I have a sneaking suspicion that he'd just as soon not take up delivering babies as a hobby!"

Drew smiled at her teasing, but there was a fine edge of bleakness about it that silently told Lynn he was forcing himself to be pleasant for Gwen's sake alone. He patted Gwen's arm, then turned to Lynn and said, "I've got to go out to the field and find Cal, but I didn't dare leave her until you came."

Lynn nodded and asked, "Where are the kids?"

"I sent them to play in the backyard as soon as I realized what was happening. I didn't want them to hear, well . . . you know," he ended faintly.

He looked almost as faint as he sounded and Lynn

glanced at him with sharp concern. It was as though now that the crisis was over and she was here to take his place, he was almost reaching a point of collapse.

She followed him out of the bedroom and asked softly, anxiously, "Drew, are you all right?"

"I'm fine," he snapped curtly. "Just get back in there with her, will you? Those sheets need changing and I just . . ." his voice cracked and his eyes glazed before he half-turned away from her, "I just can't do anymore."

"You've already done more than enough," Lynn said, trying to comfort him. She placed a hand on his arm, but he jerked back as though he resented her touch.

"I'll go for Cal," he said abruptly. "You get Gwen ready to leave for the hospital." Swiftly, he strode through the house and out the door.

Lynn was hurt by the way he had pulled back from her touch. He had acted as though he were furious with her about something and yet as far as she could see, she had done nothing to anger him. Unhappily, she watched him go. Then, with determination, she went briskly to the back of the house to check on the children before returning to Gwen.

She found them at the swing set. With hunched shoulders and a melancholy air, Pat was pushing little Kenny on a swing while Penny sat still, lost in somber thought, in the other swing.

As soon as she walked out the door and they saw her, Pat helped Kenny out of the swing and he and Penny raced to join her.

"Mommy?" Pat looked at her questioningly. His eyes were wide and serious. "Is she hurt?"

"Is she still crying?" Penny asked. Dried tears streaked her face, mute testimony to her anxiety.

Drew had sent them outside, hoping they would

LOVE'S GENTLE CHAINS

not hear any of what had been going on with their mother, but obviously they had heard more than anyone had dreamed and now they were terrified that something bad had occurred.

Lynn bent to gather both children into her arms and she planted a loving kiss on each of their foreheads. "Your mother's just fine," she assured them with a bright smile. "And what's more, you now have a brand-new little baby sister!"

Penny pulled back from her in surprise. "We *do?*" she asked in amazement.

Lynn nodded and smiled.

"Can we go in and see her?" Pat asked.

"In a little while, honey," Lynn answered gently. "She needs a few minutes' rest just now and I've got to help her get ready to go to the hospital as soon as your daddy comes home. But I promise you'll get to see them both before they go. Right now I want you to stay out here and take care of Kenny while I help her, okay? And after they leave, I'll fix us all some supper."

"We been takin' good care of Kenny," Pat said. "Uncle Drew told us to an' we did it."

Lynn smiled and ruffled his hair. "You've done a very good job of it, too," she assured him. "I'm proud of you both."

She went back inside to Gwen and set to work. She managed to remove the soiled bed sheets without disturbing Gwen and the baby too much and then brought warm water to bathe them both.

By this time, Gwen was a bit more rested and alert than before and was able to sit up in bed and dress herself in a fresh gown while Lynn cuddled the newborn in her arms.

"She's perfect, Gwen," she said softly. "She's got the loveliest, darkest eyelashes! And look at her

225

hands. Long fingers! I'll bet she'll be the musician in the family."

Gwen smiled with maternal pride. "Or maybe a surgeon." Then she laughed. "Poor baby! Not an hour old even, and here we are trying to decide on a career for her!"

Lynn laughed, too, and replaced the infant in her sister's arms. "You're right. I guess we are getting ahead of ourselves, aren't we? Have you and Cal decided yet on a name for a girl?"

Gwen nodded. "Her name is Angela."

Lynn smiled down at her new niece. "Hi, Angela," she said. "Your brothers and sister are waiting to make your acquaintance."

Gwen settled back against the pillows. "Go ahead and bring them in," she told Lynn. "We're ready for company now."

Lynn moved toward the door, but Gwen stopped her before she could leave the room.

"Lynn?"

Lynn paused and turned back. "Yes?"

Soft color stained Gwen's face. "I don't know how I would have managed," she began slowly. "Without Drew, I mean. Here I was all alone with three small children and I could tell this labor was different from the others. It was too hard and too fast. I knew the baby was going to be born soon and I didn't dare even get into the car to drive as far as your place so that I could send Pat out to the field for Cal. I had called your house and gotten no answer and I was frantic. I suppose Drew just came straight here from town, but anyway I just don't know what would have happened if he hadn't come. The kids were terrified . . . I'm sure they thought I was dying, but Drew calmed them down, got them out of the house and then he tended to me." She paused, then went on more softly. "It wasn't easy for him, Lynn. The man is truly afraid of childbirth. I could see it in his eyes and by the set of his jaw even though he tried his best to keep me from knowing it. I just want you to be aware of how traumatic it's been for him. Much more than he will let you see, I think. So if he acts moody for a while, just be patient and kind and understanding with him, okay? This thing was just thrust upon him and I think the shock of being forced to deliver my baby, being *confronted* physically with his own private fears, was all just a bit much for him."

Lynn nodded, wondering if perhaps Gwen had watched through the doorway when Drew had jerked away from her and that was why she was warning her to be patient. After a moment, she smiled and nodded. "All right, sis. I get your meaning," she agreed in a low voice. "And now, can I bring the children in to meet their baby sister and see for themselves that you're okay?"

Gwen laughed. "Go get them!" She smiled down at the baby and said softly, "We're about to have a little birthday party for you, Angela."

The children came and while they were not allowed to touch the tiny being in their mother's arms, they were ecstatic just to see her. The older ones were thrilled and filled with awe, while even little Kenny's eyes were large with wonder. "Baby?" he asked. He pointed toward Angela. "Baby?"

The men arrived, and as soon as Cal entered the room, Lynn quickly herded the children out to the living room so that for a minute, at least, husband and wife could be alone with their new child.

Drew was in the living room, an altogether different man than the one she had parted from only that morning. He was tense and there was a distant expression in his eyes as he looked at her that chilled her heart.

"Are they all right?" he asked stiffly.

"As far as I can tell, they're doing fine," she answered.

Drew nodded. "Cal's going to grab a quick shower and then we'll take them to the hospital. He asked me to drive so he can sit in back and be with Gwen."

"Good," Lynn said with approval. "I'll stay here with the children, of course."

"It'll probably be extremely late when we get back," Drew said.

"I know," she replied softly. "I'll have some supper waiting for you both. I'd take the kids home with me tonight, but they've been so upset already that I think it's probably best if I just stay here with them overnight."

Drew nodded. "I think you're right. Poor little tykes. They don't really understand what's been going on."

"I may be asleep when you get back," Lynn said. "Why don't you plan on coming back here for breakfast in the morning? I imagine Cal will leave early to go back to the hospital and you and I can pack up the kids and take them home with us then."

Drew didn't answer because just then Cal came out of the bedroom and they both turned toward him.

Cal's face was a dull, self-conscious red. "They both seem fine," he said on a sigh of relief. "All the same, I'll be glad when I've got them in the hospital.

I'm going to take a shower now and then we can leave. While I'm doing that, Drew, would you call the hospital and alert them that we're coming?"

Lynn had no further private conversation with Drew. While he made the phone call, she returned to the bedroom, added a toothbrush and cosmetics to the small suitcase Gwen had packed for the hospital a couple of weeks ago, then helped her sister into her robe. By the time she did those few things, Cal, who had showered and dressed so quickly that he had probably set a world's record, came to join them.

They made an odd procession outside to the station wagon where Drew had placed blankets and pillows for the drive ahead. Cal carried his wife in his arms; Lynn carried the baby; Drew carried the suitcase and the older children tagged along to say good-bye.

While the children kissed their mother, Lynn walked around to the driver's side of the car where Drew was about to get in.

There was still that disturbing, remote expression on his face. She had the oddest impression that while he was physically present, his mind had withdrawn from what was actually going on around him, even withdrawn from her.

She swallowed hard and whispered, "I just wanted to tell you how much I appreciate what you did for Gwen. How proud I am of you."

"Proud?" The word came out harsh and derisive. "What's to be proud about? I had no choice in the matter." He opened the door and slid behind the steering wheel. Only then did he look up at her again. "You'll be all right?" he asked in a flat, emotionless voice.

There was an alien note to his voice. Lynn got the strange sensation that there was a certain finality to his words, as though they extended over a far broader range than just this one night.

She was right. The next day Drew had gone—for good.

Chapter Thirteen

The warm summer sun beat down on Lynn's body. She wore a strapless knit top and a pair of blue shorts, and her hair was caught at the nape of her neck by a ribbon. In the six weeks since school had been out, she had spent much time out of doors and now her slender limbs were a soft golden hue.

She was in the garden, bending over a tomato plant. The bush was loaded with fruit and even a few yellow blossoms still, and the largest tomatoes were a light pink. Only another day or two and they would be ripe enough to eat.

She tried to take pleasure in that simple knowledge, pleasure in the rest of the garden, in the growing chicks, the good stand in the fields Cal had planted. But she failed. She had found little pleasure in anything since Drew had gone away nearly two months ago.

For the thousandth time she asked herself why, but the answer never came. The night Gwen's baby had been born, Cal had returned home late, close to midnight. Drew had said he was tired and had asked to be dropped off at their house before Cal went to his own. Lynn had thought little of it at the time, for they were all exhausted. While Cal had gone to his bedroom to snatch a few hours' sleep before heading back to Savannah and the hospital, Lynn had stretched out on the living room sofa.

In the morning, Cal was already gone again by the time Lynn awoke. She went into Gwen's kitchen and began breakfast for the children. When Drew didn't arrive, she called home to remind him to join them. There had been no answer to the phone and even then she had not been alarmed. She had merely supposed that he was probably outside feeding the chickens, pony and dog.

By ten he still had not come. Lynn straightened the bedrooms, cleaned the kitchen and then packed the children's clothes so that she could take them home with her until Gwen returned from the hospital and was back on her feet again.

It was only after she reached the house and walked into her bedroom to find the note on the bed that she realized the truth.

Drew's note had been brief. He said he had been called back to L.A. by a business emergency and that he was leaving her a second set of keys to the truck, which would be waiting for her at the airport. She was to pick it up and keep it, for he knew she needed a truck around the farm. That, more than anything else, told her he did not intend to return.

A week later she received a letter from a lawyer stating that an account had been set up for her. Each month she would be mailed a generous check for

Joy's child support. Further, trust funds had now been established for each of them. Beyond that, Lynn heard nothing—from the lawyer or from Drew. As abruptly as he had reentered her life, he had left it again.

She had too much pride to call him. If Drew could walk out on her and Joy without a single word, it proved only one thing. That despite his talk of their permanent reconciliation, he had had second thoughts. He didn't love her enough. He no longer wanted her.

The bottom had fallen out of her world. After having been raised to the heights of happiness she had, with no warning, been plunged into the depths of loneliness, confusion and pain. And gradually, as the numbing shock had worn off, a bitterness crept through her being. Drew had come and deliberately lured her into loving him again, giving her a false sense of security about their relationship, just so he could have the satisfaction of walking out on her this time, the way she had once done to him. He had told her once that she would pay for what she had done to him. Well, she was paying indeed.

Particularly cruel though, was the fact that this time Joy was also paying. In the first weeks after Drew went away, she had asked incessant questions about when her daddy was coming back and why he didn't call her on the telephone like he had done the time before when he had gone away. Lynn, of course, had no real answer. She could only offer the lame excuse that he was far too busy to call and add that she was sure he would whenever he had the time. It was a lie meant to soothe and comfort her child, though in truth, she didn't believe a single word she was saying.

As the weeks went by with no word, Joy's questions became more infrequent, much to Lynn's deep relief. *Thank God,* she thought now, *that a young child's memory was mercifully short, that they could be so quickly distracted by current events.*

If only it were so easy for herself! Lynn left the garden and walked slowly back toward the house, her heart heavy with the dull ache that never left her these days.

Joy and Penny were playing house in the shade cast by the garage. Joy was cuddling her doll, Mary Louise, while Penny arranged the plastic toy dishes on a tea towel.

"Mommy," Joy called, "can we have some cookies?"

Lynn forced a smile to her lips and nodded. "A tea party calls for some, I think. Come into the house and I'll get them for you."

A few minutes later the girls returned to their outdoor "house" armed with cookies and grape juice, and Lynn was alone again.

Alone. Such a bleak word. Such a bleak existence. If it weren't for Gwen and Cal nearby, Lynn knew she would already have gone mad with loneliness. The farm had seemed like such a wonderful idea when she had bought it and she had loved it more each day while Drew had been here. His presence had made it exciting and interesting, and all the chores had seemed like fun rather than work, but now she felt burdened by all that needed to be done and the weight of her responsibilities depressed her even more.

She went into the bathroom to wash her perspiring face and grubby hands. A glimpse of her face in the mirror jolted her. Her eyes were cloudy and troubled, set deep in her face with dark pockets beneath them. There was no spark of liveliness to the eyes, no hint of animation to the rest of her somber face. There was only a deadness, a replica of how she felt inside.

That evening after supper for herself and the two little girls, Lynn drove Penny home. In the distance beyond the house she could see a cloud of dust rising from the field. Cal was still at work and would probably not come home until after dark.

She found Gwen in the living room nursing Angela while she watched the news on television.

"Hi," Gwen greeted her warmly. She waved her free hand toward the television set and said, "Turn that off for me, will you?"

Lynn complied and sat down on the sofa while Penny kissed her mother hello before she and Joy scampered off through the house toward the backyard to find Pat.

"Cal's working late again, I see," Lynn observed idly.

Gwen nodded. "He's rarely in the house before nine every night."

"He works so hard," Lynn mused. "I'm sorry the deal about running my farm fell through. Now he still has to keep on with that job in town."

"Don't worry about that," Gwen told her. "It's what he was doing all along, anyway, so nothing's changed." She paused, lifted the baby to her shoulder and began patting gently on her back. Thoughtfully, she looked across at Lynn and asked, "When are you going to tell Drew that you're pregnant?"

Lynn's shoulders sagged. "Soon."

"When?" Gwen insisted softly.

"Soon," Lynn repeated.

"What are you waiting for?" Gwen asked. "You said yourself you wouldn't hide it from him this time, but you've known for certain for over a month."

235

"I know." Lynn looked at her twin with tortured eyes. "I guess I'm just waiting until I feel I can talk to him without breaking down and crying or else shouting furiously at him."

Gwen smiled. "Can't make up your mind which?"

Lynn shook her head. "No, I really can't. Oh, Gwen, one minute I hurt so badly and I miss him so and then the next I'm angry enough to kill him for going off and hurting Joy." She spread out her hands in a gesture of uncertainty. "What I just can't understand is how he could do that to her. Me, yes. Maybe I deserved it, I don't know, but I do know Joy didn't deserve that kind of pain."

Angela burped loudly and for a minute it disrupted the serious conversation. Both women laughed and Gwen left the room to place the now-sleeping baby in her crib.

But when Gwen returned, she picked up the subject again just as though there had been no interruption at all. "Lynn," she began as she curled her legs beneath her at the opposite end of the sofa, "I've given this matter a lot of thought and I really believe you should go out to California and see Drew face to face when you tell him. And Cal agrees with me."

Lynn stared at her in horror. "You've got to be kidding!" she gasped. "After he just walked out on me like he did?"

Gwen nodded. "Especially because of that."

"You're not making sense," Lynn flared. "Not that it makes any difference. I won't do it. I have no desire to ever see him again."

"Listen to me," Gwen said patiently. "Drew had a great deal of resentment in him because you hid your first pregnancy from him and walked out on him. Well, now he's done the same to you. Maybe it's because he is paying you back, I don't know. Or maybe it has something to do with the fact that he had to deliver Angela and . . ."

"That's just absurd!" Lynn snapped. "Why should that have anything to do with our marriage? I could see him maybe being upset enough to leave if he knew *I* was pregnant again, since that's what started all our problems in the first place, but he didn't know! He left out of revenge and . . ."

Gwen held up a hand and when Lynn fell silent, she said, "Why he left like he did isn't the point. Not at the moment, anyway. The point is that you've got to tell him this time and there's no sense putting it off any longer. And telling your husband that you're going to have his baby really isn't the sort of news that should be put into a letter or told over the telephone. You *did* cheat him of that knowledge the first time around; this time you owe him better, no matter what has happened between you in the meantime. Play fair, Lynn," she pleaded. "Go to see him and tell him. You owe it to this child, too. Drew has a right to know about it and the child has as much right to receive his financial support as Joy does."

"I agree about that part," Lynn said, "and I will let Drew know. But I see no reason to have to go there and face him."

"Are you afraid?" Gwen asked.

Lynn started. "Of what?"

Gwen shrugged. "Of Drew. Of his possible reaction."

"I suppose in a way I am." Lynn grimaced. "I'm sure he'll be angry when he finds out. After all, he never wanted Joy, remember?"

Gwen smiled and shook her head. "Correction," she said gently. "He never wanted a baby, period, for some unknown reason. But once he learned about Joy as a fact, as a living, breathing person, he couldn't get here fast enough. And there's no question in my mind that his love for her is sincere. From what I've observed, I can't even imagine Drew not loving this child as well."

"Then why did he leave?" Lynn burst out in exasperation. "Even if he doesn't want anything more to do with me, why doesn't he keep in contact with her?"

Gwen shook her head. "I don't know the answer to that. Only one person does. Why don't you ask Drew that when you get there?"

One week later, still against her own better judgment, Lynn was on her way to California. For a person who was generally agreeable and seldom demanding, her sister had continued to badger her daily. Cal, whenever he was around, added the weight of his opinion solidly behind his wife's. Lynn offered as many reasons as she could contrive in her own defense, only to have each one knocked down by quiet logic and relentless persuasion. Finally, as much to get away from them as anything else, Lynn gave in and now the plane carried her closer, moment by moment, to her destination.

She did not warn Drew she was coming. It would only have given him time to marshal his rationalizations for what he had done and she was in no mood to listen to a pack of lies. Quite frankly, she was in no mood to listen to him, period. She simply planned to confront him, tell him what she had come to say and go away again. The entire process should not take up more than a few minutes of their time and then she would never have to see him again.

At the L.A. airport, Lynn rented a small car and

drove to the hotel where she had booked a reserva-
tion. By the time she reached it, it was nearing five in
the afternoon.

She had brought a small overnight bag with her,
which contained only one change of clothes. She was
hot and tired and feeling a little frayed around the
edges, but the soft blue lightweight dress she was
wearing would have to do for her interview with
Drew. Lynn contented herself with slipping out of it,
taking a quick shower and then, dressed only in a bra
and panties, resting on the bed for an hour.

At six-thirty she finished dressing and called room
service for soup and a sandwich. She wasn't hungry.
Her stomach was tied up in knots from dread over
the coming confrontation, but she was carrying
another life within her that required proper nourish-
ment and so she forced herself to eat.

By seven-thirty, there was no further excuse to
delay. Lynn double-checked her appearance in the
mirror. The blue dress cast bluish highlights to her
gray eyes, softening the troubled expression they
held. She wished there was a bit more healthy color
in her face, but inexplicably, the tan seemed to have
faded. Her face was pale, framed by hair that
seemed darker, a harsher tone than usual. The dress
itself was elegant and simple, for Lynn had chosen it
carefully for this particular evening. However briefly, she was returning to a more affluent environment
and the occasion demanded that her own appearance match it. The casual attire she wore around the
farm had no place in Drew's home here.

When she reached the white-bricked fence and
turned into the curving drive, every nerve in Lynn's
body was tense. She told herself suddenly that she
should have called first. What if he wasn't even
here? Then she would just have to go through the

entire process of gearing herself up once more to come a second time. Or worse, what if he had a woman here with him? It was entirely possible, of course, and how could she bear it if she were required to deal with that? The questions, the doubts, hit her hard and fast and it was only with supreme willpower that she was able to force herself to bring the car to a halt and actually walk up the steps to the massive double front doors.

She pressed the bell and waited with a pounding heart. It was still light enough in the early evening for her to easily see that the exterior of the house, at least, looked the same as she remembered it: white, two-storied, with black shutters at the windows. The entrance porch boasted huge urns with topiary shrubs, very beautiful, precisely sculpted, with understated refinement.

One of the doors swung open and Lynn, expecting to be greeted by a black-clad maid, was met instead by the cook she had remembered. Mrs. Watson's ample bulk filled the doorway. Her short gray hair was tidy and she wore a neat dark blue dress and a large white apron.

"Why, Mrs. Marcus!" she gasped. "Come in, come in!" She stepped back so that Lynn could enter the hall.

The marble floors gleamed beneath the chandelier and well-tended plants gave a lush, inviting appearance to the foyer, again, just as Lynn recalled. But she took it all in at a single glance because the focus of her attention was on the woman who smiled at her.

"It's good to see you again, Mrs. Watson," Lynn said with a smile of her own.

"It's *real* good to see you," Mrs. Watson responded. "Maybe now things will settle down around here and be normal again." She shook her head sadly. "We've had a bad time here ever since Mr. Marcus came back from Georgia."

"You knew he was with me?" Lynn asked. Somehow, she was surprised.

Mrs. Watson nodded. "Sure. He told me the first time he came back . . . when he was here that two or three weeks. Told me all about your little girl. I'd love to see her. Did you bring her with you?"

Lynn shook her head. "No. I left her with my sister." She didn't add that she had seen no sense in disrupting Joy's life by bringing her to see a father who apparently wanted no more to do with her. Now she asked, "What do you mean about having a bad time with Mr. Marcus? Has he been ill?" she ended anxiously.

Mrs. Watson shook her head and grimaced. "To put it plainly, he's hell to live with these days. He snaps everybody's heads off, he doesn't like whatever I cook and half the time he won't eat at all. Just today one of my maids quit because he yelled at her one time too many. It's getting so bad, *I'm* almost ready to quit, too."

Lynn was shocked. Mrs. Watson had been with Drew for years and had enjoyed her privileged position as ruler over the entire household. "I'm sorry to hear this," she said with genuine concern. "But I hope you won't do anything too hastily. I'm sure Drew would be very upset to lose you."

Mrs. Watson sniffed as though she were near tears. "Well, I'm upset, too."

"Where is he now?"

"Shut up in his study like he is every night when he's home. He won't answer the telephone and I have orders to tell any visitors that he's not home." She gave Lynn a dubious look.

Lynn smiled and summoned up her waning courage at this piece of news. "Well, I'm not precisely a visitor, am I?"

Mrs. Watson shook her head. "You want me to go tell him you're here?" She clearly did not relish the task.

Lynn shook her head. "No, thanks. I'll announce myself." She started to move away.

"Will you be staying the night?" Mrs. Watson asked. "Are your bags outside?"

"No," Lynn said. "I won't be staying." She forced one more smile. "If I don't see you again before I leave, it was nice seeing you, Mrs. Watson."

The older woman nodded. "Same here, but I sure wish you were back for good."

Lynn went to the door of the study and paused, hand on the knob, to suck in a deep breath. Then she quietly turned the knob, pushed open the door and went inside.

Drew sat behind his desk with his chair turned facing the window. At his elbow on the desk was an untouched drink.

For a long moment Lynn stood frozen, studying his profile. One lock of his jet black hair fell across his forehead, a stark contrast against the whiteness of his face. His features seemed leaner, gaunter and more roughly chiseled than they should have been. He wore dark slacks and a white business shirt that was opened at the collar. He sat still and unmoving, lost in brooding thoughts and Lynn had a swift instinct that he had been like that for a long time.

In spite of everything, a vise squeezed her heart at the sight of him. She had told herself for weeks that she hated him, but now she knew she had only been kidding herself. She could see at a glance that Drew was just as unhappy as she was and it tore at her. She still loved him, had never stopped loving him for a single instant and in this moment she would have given anything to make his world right again, whether or not it also included her.

Softly, she closed the door behind her and as the latch clicked, Drew roused from his meditation and turned his head toward the sound.

A glimmer of shock flashed in his eyes, but was quickly concealed as he got to his feet and came around the desk to where she stood. Lynn waited, saying nothing, warily taking in his reaction to her unexpected presence. She did not have long to wait.

"How did you get in here?" he asked brusquely.

"Mrs. Watson let me in," she answered truthfully.

"Damn her! She deliberately disobeyed me!"

Lynn smiled grimly and nodded. "Yes, I know. She told me. Why don't you fire her for such insolence at actually allowing your own wife into the house? I doubt it would bother her much. She's thinking about quitting her job, anyway."

Drew's brows snapped down over his eyes. "How the hell would you know? Did she say that?"

"Yes, she did. It seems you're a very disagreeable employer these days. Did she tell you one of the maids quit today?"

He gave her a baffled look. "What?"

Lynn moved away from him and the door and went to the desk where she placed her white purse. "Yes," she went on casually. "One you've been yelling at, I understand. Now maybe this maid is easily replaced, I don't know, but I *do* know you're a fool if you let your temper drive Mrs. Watson away. I really can't believe her cooking standards have suddenly fallen so low as to deserve constant criticism."

"Is that what she told you?" Drew gave her a

thunderous look. "I damn well *should* fire her if she's gossiping behind my back!"

Lynn shrugged her shoulders, perched on the edge of the desk and picked up a pen that lay on it and began tapping it against her palm. "I've done a bit of gossiping behind your back lately myself," she taunted sweetly. "Do you plan to fire me, too?"

Drew made a sound of exasperation and turned his back on her. "What did you come here for?" he asked in a muffled voice.

"To tell you something," she replied in a hard, cold voice. "And to ask you something." She paused, then asked, "Have you enjoyed your little revenge?"

Drew swung around to face her and his eyes blazed as he stared at her. "What's that supposed to mean?"

Lynn dropped the pen back to the desk with a little thud and got to her feet. "It's why you left me, isn't it?" she demanded. "It was your plan from the beginning to get me to trust in your love again, to be ready to reconcile, so that then you could have the pleasure of walking out on me this time."

Abruptly, Drew crossed the distance between them. He grabbed her arm and held it so tightly she winced in pain. "You don't believe that!" he said harshly. "You can't!"

Lynn managed to free her arm and rubbed it gingerly. "Of course I do," she retorted. "Why else would you leave me without a word? But what is really unforgivable, Drew, is how you hurt Joy!"

"Oh, my God!" he moaned. He turned from her again, thrust his hands in his pockets and walked over to stand dejectedly before the window. "I didn't want to hurt her. Or you."

"Then why?"

He shook his head. "I just . . . I just realized it wasn't going to work out between us after all! I guess the truth is I'm just not cut out for marriage!"

Spasm after spasm of pain assaulted her and Lynn suddenly felt so weak she actually had to return to the desk just to lean against it. Gone now were her last hopes. Insane though it had been, illogical and crazy, still she had harbored the faint hope that coming to see him might somehow bring Drew back to her. But no more. He couldn't possibly make it any plainer that he no longer wanted her!

Her lips trembled, her voice shook and yet she couldn't help it. "If that's the way it is," she said at last, "that's the way it is. But what about Joy? You haven't even called her!"

Drew shook his head. "I couldn't. I decided that splitting her between us would be too hard on her, too confusing, too unsettling." He turned around to meet her gaze then and she saw unmistakable anguish in his eyes. "You're a good mother, Lynn. You've got far more to offer her than I ever could. Hell," his voice grew raspy, "I don't know the first thing about raising children the right way. I realized that all those weeks watching you with her. You give love and encouragement and that's what she needs. I never had that when I was a child and maybe I don't know how to give it, either. So . . . I don't want to harm her in any way by taking her away from you, even on a temporary basis. If I did, I'd just be selfish."

Lynn swallowed hard and blinked back the tears that scalded her eyes. "You're being unfair to yourself, Drew. And to Joy. You've already proved what a wonderful father you can be. Joy adores you and she misses you. She needs . . ." her voice was husky, "she needs her daddy as much as she needs me."

"Don't!" The word came out tortured and choked. "I'll give you a divorce, Lynn. You need to remarry. A woman like you deserves a good husband, the sort of life you really want. And when you do, Joy will have herself a new father. She won't need two of them."

"No, Drew," she said quietly. "A divorce is impossible just now. I told you I had come here to say something and it isn't easy for me. But I didn't have the courage to face you with it the first time, so in my own way, I'm trying to make amends by doing what's right this time." She sucked in a breath, then added in a rush, "I'm pregnant again. I'm going to have your baby."

A stunned look crossed Drew's face, and then it was swiftly displaced by absolute horror. His face went ashen and he gasped, "Oh, my God, no!" Then he buried his face in his hands.

Lynn went to him and put a hand on his arm. "Drew?" she asked uncertainly. "Drew, are you all right?"

"I never meant this to happen!" he said in a low, shaken voice. "I'm sorry! I never meant this! Not again! Not ever!"

Lynn recoiled and stared at him with sudden abhorrence. Her lips felt stiff as she managed to say, "Don't worry about it, Drew. Since you obviously hate the idea so much, you don't need to ever even see the child. I'm not asking you to see it or love it or even s-support it." Now she was breaking. "I only came to tell you b-because I owed it to you. But it's done now and you can for-forget I ever came."

Half-blinded by tears, Lynn turned, snatched up

her purse from the desk and made for the door. She was almost there when Drew caught her arm and halted her flight. Like a wild woman, she began to fight. She lashed at him with her hands and caught him smack on the cheek. The dreadful sound of it stilled them both.

"I'm sorry," she whispered raggedly. "I didn't mean . . . just let me go, Drew!"

He shook his head and his eyes were dark as a stormy night. "I'm the one who's sorry, Lynn," he said bleakly. "Please . . . don't go yet. I . . . I know I owe you an explanation." His hand on her arm was gently persuasive now and he lead her to his chair behind the desk. Once she was seated, he resumed his position at the window, looking out.

"I never told you . . ." he began. "I never told anyone before because I've been so ashamed all my life. My mother . . . died on the night I was born." Lynn gasped softly, but Drew ignored her, intent on his story. "She never wanted any children at all, my father said. When she discovered she was pregnant she cried and raged for weeks. She hated growing bigger, losing her beautiful shape, knowing she would lose her freedom when she became a mother. Only instead, she lost her life. She hemorrhaged to death. My father . . ." Drew stopped and was silent for a long time before he finally continued, "My father loved her very much and because she disliked it so much, he wished she hadn't become pregnant, either. And then she suffered so much in labor before I came, two days of it and then when it was all over, she died and he was left with only me." His voice was muffled as he forced himself to finish. "Don't you see, Lynn? It was *because* I loved you so much that I didn't want you to bear children. I've already taken one woman's life; I knew I couldn't

247

live with myself if I ever lost you the way my father did my mother!"

Lynn was scarcely even aware of leaving her chair as she went to him and put her arms around his waist, resting her face against the broad strength of his back. "It wasn't your fault, Drew," she said gently. "It was just something that happened . . . that couldn't be helped. Your father was a cruel, cruel man, darling. He had no right to tell you such horrible things and to place such a burden of guilt on you. No wonder you've been so set against our having children." She rubbed her cheek lovingly against his back. "I could never reconcile your attitude with the love you showed for Joy, but now I think I understand. The day Gwen's baby was born . . . it just brought all the old fears back to you, didn't it?"

"Yes." Drew's voice was thick. "I tried to keep control for her sake, Lynn. Honest to God, I did. But whenever she cried out in pain, it was like a sword going through me, slicing me to bits and pieces and I kept thinking, 'What if she dies? What if I do the wrong thing and she dies?'"

"But she didn't," Lynn pointed out softly. "Yet you left me, anyway."

Drew removed her arms from around his waist so that he could turn to face her. Pain glazed his eyes and stamped his features with grim lines. "I was afraid if we stayed together that *this* would happen! I didn't want to be responsible for making you pregnant again, Lynn. I love you too much to want to be the cause of your death!"

Lynn smiled through a haze of tears and cupped his face with both her hands. "Listen to me, darling, and listen well. I love you with all my heart. And part of my loving is wanting your children. Unfortunately it's true that a small percentage of women do have complications from childbirth and die, like your mother. An even smaller percentage never wanted their children in the first place. But I do want mine and like my sister once told you, I'm willing to take the slight risk of danger to me and the temporary pain in order to have them. Drew, please, don't be afraid for me. I was in excellent health when I carried Joy and I had a perfectly normal delivery. There's no reason in the world to believe this time will be any different. But even if it happened, even if by some quirk of fate I did die, I want you to know that I would never feel you were to blame in any way, nor would I ever want my child to have to live under such a burden of false guilt as your father forced upon you. I'm doing this willingly and happily. Please . . . accept that."

"I guess," Drew said humbly, "I just never thought about how you felt about it . . . that you really wanted children badly enough to take risks. You even wanted Joy enough to leave me because you just couldn't get *through* to me. I'm sorry, Lynn," he said in a low tone. "I just didn't understand a genuine, loving woman's attitude."

Lynn smiled through a haze of tears. "How could you?" she asked tenderly. "You had been raised with such a harsh concept of it. You couldn't know that for a woman in love, giving a man his children is her ultimate fulfillment. Now," she laughed throatily, "tell me the truth . . . doesn't it excite you and make you happy, too, even just a little bit . . . that we're going to have another child? Maybe a son this time?"

Drew crushed her to him and kissed her with starving passion. His lips were hard with desire but as they moved hungrily over hers and he felt her giving in return, his mouth softened. The kiss grew gentler.

Then with their cheeks pressed together while Drew held her close as though he would never again release her, his voice quivered. "You're the most wonderful woman in the world to give me so much happiness—especially since I don't deserve it. I'm sorry I put you through so much because of my irrational fears. I swear I'll spend the rest of my life making it up to you, if you'll only let me. Can you ever forgive me?"

"Only on one condition," she teased.

Drew pulled back enough so that he could look down into her eyes. He saw the twinkle there and it brought a soft smile to his lips. "What's that, darling?"

"That you promise never to leave me again," she whispered.

He pressed her body to his once more. "That's the easiest promise I'll ever make," he said. His voice trembled with deep emotion. "I'll never let you—or my children—away from me. Just be patient with me, darling. Teach me the things I never knew—about life and love." His hand went to her midsection and a light glowed in his eyes. "I love you," he said softly. "And Joy. And now this new precious life that's growing inside you. What more could any man ever ask for than to have all these riches?"

Lynn felt a happiness so great that it brought a lump to her throat. At last the cruel chains of the past were broken. Love's gentle chains bound them now—to one another, to their child and to their unborn baby . . . and nothing that lay before them in the lifetime ahead could ever sever this one.

As Drew kissed her once more, neither of them heard the soft whisper of the door opening. Mrs.

Watson had come to ask if they wanted any refreshments, but she could see at a glance that they needed nothing at the moment except each other. She smiled to herself with satisfaction as she closed the door again. She had a feeling that now her job was secure—and that the household was about to become a home once more.

MORE ROMANCE FOR
A SPECIAL WAY TO RELAX
$1.95 each

2 ☐ Hastings	21 ☐ Hastings	41 ☐ Halston	60 ☐ Thorne
3 ☐ Dixon	22 ☐ Howard	42 ☐ Drummond	61 ☐ Beckman
4 ☐ Vitek	23 ☐ Charles	43 ☐ Shaw	62 ☐ Bright
5 ☐ Converse	24 ☐ Dixon	44 ☐ Eden	63 ☐ Wallace
6 ☐ Douglass	25 ☐ Hardy	45 ☐ Charles	64 ☐ Converse
7 ☐ Stanford	26 ☐ Scott	46 ☐ Howard	65 ☐ Cates
8 ☐ Halston	27 ☐ Wisdom	47 ☐ Stephens	66 ☐ Mikels
9 ☐ Baxter	28 ☐ Ripy	48 ☐ Ferrell	67 ☐ Shaw
10 ☐ Thiels	29 ☐ Bergen	49 ☐ Hastings	68 ☐ Sinclair
11 ☐ Thornton	30 ☐ Stephens	50 ☐ Browning	69 ☐ Dalton
12 ☐ Sinclair	31 ☐ Baxter	51 ☐ Trent	70 ☐ Clare
13 ☐ Beckman	32 ☐ Douglass	52 ☐ Sinclair	71 ☐ Skillern
14 ☐ Keene	33 ☐ Palmer	53 ☐ Thomas	72 ☐ Belmont
15 ☐ James	35 ☐ James	54 ☐ Hohl	73 ☐ Taylor
16 ☐ Carr	36 ☐ Dailey	55 ☐ Stanford	74 ☐ Wisdom
17 ☐ John	37 ☐ Stanford	56 ☐ Wallace	75 ☐ John
18 ☐ Hamilton	38 ☐ John	57 ☐ Thornton	76 ☐ Ripy
19 ☐ Shaw	39 ☐ Milan	58 ☐ Douglass	77 ☐ Bergen
20 ☐ Musgrave	40 ☐ Converse	59 ☐ Roberts	78 ☐ Gladstone

MORE ROMANCE FOR
A SPECIAL WAY TO RELAX

$2.25 each

79 ☐ Hastings	84 ☐ Stephens	89 ☐ Meriwether	94 ☐ Barrie
80 ☐ Douglass	85 ☐ Beckman	90 ☐ Justin	95 ☐ Doyle
81 ☐ Thornton	86 ☐ Halston	91 ☐ Stanford	96 ☐ Baxter
82 ☐ McKenna	87 ☐ Dixon	92 ☐ Hamilton	
83 ☐ Major	88 ☐ Saxon	93 ☐ Lacey	

LOOK FOR *WILD IS THE HEART* BY ABRA TAYLOR AVAILABLE IN JULY AND *THUNDER AT DAWN* BY PATTI BECKMAN IN AUGUST.

SILHOUETTE SPECIAL EDITION, Department SE/2
1230 Avenue of the Americas
New York, NY 10020

Please send me the books I have checked above. I am enclosing $_____
(please add 50¢ to cover postage and handling. NYS and NYC residents
please add appropriate sales tax). Send check or money order—no cash or
C.O.D.'s please. Allow six weeks for delivery.

NAME _____

ADDRESS _____

CITY _____ STATE/ZIP _____

If you enjoyed this book...

...you will enjoy a Special Edition Book Club membership even more.

It will bring you each new title, as soon as it is published every month, delivered right to your door.

15-Day Free Trial Offer

We will send you 6 new Silhouette Special Editions to keep for 15 days absolutely free! If you decide not to keep them, send them back to us, you pay nothing. But if you enjoy them as much as we think you will, keep them and pay the invoice enclosed with your trial shipment. You will then automatically become a member of the Special Edition Book Club and receive 6 more romances every month. There is no minimum number of books to buy and you can cancel at any time.